E.R. PUNSHON
SECRETS CAN'T BE KEPT

ERNEST ROBERTSON PUNSHON was born in London in 1872.

At the age of fourteen he started life in an office. His employers soon informed him that he would never make a really satisfactory clerk, and he, agreeing, spent the next few years wandering about Canada and the United States, endeavouring without great success to earn a living in any occupation that offered. Returning home by way of working a passage on a cattle boat, he began to write. He contributed to many magazines and periodicals, wrote plays, and published nearly fifty novels, among which his detective stories proved the most popular and enduring.

He died in 1956.

The Bobby Owen Mysteries

E.R. PUNSHON

SECRETS CAN'T BE KEPT

With an introduction
by Curtis Evans

DEAN STREET PRESS

INTRODUCTION

IN HIS WEEKLY book review column in the *San Francisco Chronicle*, the influential American mystery critic Anthony Boucher brought in the year 1946 with a ringing notice of the twentieth E.R. Punshon Bobby Owen detective novel, the memorably titled *Secrets Can't Be Kept* (1944). "Nineteen forty-six starts off well with this specimen of the leisurely detailed school at its soundest, with an ending which, if somewhat chancy, may yet chill your blood," pronounced Boucher, who had become rather a Punshon fan since the publisher Macmillan had begun issuing the author's mysteries in the United States a couple of years earlier. Boucher's term "leisurely detailed school" was a catchall for Golden Age detective novelists, mostly British, who specialized in the devising of extremely intricate puzzle plots. Typically included as well in this group of detective novelists were Punshon's Detection Club colleagues Freeman Wills Crofts, J.J. Connington and Cecil John Charles Street (who wrote mysteries mostly under the pseudonyms John Rhode and Miles Burton). All three of these men were, like E.R. Punshon, supremely accomplished puzzle purveyors, yet where Punshon exceeded them, in my view, was in his treatment of character and atmosphere. In Punshon's hands the detective story, while retaining the complex puzzle plotting which readers of Golden Age detective fiction expected, successfully moved in a more serious direction, toward what we today call the crime novel, attaining greater psychological depth and everyday realism.

It is of literary realism that I suspect *New York Times Book Review* critic Isaac Anderson was thinking when he praised *Secrets Can't Be Kept* as "a fine example of sound detective work without sensationalism." Punshon's people are not improbable caricatures but believable men and women, and they are, to borrow from Raymond Chandler, people who commit murder "for reasons, not just to provide a corpse. ..." To be sure, Punshon was not a hard-boiled writer in the manner of Chandler or Dashiell Hammett, but often in his detective fiction he, like Chandler and Hammett, compellingly portrayed the dark and violent passions that all too often have lethal consequences not only in crime fiction but in real life. It is in this respect, in my view, that *Secrets Can't Be Kept* constitutes one of Punshon's most noteworthy mystery tales. If its ending does chill the blood, it does so not simply because it is horrifying, but because it is credible.

The detective novel opens with Inspector Bobby Owen receiving a rather singular visitor in his office in Midwych, the market town of Wychshire: clubfooted Ned Bloom, a splenetic young man from the picturesque town of Threepence, located "in a valley between Wychwood Forest proper and the high-lying moorlands west and north," atmospheric locales with which readers of the earlier Punshon novels *Diabolic Candelabra* and *The Conqueror Inn* should already be familiar. In Threepence Bloom's taciturn mother owns and manages the Pleezeu Tea Gardens, an establishment which before the war was much patronized by hikers and cyclists in need of refreshment and currently manages still to do a good business, even though customers find that there is something vaguely off-putting about Mrs Bloom.

Young Ned Bloom claims that he has valuable information for the Wychshire police, but only at a price: not money, but a job as a police detective. Bobby immediately demurs, explaining, in a tacit reference to Bloom's clubfoot, that "[p]oliceman have to be fit," which prompts an infuriated Bloom to make his exit while vowing to Bobby, "I'll get my start in private practice instead. ... More scope. No hidebound rules and regulations." Bobby is inclined to dismiss the odd Ned Bloom affair, but that same day at the Midwych police station three telephone calls are received from individuals anxiously inquiring whether Ned Bloom has been there. When Bobby, now somewhat intrigued, gets around to checking on Bloom's whereabouts, he learns that his disgruntled visitor is nowhere to be found. Now Bobby is tasked with determining whether Ned Bloom's penchant for nosing out other people's secrets has proven fatal for the desperately inquisitive young man.

Bobby catalogues his unlikely list of likely suspects in the Ned Bloom disappearance when discussing the case, as is his wont, with his closest confidant, his wife Olive: "[Ned's] mother. The vicar of the parish. A most superior waitress in a local tea garden. Her invalid father. A highly successful music-hall comedian. An artist with a steady market in water-colours of Wych Forest. The artist's niece with a fancy for ordering teas she never touches. An Army captain on leave with a wounded arm." Olive pronounces the group a "scratch lot." Could one of these seemingly innocuous individuals really have been willing to kill to keep a secret?

It was a stroke of brilliance on Punshon's part to make the cozily named Pleezeu Tea Gardens every bit as eerily haunted a place as his earlier depicted Conqueror Inn, or even the great Wychwood Forest itself. "It sounds silly, doesn't it," ruminates Olive about the paradox presented by the Pleezeu Tea Gardens. "Just a lot of people having tea out of doors, just a pleasant Sunday afternoon, every one trying to forget the war for half an hour, and why should that give you the jitters?" Down these mean tea gardens a man must go, to paraphrase Raymond Chandler, in search of secrets that can't be kept--some of which belong more to the world of noir than to the cozy.

Curtis Evans

CHAPTER I

A VISIT

GENTLEMAN TO SEE you, sir," announced Constable Watts, putting his head into the sanctum where sat Inspector Bobby Owen, chief of the still embryo Wych County C.I.D., that the war had prevented from coming to full birth—and alas for Bobby's beautifully complete plans, all carefully pigeon-holed till the war should be over and for goodness knows how long afterwards as well, most likely.

Bobby looked up from the piles of orders and counter orders, instructions and counter instructions, directions and counter directions that multitudinous authority showered upon him day by day. His head was still a little dizzy from his efforts to reconcile so many and so varying demands. He was almost grateful for an interruption that was at least straightforward and simple. He said:

"Who is it? What's he want?"

"Name of Bloom—Mr Ned Bloom," answered Watts. "Comes from Threepence. Says he has important information to give, but won't say what. Sergeant said to report."

Bobby hesitated, aware of a table piled high with papers, all of which would have to be disposed of that afternoon so that the way might be clear for the sure and certain renewal of the flood next morning. But a policeman is at the beck and call of every citizen, and it is never safe to dismiss any complaint as trivial, any information as insignificant. The complaint may be anything but trivial in some one's eyes, the information may turn out to be of life-and-death significance.

"Oh, well, fetch him in," he said at last. "May as well hear what he has to say."

Watts retired and returned to introduce the visitor. This was a youngster of about twenty with a pale, handsome, discontented face, a small, angry mouth, eyes of a curious greenish tint but bright and soft as a girl's, and eager, sensitive hands, long and narrow—temperamental hands, Bobby thought, and hands with which their owner seemed to express his meaning almost as plainly as with his tongue. A spoilt, wilful, not unattractive personality, Bobby told himself, and then he noticed that the new-comer was lame, suffering from the unfortunate disability known as a club foot. It was perhaps this unhappy deformity that accounted for the slightly provocative impression he managed to convey, as though the grudge he had against fate for so ill-using him he extended towards all mankind.

"Sit down, Mr Bloom—isn't it?" Bobby said. "I understand you have some information to give us."

Bloom did not answer at once. He was watching Bobby closely, and those soft and lustrous eyes of his had grown hard, shrewd, calculating. Bobby was reminded somehow of the 'gold-digger' type of young woman, forgetting her charm and glamour as she calculated how much and what she is likely to get out of her newest acquaintance.

"Not to give, to sell," Bloom said abruptly.

Bobby raised surprised eyebrows. Police certainly do pay on occasion for information brought to them. But this young man did not look like those who sometimes come to the police, offering to sell a pal for the price of a drink. Bobby was puzzled, but his voice had a sharper edge as he asked:

"What do you mean? What do you want?"

"Oh, not money," Bloom explained. "A job."

"A job," Bobby repeated, still more puzzled. "What do you mean? This isn't an employment agency."

"Aren't there any vacancies in the police force?" demanded Bloom.

"We want men badly," Bobby agreed. "There's a fairly high physical standard though, you know. Policemen have to be fit."

"You mean—that," Bloom said aggressively, pushing forward his deformed foot, at which Bobby had been careful not to look. "Why can't you say so? I'm not a fool. I don't mean I want to pound a beat and yell 'Move on'. I've heard of you. You're a detective. That needs brains, doesn't it? Brains. Not brawn. You aren't sitting there, looking superior, because of brawn. You're supposed to be clever, aren't you?"

"Only supposed," said Bobby sadly. "A detective needs brawn, too, you know. I've had to fight for my life before to-day."

"Then you fell down on your job," his visitor informed him. "Not a detective's business—to fight. Your job is to find out things, and leave the rough-and-tumble stuff to others."

"Dear me," said Bobby, beginning to be a little amused by his self-assured young visitor. "You know all about it, don't you? But don't you think that often enough it's only by the rough stuff that you can find out things?"

"Nonsense," pronounced Mr Bloom. "Not if you know your job."

"Oh, well," said Bobby, slightly less amused now. "If you mean you want to join the police force, either this or any other, I'm afraid it's not possible."

"The detective branch," interposed Bloom. "The special branch."

"We only take men from the ranks," Bobby explained. "Every one has to go through the uniformed ranks. Necessary. Where you learn your job. And for that the physical standard has to be high. Sorry, but there it is."

"In that case," said Bloom, "I'll take my information some-where else, and when the case breaks, the sickest man in all England will be Inspector Bobby Owen, who muffed the biggest chance that ever came his way and he hadn't sense enough to see it."

Bobby looked up sharply. He had not been very favourably impressed so far, but there was something about the boy—a mixture of sulkiness, determination, assurance—that made its mark.

"You live at Threepence, don't you?" he asked. "What's your address there?"

"The Pleezeu Tea Rooms."

"Oh, yes, I know;" Bobby said.

He had in fact occasionally patronised the Pleezeu Tea Rooms when routine duty or visits of inspection had taken him in the direction of Threepence, a favourite holiday resort for Midwych trippers and hikers. It lay in a valley between Wychwood Forest proper and the high-lying moorlands west and north, and was in process of being transformed from a picturesque, isolated, self-contained little community into a dormitory for prosperous

Midwych citizens and a place for them to retire to when their active business life was over. Though no railway served it, a line of motor-'buses had before the war brought it into close touch with the city, and even in days of petrol shortage an attenuated service was still maintained. Bobby retained an agreeable memory of the excellence of the tea, the home-made jam, the scones, and cakes provided at the Pleezeu Gardens, and of how pleasant and well arranged had been the garden where the outdoor teas were served. How Threepence itself had come by its odd name no one seemed to know, though local antiquarians loved to propound and wrangle over rival theories. That put forward by a jealous and rival community, attracting fewer visitors, that the name was the result of a general conviction that the whole place, inhabitants and all, was worth exactly threepence, neither more nor less, had won general acceptance only in the place of its origin.

Bloom was on his feet by now. He said:

"Well, if you don't care to have the information I've got, it's your own affair. I'll go to a private man instead. O.K. by me. Private work gives you much greater freedom, once you get a start. I thought I would give you first chance, but if you only want the prize-fighter type—" He pushed forward his deformed foot and looked challengingly at Bobby. "I knew—that—barred me," he said. "I thought I could show you—but if you don't want to be shown, not my fault. It just means I'll get my start in private practice instead. Better from my point of view. More scope. No hidebound rules and regulations."

He flung this out with mingled triumph and defiance, gave Bobby a nod which plainly meant 'what do you think of that?' and was moving towards the door when Bobby called him back.

"One moment, Mr Bloom," he said, though still not sure whether to take this odd youngster seriously or not. "Please remember that if you know, or think you know, anything affecting public security or welfare, and you keep silent about it, then you may find yourself an accessory before the fact and may become liable to severe penalty."

The young man laughed scornfully.

"When my story breaks," he said, "I think—I rather think—that'll be all right. I don't know whether you will think so, though." He turned towards the door and then turned back. "By the way," he said, "ever go to see McRell Pink at the New Grand?"

Therewith he gave Bobby a nod charged full—overflowing, in fact—with mystery, warning, and significance, and so departed, while Bobby, puzzled, amused, and just the merest trifle worried as well, returned to all those piled-up forms, inquiries and reports heaped so high upon his desk.

CHAPTER II
THREE 'PHONE CALLS

BUSY AS BOBBY was with all this clerical work, there remained in his mind from his talk with Ned Bloom a small point of irritation, nagging continually. He found himself writing in answer to question 3A64 the response appropriate to inquiry XX4, and he was annoyed. Not that he supposed it would make the slightest difference or that any one would ever know, but it offended his passion for the tidy—a passion which Olive, his wife, had more than once informed him was a flaw in his otherwise imperfect character.

He began even to regret having let young Bloom go.

"I wonder," he said aloud, "if the kid really does know something."

The door opened again, and once more Constable Watts appeared on some fresh errand. To him Bobby said:

"Watts, have you ever seen McRell Pink at the New Grand?"

On Constable Watts's large moon-like countenance a smile dawned. It spread. Slowly it spread and spread, and Bobby watched fascinated as the whole of that enormous countenance became transformed into the very image of transcendent mirth. Then the huge Wattsian body—all eighteen stone of it—started tremendously to shake and quiver. Finally, a mouse from a mountain, emerged a tiny chuckle.

"Well," said Bobby, "does that mean you have?"

"Begging your pardon, sir," said Watts, returning suddenly to his customary official gravity, "every Friday, sir, as and which duty allows."

"What's he do?" asked Bobby, who himself had never patronized the New Grand, though he had often seen posters advertising the name 'McRell Pink' in large letters.

"Well, sir," Watts answered slowly, "he—you see, sir—he—it's like this, sir, it's not so much what he does as the way he does it."

"Sing, dance, what?" Bobby asked, still curious.

Watts didn't seem quite sure, but did show signs of breaking into reminiscent mirth once more.

"There's times," he said presently, "he's that funny you're fair apt to cry being so sorry for him."

"I think I'll have to go and have a look," Bobby remarked.

"Yes, sir," said Watts. "You'll enjoy it, sir. That young fellow's mother what was here just now has been ringing up to ask about him. Seemed fair worried like."

"What about?" asked Bobby. "What did she say?"

Constable Watts didn't succeed in making that very clear. Solid and trustworthy as the Rock of Gibraltar, he was not highly gifted in the way of exposition. All he managed to convey was that Mrs Bloom seemed excited and alarmed—more than alarmed, frightened indeed. Apparently she had meant to ask that if the boy paid a visit to county headquarters he should not be allowed to leave till her own arrival. She had sounded very upset on hearing that she was too late and that the boy had already made his visit and departed.

Watts withdrew, and Bobby looked up the 'phone number of the Pleezeu Tea Gardens. He put through a call, only to learn that Mrs Bloom was out, had been out all afternoon. She had said she was going to Midwych, but had not said when she would be back. Bobby asked who was speaking, and was told it was Miss Bates, who worked for Mrs Bloom as cashier and book-keeper and who had not seen Mr Ned Bloom all day. Miss Bates's tone suggested that this fact in no way grieved her, and so Bobby rang off. He went on with his work, and after a time his chief assistant, Sergeant Payne, appeared on some routine errand or another.

"By the way, sir," he said, this disposed of, "wasn't there a young fellow, Ned Bloom, in here just now?"

"Yes. Why?" Bobby asked.

"Watts seems worried," Payne answered. "He says Bloom's mother rang up to ask about him, and now she's rung up again."

"What's she want this time?" asked Bobby, mildly interested.

"Watts wasn't very clear about that. Something about had the boy come, and, if he had, what had he told us, and was he here still? What worried Watts is that he's sure it wasn't the same voice. Quite different this time, and when he said so, whoever was speaking shut down in a hurry."

"A bit odd," Bobby commented. He hesitated and then on the intercom. system rang through to the outer office, telling them if Mrs Bloom 'phoned again to put the call through direct to him. "By the way," he went on to Payne, "do you ever go to the New Grand? Know anything about a McRell Pink appearing there?"

Payne smiled, though not quite so all-embracingly as the massive Watts.

"Comic, sir," he said. "I've seen him once or twice. Very good, too. Has the whole house in a roar in no time."

"What's he do?" Bobby asked. "Sing, dance, or what?"

"Well, pretty nearly everything in turn and never the same twice. One time I saw him he was giving an imitation of a man in the kitchen after listening to Freddie Grisewood of the B.B.C. on the kitchen front, as they call it." Payne paused to grin. "Killing," he declared. "He has a ventriloquist act sometimes—clever patter. There's a long argument he does with Lord Haw Haw, and you could almost swear it was the Joyce skunk answering him. Then there's a song of his that made quite a hit, something like this: 'Eire's a new, new, new land, so she is; and she wants to be neu-neu-neu-tral, so she does.' I forget how it went exactly. About how nice it is to be neutral and safe. Catchy tune." Payne tried to hum it, not very successfully. "Never the same thing twice, though. Oh, and only three days a week—Mondays, Fridays, and Saturdays."

"You mean he only appears those three days?"

"That's right."

"How do they manage the rest of the time?"

"There's a sort of fill-in act those three nights—bar turn generally. When McRell Pink is on you can hardly get a seat. Other nights it's different, though of course anything goes in the theatre just now."

Bobby knew enough to realize that for a turn to be put on three nights only was unusual. What was the reason, and where was Mr McRell Pink the other three nights? And why had young Ned Bloom asked in that significant tone if Bobby had ever seen him?

"Doesn't he appear somewhere else when he's not on at the New Grand?" Bobby asked.

Payne had no idea. Puzzling, all this, Bobby thought, and he didn't like being puzzled. In fact, there was nothing he disliked more. Payne was feeling a little puzzled, too, by these inquiries. He said:

"Nothing against him, sir, is there?"

"No, no," Bobby answered. "It's just that his name happened to crop up and made me wonder."

"The New Grand makes a bit of a mystery about him," Payne went on. "Advertisement most likely. They sort of smuggle him in and out; and he never mixes with any of the other performers, though you know how pally music-hall people are as a rule. If any of them speaks to him he just mumbles something and bolts like a frightened rabbit. Publicity stunt, I expect, but it does seem to be a fact that quite big noises in the Variety line have tried to get in touch with him and failed. He doesn't answer letters or telegrams. Even when a well-known agency wrote, offering to book him on a swell circuit, he didn't reply."

"Funny," Bobby said thoughtfully, "but I suppose he knows his own business best. Doesn't want to leave Midwych most likely."

"And that," commented Payne, "is more than funny. It's the only tiling most Midwych people want, even if they want to come back again as soon as they have."

The 'phone rang. Bobby answered it. A voice said:

"Are you the county police? This is Mrs Bloom speaking, from the Pleezeu Tea Gardens, Threepence. I believe my son, Ned, wants to see you. Can you tell me if he has been yet?"

"Hold the line a moment. I'll inquire," Bobby said. He put his hand over the receiver. He said quickly to Payne: "Ask Exchange to check up. Three mothers to one son is two too many."

He uncovered the receiver and spoke again: "Are you there?" he asked. "Is it Mr Ned Bloom you are asking about? Have you rung up before?"

"No. Why?" the voice answered. A woman's voice, Bobby thought, and yet a disguised voice, he thought as well, for it did not sound to him quite natural. The voice went on: "You haven't answered me. Has Ned been?"

"Hold the line, please, and I'll inquire," Bobby repeated.

Payne came quickly into the room. Bobby put his hand over the receiver again. Payne said:

"Exchange reports Call Box, Love Lane, Threepence, speaking. I've 'phoned our man there to check up who it is."

"Good," said Bobby, and uncovering the receiver, put it to his ear again. By one of those tricks the 'phone sometimes plays, he heard distinctly a man's voice say:

"Aren't they answering?"

"No," replied the first voice. It sounded hurried. It said: "There's something up. I can hear them talking. They've rumbled something."

Said the man's voice, distinct over the line:

"The young swine's been already. We'll have to out him pronto."

"Are you there?" Bobby asked, but this time there was no reply, only a silence complete and ominous.

CHAPTER III
MISSING

LATER ON THAT day there arrived a report from Sergeant Young, the officer in charge of the Threepence police station. This was to the effect that when the sergeant, who had undertaken the duty himself, arrived at the Love Lane call-box, it was empty. On one side of Love Lane were open fields. On the other was a small spinney. No one was in sight in the fields. Young had made as quick a search as possible of the spinney, but without success. Then he had gone on to where Love Lane joined the high road and had found Mr Roman Wright, the artist, sketching in the garden of Prospect Cottage, where he lived with his wife and niece.

He had questioned Mr Wright, but Mr Wright was sure no one had gone by there down Love Lane that afternoon. Then Young had returned to the other end of the lane to make inquiries at a small group of labourers' cottages there situate. But none of the inhabitants had noticed any stranger nor had the vicar, the Rev. Martin Pyne, who chanced to be making a parochial visit at one of the cottages.

"Painstaking man, Sergeant Young," observed Bobby approvingly. "Whoever it was must have slipped off in quick time, across the fields perhaps, dodging behind hedges, or else through the spinney. Time enough before Young could get there. But why should they unless there's something queer going on?"

"Yes, sir. Only what could that be?" Payne countered, and Bobby answered thoughtfully that he hadn't an idea in the world.

"Young Ned Bloom certainly thought he was on to something," he went on, "and I didn't much like what I heard on that third call. Sounded nasty somehow. And why did three people ring up, each claiming to be the boy's mother? Exaggerated claim in two cases anyhow. May not amount to much, of course. Storm in a teacup, very likely. You never know. You might ring up Young, thank him for his report—his very complete report—and ask him to get in touch with Bloom. Tell him to tell Bloom I would like to see him again. You might tell Young, too, to keep an eye on the Pleezeu Tea Gardens for the present."

Payne, though evidently thinking all this was making mountains out of molehills, went away to put through the suggested instructions. Sergeant Young, inwardly wondering what it was all about, undertook to carry them out. It was much later—nearly midnight, in fact, and both Bobby and Payne had gone home—when Young rang up again to say that Ned Bloom had not returned and that Mrs Bloom was uneasy at his unexpected absence.

The officer on duty made a note for Bobby's information next morning, but saw no reason to do more. The wise and prudent sergeant does not disturb inspectors off duty save for very good cause. It was getting on for eleven next morning before Bobby, overwhelmed as usual by a fresh batch of correspondence, every single item marked urgent, secret, very confidential, or something similar, arrived at the note recording Young's report. He found it worrying. He rang up Threepence and heard that Ned was still missing, that Mrs Bloom had sat up most of the night waiting for him, that the constable on the beat—the one beat that included the whole of Threepence—had seen a light in the small hours in a shed at the bottom of the tea gardens, the part farthest from the house and used chiefly for growing vegetables and herbs. It was separated by a hedge from that portion of the gardens where teas were served in fine weather. The constable, shocked by such a breach of the black-out regulations, had investigated, but without success. He found no one and no sign that there was or had been any one in the shed in which he thought he had seen the light. He had, however, gone on to the house, and Mrs Bloom, still sitting up in the hope that Ned might return, had accompanied him back to the shed. It was one used by Ned for his own private purposes, and there was nothing to show that it had been entered or any of its somewhat miscellaneous contents in any way disturbed. True, the door was unlocked, but Mrs Bloom had not seemed to think that very unusual. So she went back to the house, there to resume her vigil, the constable had continued to give the Pleezeu Tea Gardens his special attention, and nothing else had happened. If indeed anything at all had happened, for nothing is easier than to imagine a light where no light is.

Another day went by and still there was no news of Ned Bloom. Officially it was not a police matter. No complaint had been made, and there may be many reasons why a young man should wish to absent himself from home. None the less, Bobby was uneasy. He could not get from his mind the memory of that whining threat he had seemed to detect in the snatch of conversation overheard from the Love Lane call-box. Finally he decided to spare time for a visit to Threepence, a talk with Mrs Bloom, and perhaps a look at the shed or out-building or whatever it was where a mysterious light had been seen and then, like Ned himself, had disappeared. If Mrs Bloom's cakes and scones and her home-made jam remained anywhere near pre-war standard, the visit would not be entirely without compensatory features.

After lunch accordingly, he cycled out to Threepence. A pleasant ride and a pleasant change from office work. He turned off the main road down Love Lane, though that was hardly the nearest way. At the corner stood Prospect Cottage, where lived Mr Roman Wright, generally referred to in Threepence as 'the artist', and mentioned by Sergeant Young as declaring that he had seen no one pass that way about the time of the 'phoning from the callbox. Professional artists are somewhat rare birds in the Midwych area, and Bobby wondered vaguely who Mr Wright was and what his work was like. A pleasant little home he seemed to have, newly built—a product, indeed, of that 'ribbon development' along the new highways that so many deplore and condemn. For the present, until building took place opposite, as no doubt it would the moment the war was over, the cottage commanded a wide view over open country, towards the south. At the back a row of tall trees, oaks and beeches, the border of a small spinney, grew so close to the house as to deprive it of any rear garden, but gave good, if overshadowing, shelter against winds from the north.

At the front door a tall, buxom young woman was standing, smoking a cigarette in a long holder. Something of a chain smoker apparently, and extravagant as well, for Bobby saw her jerk from her holder a cigarette but half smoked and immediately light another. Or, rather, try to, for her match broke off short, without catching. She tried again, with the same result. This seemed, quite in the Hitler style, to exhaust her patience. She swore aloud so that Bobby heard her plainly—she used a word young women do not often employ, even in the most advanced circles—flung the match-box on the ground, stamped on it, kicked it away, and retired indoors, banging the door angrily behind her.

A young woman in a highly nervous state, Bobby told himself, and had she been a young man he would have been tempted to diagnose a hangover of some sort. Only after her disappearance did he become aware of another woman in the small front garden, near some bushes; a woman so oddly inconspicuous, so motionless and silent, that even he, accustomed and trained to quick observation, had not at first perceived her presence. An elderly woman, small, thin, pale, giving an impression somehow of looking much older than her age. Bobby wondered in what relationship she stood to the impatient damsel who had just retired indoors. Payne had spoken of aunt and niece, Bobby remembered. But not many aunts, not even in these days of the rule and supremacy of youth, would have suffered such a display of temper and impatience to pass without some sort of comment or sign of surprise or disapproval. But she had given none, had not even seemed to notice. Nothing to do with him, Bobby thought, and when he looked again he was surprised to see that this possible, hypothetical aunt was no longer there, though he had not seen her go. Then he saw that she had merely changed her position slightly, but seemed somehow to have so great a gift for being inconspicuous that not till he looked twice did he distinguish her where she was now standing, as still and silent as before.

"Sort of cap of invisibility she must possess," he told himself smilingly as he continued on his way.

A little farther on he saw a man whom he supposed must be Mr. Roman Wright himself—at any rate an artist engaged in painting the scene before him.

Bobby got off his bicycle and stood looking on with deep envy. A wonderful life—nothing to do but sit on a campstool all day watching the play of light and shade on all the loveliest bits of landscape in the neighbourhood. How bitter, bitter a contrast with the toilsome existence of a C.I.D. inspector! How spiritually elevating, this daily communion with Nature at her best, as compared with his own dusty job of struggling ever to protect a society that sometimes he was moved to think but little deserved protecting. Sighing, he remembered his own youthful dreams of an artist's life, ended for ever by realization of the fact that, though he could draw well enough, his colour sense was poor. Nor is drawing well enough much of a foundation on which to build hopes of earning a living. None the less the sight of an easel still drew him as a honey-pot draws flies. But, since he was on duty, he would certainly have ridden on, had not his passing glimpse of Prospect Cottage aroused in one detail a faint surprise in his mind. Nothing much, but anything that puzzled him and roused his curiosity was always to him quite irresistible. The two women, too, remained in his memory—one with her display of temper and exaggerated nervousness, the other with her odd gift for escaping notice.

So he leaned his bicycle against the hedge and, passing through a gap in it, approached the artist: encouraged, when that gentleman looked up, by a friendly smile.

Bobby expressed a hope that he was not intruding, not interrupting. The artist, who was working in water-colour, added a fresh touch to his sketch and said 'Not at all'. Bobby gave his own name and wondered if he was speaking to Mr Roman Wright, and Mr Roman Wright appeared much gratified and said that was so and how did—Mr Owen, was that the name?—how did Mr Owen know? So Bobby explained he had heard a friend of his resident in Threepence mention Mr Roman Wright, but did not add that the friend in question was the local sergeant of police. He had no wish to emphasize his profession, mention of which, he knew, often made people shy and embarrassed. Instead he passed some remarks on the work in progress—remarks more laudatory than candid, for privately he thought the composition poor. Besides, he knew enough of drawing to know a good line when he saw it, as he did not in Mr Roman Wright's work. He decided inwardly that Mr Roman Wright must be one of that wise band of artists who have taken the precaution to provide themselves with a sufficient private income before embarking on their profession. Rather a surprise to learn casually, in the course of conversation, that Mr Roman Wright had been commissioned by a London dealer to provide him with half a dozen water-colours of Wychshire scenery.

"It's what a business man would call my speciality," Mr Wright explained genially. "Wychshire scenery, I mean. Especially the forest. Out there you'll find me at all hours—morning, noon, and night when all you other lucky people are snug in bed. I suppose you don't know my 'Winter Dawn—a forest scene'?"

Bobby had to confess ignorance. Mr Roman Wright looked sad.

"I never knew who bought it," he said. "Dealer, I suppose. Resale in the U.S. most likely. Anyhow, it stopped all sale of engravings. Some dodge under copyright law. Engravings doing quite well at the time, too."

Bobby expressed sympathy. He remarked that copyright law was a jungle through which only experts could find their way—and often even they got lost therein. He asked if Mr Wright ever did portraits, and Mr Wright shook his head.

"John told me once I ought to," he said thoughtfully. "Sometimes I wish I had taken his tip. Portraits pay. But I've stuck to my landscapes, and I suppose I've not done too badly. Even John admits that."

"John?" repeated Bobby questioningly.

"Augustus John," explained Mr Wright. "Quite well-known man. I don't see much of him nowadays. Drifted apart somehow."

"I know the name," Bobby said, knitting his brows in an evident effort at recollection. "Once when I was having a holiday in London I went to the Tate Gallery. Very interesting. I remember a John painting there—my friend said it was one of his best things. Sort of resurrection-day scene. Lot of corpses getting up out of their graves, all very stiff. Very clever, I suppose."

Mr Roman Wright nodded.

"I know," he said. "I remember seeing it in his studio when he was working at it years ago. 'You've got something there, John,' I said. Other people had been running it down, so it bucked him up no end to hear me say that."

"I am sure it would," agreed Bobby politely. "All the same, I like his 'Shrimp Girl' in the National Gallery much better. Well, I must be getting on."

"So must I," smiled Mr Roman Wright. "I've to get this lot delivered by the end of the month—£50 each for the six." He shook his head sadly. "And probably the dealer will ask twice as much. That's what we poor devils of artists have to put up with. You can't find your own customers, so there you are. In the hands of the dealers."

Bobby said sympathetically that it was hard lines, hinted he himself would have liked a specimen of Mr Wright's work. But £50—he, too, shook his head sadly. Altogether beyond him, a figure like that. So Mr Roman Wright laughed genially and explained he was under contract to his dealer not to sell privately.

"Thinks I should let 'em go too cheap," he said. "Says he means to hold for the coming boom—maybe years, maybe never, I tell him. Anyhow, there it is."

CHAPTER IV

TEAS

IN THOUGHTFUL MOOD Bobby rode on, and came presently to that small group of cottages where Sergeant Young had seen the vicar, Mr Martin Pyne, making his call. Farther on, at the entrance to the village proper, in the High Street, where already some of the big multiple shop concerns were beginning to establish themselves, Bobby saw coming towards him a small man in clerical dress. An odd-looking little man, Bobby thought, with an enormous, nearly perfectly bald head, a thin almost shrunken body, and disproportionately long arms and legs. The Threepence vicar, Bobby supposed, the Mr Pyne of whom Sergeant Young had spoken. He turned into one of the shops as Bobby drew nearer.

Not much farther on was the Pleezeu Tea Garden. There Bobby alighted. The day was fine, and the tea-rooms seemed to be doing a good trade. The falling off in hikers and cyclists that had marked the opening phase of the war, in the black Dunkirk days, had now been more than atoned for by soldiers from a nearby camp, glad of any change from the barrack room; by residents in the neighbourhood ready to pay for an outside meal that would help them to eke out their tea and sugar rations; by others who did their shopping in Threepence rather than make the longer journey to Midwych, and who, that task accomplished, felt they had both earned and deserved rest and refreshment.

Bobby had to wait some time before his modest wants could be attended to. The Pleezeu Gardens seemed to be suffering, like every other establishment of its kind, from shortage of staff. The only waitresses in evidence were a willing but apparently inexperienced and certainly extremely clumsy child of fifteen or sixteen; and an unusually tall and handsome girl, who, with her stately carriage and a certain native dignity of bearing, seemed as much out of place, taking orders and carrying trays, as did, though in another sense, the child who had just dropped a tray of scones and tea.

"Oh, Liza," said the tall girl resignedly, "there's another cup broken, and you know how hard it is to get replacements."

"Please, Miss Kitty, it just went out of my hand," protested Liza.

"So I see," the tall girl agreed. "Gracious," she added presently as Liza, having picked up the scattered scones and given them a perfunctory wipe, showed signs of continuing on her way with them to the waiting customer, "you mustn't serve those. Take them back to the kitchen and get fresh."

Liza, looking slightly surprised, as if she found it difficult to grasp the reason for this command, obeyed, however; and the tall girl came to Bobby and took his order, though a little with an unconscious air of not so much taking an order as of receiving homage. He said to her:

"I noticed a clergyman in the High Street—a smallish man, rather thin, with an enormous, quite bald head. Would that be the vicar here?"

The tall girl looked at Bobby disapprovingly. He had a feeling that she considered his description lacking in courtesy.

"I couldn't say," she answered coldly. "If you wish to see Mr Pyne you can call at the vicarage. It is near the church. But Mr Pyne is nearly always out visiting in the parish at this time."

She went away then, leaving Bobby feeling that he had been well and truly put in his place. When his tea arrived he noticed it was brought him by the child, Liza, not by the tall girl she had called Miss Kitty. Miss Kitty herself seemed very busy at the other end of the garden; and Bobby, noting her swift efficiency, told himself that the young woman, however superior in manner, did not at any rate hold herself superior to her job. He took an opportunity when she, not Liza, was near, to ask for his bill and to say something complimentary about the scones.

"Like pre-war," he declared, and Miss Kitty smiled—her clear-cut, perhaps too prominent, distinctly aristocratic features took on a very pleasant expression when she smiled—and said it was really wonderful what Mrs Bloom could do with the materials available.

Bobby said it was rather jolly there, and might he sit on for a while and smoke a cigarette; and Miss Kitty said, of course, as long as he liked. Then she departed to attend to a fresh customer, and on the way met yet another, a young man in the uniform of an army captain, who seemed to have suffered some recent injury, as he had one arm in a sling.

"Oh, good afternoon," he said cheerfully.

"You've had one tea already, Captain Dunstan," said Miss Kitty, not without severity.

"Oh, that was yesterday," he declared.

"Yesterday and today," she retorted.

Captain Dunstan looked depressed.

"You've such a good memory," he sighed. "Nearly as good as a quartermaster's for the stuff he's issued and you've never had." He sat down at the nearest table, close to Bobby's. He said firmly: "Tea, please, and one scone. No sugar and lots of hot water."

Miss Kitty turned her back on him, and Bobby observed that he, too, when his tea arrived, had it brought to him by the Liza child.

"Please, sir," she said, "Miss Kitty says it's all the scones there is to spare and it's been on the ground because of the tray going sudden like out of my hand, but I've wiped it careful."

"I'm sure you have," said Captain Dunstan, "and tell Miss Kitty that if she thinks to scare a soldier of the king by a little thing like that, she little knows army rations."

Therewith he took an enormous bite, grinned at Liza, filled his cup from the teapot, and looked with some surprise at the result. Then he called to the retreating Liza.

"Tell Miss Kitty, too," he said enthusiastically, "the finest cup of aqua pura, heated, I've seen for months, even years."

Liza, looking puzzled, returned, stared at the teapot and cup, gasped and explained:

"If she ain't gone and been and forgot to put in the tea."

Therewith she snatched up the teapot, and scuttled away, and Captain Dunstan shook his head sadly and remarked aloud:

"Not forgotten, I fear, but served before."

He lighted a cigarette. Liza did not reappear. Miss Kitty was nowhere visible. One of the few remaining customers began to show signs of wishing to pay, and Miss Kitty emerged. Probably calculating the amount due was a task slightly beyond Liza. But she made an appearance now, blundering energetically from one to another of such customers as still required attention. Captain Dunstan called 'waitress', and Kitty came at once towards him.

"Your bill, sir?" she asked formally.

"You needn't be so beastly stuck up," he grumbled. "I may be dirt, but why wipe your feet on me quite so hard?"

"Well, I like that," she gasped.

"Of course," he admitted, "I'd rather you wiped your feet on me than nothing at all—like that teapot."

"Tea is rationed," she said. "I'm not going to waste it on people who don't want it. Oh, and there's no bill."

She turned and was going away, looking statelier than ever. He got to his feet and stopped her. He said:

"Why are you being like this?"

"Have you been quarrelling with Ned?" she asked.

He looked very sulky.

"I would have knocked the young fool's head off," he admitted, "only you can't, a chap like that."

"Mrs Bloom is very worried," Kitty said. "He's all she has. What did happen?"

"Nothing much. He wanted to fight. I told him not to be a fool. I told him to shut up, to go home and play. He said he might be a cripple but I was one-armed, so we were quits. That's all."

"What happened?" she repeated, as if somehow she were not fully satisfied.

"Oh, well, he came at me, squaring up. I had to give him a push to keep him away. He was trying to hit out. Well, he went down. I couldn't help it. It wasn't my fault. You have to do something if a bloke comes squaring up at you. I told him I was sorry, and then I just cleared off fast as I could. If I hadn't I believe he would have gone for me again as soon as he was on his feet. He wasn't hurt, not really. Only rather surprised, and so was I. He went over so easily."

"Well, I think it was a great shame and very disgraceful," she told him with severity. "A boy like that."

"You seem very concerned about—Ned," he retorted, growing angry now, and giving a very vicious snarl to his pronunciation of 'Ned'.

"Yes, I am," she snapped, "very concerned, and so is Mrs Bloom—poor boy."

These last two words were, and were plainly meant to be, a turning of the knife in the wound. Captain Dunstan went very red. Miss Kitty marched away, making her back look as haughty, offended, and aloof as ever back could look. Captain Dunstan marched away in the opposite direction. Bobby got up and went to the cash desk, where sat a severe and competent-looking middle-aged woman—the Miss Bates, he guessed, to whom he had spoken on the 'phone. He asked if Mr Ned Bloom had returned, and Miss Bates gave him a suspicious glance and said, no, he had not. Bobby asked if he could see Mrs Bloom, and Miss Bates said Mrs Bloom was resting—that is, if she had finished clearing up the kitchen, which was a long and tiring job. Perhaps the gentleman could call some other time? Was it anything special?

So Bobby produced his official card and explained that Mr Ned Bloom had been to see him in Midwych, and now, he, Bobby, had come to see Mrs Bloom in Threepence. Also there was a report of a light having been seen on the premises.

Miss Bates looked more worried and suspicious than ever.

"Ned's not been home," she said, "not since that day he went to town. We haven't any idea what's become of him."

"No suggestion at all?" Bobby asked.

Miss Bates shook her head.

"You're the police," she said abruptly.

Bobby waited silently. She was staring hard at his official card she still held in her hand, so it seemed unnecessary to reply. He had an idea that she was coming to a decision, making up her mind. She said:—

"I can tell you what she thinks, though she won't say. She thinks he has been murdered."

CHAPTER V
MURDER?

WHEN MISS BATES had said this she looked rather frightened, and turned first red and then white. Bobby, aware that unless he was careful she would probably take refuge in obstinate silence, took out his cigarette case, examined it thoughtfully, offered it to Miss Bates, and observed in a meditative manner:

"I'm pretty badly worried myself. I don't know why. Not much to go on. Still, you never know. What makes you think it may be that?"

She made no effort to accept the cigarette he was still offering. Abruptly she said:

"Don't tell Mrs Bloom I said so."

"Oh, no," he assured her. "Police never tell any one anything unless they have to in the way of duty. Had the boy any enemies?"

"Nobody liked him," she answered. "Bone lazy. Poking. Prying. Showing off how clever he was finding out things about you. Read your letters as soon as not if he got the chance. I caught him at it once. I boxed his ears for him I was that angry."

"Served him right," said Bobby heartily.

"Thought he knew it all," said Miss Bates. "He didn't. Not by a long way, not even about his mother. Wanted to set up as a private detective, as he called it. Rubbish."

"Yes, he told me that," agreed Bobby. "Silly idea. A man's got to be physically fit, for one thing. What did Mrs Bloom think about it?"

"Oh, she didn't know; she had no idea how he went about nosey parkering. That's what I call it. He just liked to show off. He liked to say: 'I met a Miss Polly Young today. Your friend at school was a Polly Young, too, wasn't she? But it can't be the same, because she's Mrs Jacks now, and this one isn't married.' Then if you looked startled and said, 'How do you know all that?' he was just as pleased as punch and would go away grinning silly like."

"Stupid trick," said Bobby. He picked up his card Miss Bates had laid down and held it casually so that she could still see it. "I don't want to 'nosey parker'," he said, "but police have got to be told if there's anything wrong. I'm sure you want to help, if anything has happened to him. What makes you think perhaps it has?"

"Oh, I don't know," she said uneasily. "I expect he's all right really."

"Murder's not a word to be forgotten," he said, looking at her.

"I don't see why you want to catch a body up so quick," she complained. "I didn't say that's what I thought. I said that was why Mrs Bloom was worrying so. Perhaps she isn't really."

"If she is, why is she?" Bobby said.

"Ned's never stayed away like this before," Miss Bates answered, "and I know he's got no money, because he never has and he's not working, and he asked me for some, and I wouldn't, not unless his mother said so special, because of the bills coming in and have to be met, and all his things in his room still—everything."

Bobby waited. He felt there was more to come. Experience had taught him that in getting hesitant and reluctant witnesses to talk, an attitude of patient and expectant waiting was often more effective than close questioning. So he remained silent, making it plain he was waiting for her to continue, and Miss Bates said:

"She said something once—Mrs Bloom, I mean. I don't remember exactly. It was when a motor car knocked him down. He wasn't hurt much, but he might have been killed, and she said some day he would be, and I said accidents weren't so common as all that, and she said there weren't only accidents, and I said, well, she didn't suppose any one would murder him, did she? and she looked at me so queer like I went cold all down my back, and she said once there was a dead man said that that would be. I didn't dare ask her what she meant and she never said another word, but last night I said I would stay with her if she was going to sit up for him. She wouldn't let me. She looked at me the way she did that other time I've never forgotten, and she said, just as if she were talking to herself and I wasn't there, she said that now

it might be that there had come about what had been said before, and I didn't dare ask her what she meant." Miss Bates took a
handkerchief from her bag and dabbed nervously at her face and
lips. She said: "It was the way she looked so like that other time
I've never forgot and never shall."

"Is that all?" Bobby asked.

She nodded.

"Sounds silly, doesn't it?" she said.

"No," answered Bobby.

After a time he said:

"I think I must have a talk with Mrs Bloom. I won't say anything about what you've told me unless it is really necessary,
and that's not likely. We always say 'from information received',
you know."

Miss Bates got up. She still seemed very disturbed. She went
through a door behind where she sat. She came back and said:

"She's in the kitchen. It's this way."

Bobby followed through the door. The kitchen was a large,
clean, light, airy room with a business-like, efficient air about it.
Along one wall was a range of cupboards with glass doors. To the
left was a big sink and still more cupboards and shelves. Opposite were a baker's oven and a household stove. Before the big
window at the farther end of the room was the Work-table, with
at one end an electric mixer. In the middle of the room was a trolley, serving both as an additional table and for fetch and carry to
and from the store-room, larder, packing-room. Everything had
a bright and polished appearance, and Bobby noticed the long
array of kettles of different sizes, all neatly arranged, side by side,
on one of the shelves.

Mrs Bloom was standing near the trolley, facing the door by
which Bobby and Miss Bates entered. Miss Bates at once retired,
closing the door behind her. Bobby felt she was still frightened
at what she had said. Mrs Bloom was a small woman with snow-
white hair combed back tightly from the forehead. She looked
fragile and had been pretty when young, Bobby thought, for
worn, emaciated even, as was her appearance now, the pattern
of her facial bones beneath the tightly drawn, dead-white skin

showed fineness and harmony. So, too, did her long, slender hands she held folded before her. These alone reminded Bobby of her son. Otherwise he saw small resemblance; except in some measure in her eyes—large and quiet and deep, of the same greenish tint as his, but with a look in them as of tragic griefs long past but still remembered.

What it was about her that gave this strange, vivid impression of tragedy and suffering beyond the common, Bobby was not sure; and yet he experienced a sensation he in no way understood, as though he had come blunderingly into a place where he had no right to be.

An artist of genius has made of the painting of a chair—a common kitchen chair and nothing more—a symbol of the eternal loneliness and solitude of all mankind; and so, too, this quiet, still woman with the tragic eyes, the deep lines about the mouth, the folded hands, waiting there in her kitchen for him to speak, seemed now in the same way the complete symbol of the tragedy of man.

So absorbed was he in these thoughts, or rather in the kind of wonder that possessed him, that he did not speak. It was she who broke the silence first, and her words were commonplace and simple.

"Is there anything I can do for you?" she said.

Bobby put from him the thought that he ought to apologize and withdraw, that he had no right to trouble those depths, aloof and hidden, in which he felt that long ago her life had drowned. He reminded himself he was on duty. He said:

"I called to ask about Mr Ned Bloom."

"He is not here," she answered.

"He came to see me in Midwych," Bobby continued. "He seemed to think he had some information he could give us. I should like to ask him more about it."

"He is not here," she repeated. "I do not know where he is."

"Have you seen him since his visit to me?"

"No."

"Is it unusual for him to be absent from home?"

"Yes."

"Did you know he intended to come to see me?"

"No. But I had a 'phone message that he had gone to see the county police and that I had better stop him if I wanted to see him alive again. I rang up to ask, and they told me he had been there and had gone again."

"Who was the 'phone message from?"

"I do not know. I asked, but whoever it was would not say. I did not recognize the voice. I thought perhaps it was a joke. It did not sound like one. Perhaps it was. I do not know."

"Didn't the message alarm you?"

"It worried me. That is why I 'phoned."

He asked her the exact time when she rang up. She had not noticed. He told her two other messages had been received as well as her own, each, too, purporting to come from herself, from Ned's mother. She listened gravely, but made no comment. Bobby felt baffled. He had an impression that her silence hid something significant, but significant of what, he did not know. He wondered if she knew more than she chose to say, and yet he did not much think so. She had an air of being indifferent, almost callous, and yet he knew it was not indifference, but endurance, endurance born of suffering. He blurted out angrily:

"He is your son, but you are not being very helpful." She made no answer, only those strange, deep eyes flickered for a moment and he felt that what he had said had been brutal. "I am sorry," he said. "Didn't you think of reporting his absence to us?"

"I thought of it," she answered slowly; "but what could you do?"

"Well," he said, feeling again oddly baffled, "we could make inquiries, institute a search."

"Please do so," she said.

"You don't sound very hopeful," he exclaimed, irritated again; and though she did not answer in words, again he saw that the calm depths of her eyes were troubled, so that he had the idea that she and hope had long since parted company.

His eye was caught by the long array of kettles standing side by side on the shelf they filled from end to end.

"You've a lot of kettles there," he said. "One and twenty."

"Are there?" she asked, without showing any surprise at the abrupt, disconnected remark. "I didn't know. I've never counted. We try to have freshly boiled water for each customer. As soon as one kettle boils, we take it off and put on another."

"Mrs Bloom," Bobby said, "the word 'murder' has been used. Have you any reason to think it possible anything like that has happened to your son?"

She seemed to ponder this, and it was a moment or two before she answered. Finally she said:—

"What is a reason? I am afraid, but I do not know of anything you could call a reason. Except that 'phone call, and that may have been nothing. Ned had been dropping hints about things he knew; but is that a reason for murder? I suppose it might be, or some might think so. He liked to find out things."

"What sort of things?"

"About people. Anything. Ned was lame. He had a club foot."

"I know," Bobby said. "He was sensitive about it, wasn't he? It struck me he made a point of pushing it out for you to see."

"He was very sensitive about it," she agreed. "I think he blamed me, thought it was my fault. Perhaps it was. It kept him out of things. He couldn't play games like other boys. He thought they looked down on him. They weren't always kind. Other boys, I mean. How could they be—so young? But if he knew things about them—if he knew who had a crib hidden in his desk, who had been up to this or that piece of mischief—then they didn't dare tease or laugh at him. Because he might tell. I think he never did, but they knew he might."

Bobby remembered that Miss Bates had said Mrs Bloom knew nothing of her son's habit of worming out other people's secrets. Evidently that was a mistake on the part of Miss Bates. Clearly Mrs Bloom knew. Bobby could not help feeling that there was much she knew and much she did not tell.

"When he came to see me," Bobby said, "he seemed to think he had got hold of something serious. If he was right and it was serious and the person concerned knew he knew—well, that might be serious, too."

She did not answer in words, but it was plain that she understood.

"You can't tell me anything more?" he asked.

She made the faintest possible negative gesture. He looked at her frowningly, more than ever puzzled, baffled. He became aware of an odd impression that between her and the living world was a barrier beyond his power to pierce. He turned away and stared at that long row of kettles again. Now he saw that he had counted wrong before—that there were, in fact, twenty-two. He said to her over his shoulder:

"One would think you did not care what happened to him."

There was a slight stiffening of the thin, worn, upright body before she answered. Then she said in a voice so low he could hardly catch the words:

"If my son is alive, he will return. If he is dead, can you give him back to me?"

CHAPTER VI
TROUBLED MOTHER

A QUESTION, this, to which there was no reply, and Bobby offered none. After a time, he said:

"If your son has been murdered—and I think you think that is possible, though you will not tell me why—don't you want his murderer found and punished?"

Hitherto Mrs Bloom had remained impassive, motionless, only a tightening of her hands folded before her, only the changing expression in her deep, strange eyes, giving any sign of what she felt. Now she moved away from the trolley and went to the window and stood there. Without looking round, as much as if she were speaking to herself as to him, she said:

"Could any punishment be worse than to go on living with such a memory?"

"I don't know anything about that," retorted Bobby, "but I do know my duty."

"Oh, yes," she agreed, turning and giving him a sudden, unexpected smile, so full of sympathy and kindness and understanding—even approval, as he thought—that for the moment he was quite bewildered. That smile, too, had taken twenty years or more off her apparent age, so that instead of the worn and elderly sixty she had looked before, she seemed for the instant to be only a well-preserved forty. The change went as quickly as it came and she continued: "It's your work, isn't it? to try to make the world safe for us all. Well, of course, you can't, but you are right to try. Perhaps you can for Ned, too, because there's no real reason to suppose anything so dreadful has happened."

"I hope it hasn't," Bobby said. "Very likely it hasn't. But it is quite plain that you think it possible. I want to know, and I am speaking as a police officer, what grounds you have for your suspicions?"

He had spoken designedly in his most formal and official manner. It often impressed people. Sometimes he even said: 'In the name of the King'. Such expressions had their effect, often went far to make people more willing to help. But on Mrs Bloom no such effect was produced. In her impassive way, she merely said:

"If I knew anything, I think I would tell you. But I don't. I mean I know nothing to explain why Ned has not come home. It has never happened before, and I don't understand it. I am not going to say anything when I don't know. It is so easy to suspect people who are quite innocent. Is there anything more dreadful than to throw suspicion on some one who is innocent?"

"Isn't it better for innocence to be proved?" Bobby asked.

"It is better for it not to be questioned," she answered. "It always sticks—suspicion, I mean. Have you never thought what it would be like for an innocent person to be put on trial, to suffer all that long agony, even if acquitted in the end?"

Before Bobby could answer the tall girl he knew as Kitty came briskly in and then stopped and looked surprised when she saw Bobby. To Mrs Bloom she said:

"One tea."

Mrs Bloom took down one of the two-and-twenty kettles, one of the smallest, and put it on the gas.

"I thought we had finished for the day," she said. "Don't wait. Mrs Skinner will be wondering what's keeping you. Liza and I can manage." Kitty hesitated and looked at Bobby as if doubtful whether he could be trusted, or perhaps it was merely human curiosity to know why he still lingered.

"Mother won't mind," she said finally. "She knows there are always late customers."

She took a tray from a pile near and began to arrange it, keeping a distrustful eye on Bobby as she did so. To Mrs Bloom Bobby said:

"I understand a light was reported in one of your outbuildings late last night."

"The policeman came about it," Mrs Bloom agreed. "He went to look. I went with him. There was no one there."

"It was used by your son, wasn't it?" Bobby asked. "I should like to look over it myself, if you don't mind."

Kitty had her tea ready now. Mrs Bloom said to her:

"Will you show the inspector where it is? I'll take the tea out. Nothing to eat?"

"No, she said only tea," Kitty answered. To Bobby she said: "It's this way."

Bobby followed her. He thought he had been handed over to her guidance because Mrs Bloom wished to avoid further questioning. Mrs Bloom puzzled him greatly. In a lesser degree, so did this young woman by whose side he was walking and who in manner, in bearing, in every way, seemed so different from the ordinary tea-garden waitress. But then there was a war on, and war, like poverty, makes strange fellowships. The tea garden was deserted now except for the one late customer. He recognized her as the younger of the two women he had seen in Mr Roman Wright's garden, the artist's niece, as he supposed.

"Isn't that Miss Wright, from Prospect Cottage?" he asked his companion.

"Yes, I think so. Why?" Kitty asked in her turn.

Bobby did not attempt to reply to the 'Why?'—to which, indeed, there was no answer. Nothing surprising in a resident of the village coming here for tea. Getting an occasional meal out was a frequently adopted expedient for saving rations—especially for saving tea, as so many people found the official two ounces sadly insufficient. Mrs Bloom was coming across to her, carrying a tray with its small tea-pot and solitary cup and saucer. Miss Wright was watching her, and paid no attention to Bobby and Kitty as they walked by.

"Your name is Skinner, isn't it?" Bobby asked Kitty.

She gave him a slightly hostile glance, rather as if she were inclined to ask what business that was of his. However, she contented herself with a slight affirmative nod, and Bobby went on:

"When people are reported missing, we have to make inquiries. Nothing in it generally. Often people, especially young people, have their own reasons for leaving home. Rather a cruel trick, but young people don't think of that. Sometimes it's more serious. Sometimes there's been an accident. Loss of memory, perhaps. I've never known a case myself. But I suppose they happen. Sometimes it's more serious, and this time there do seem to be some disturbing features. Mrs Bloom evidently feels uneasy." He added: "I don't like her uneasiness."

"I know she's worrying," agreed Kitty. "I don't see why. He's a queer secretive boy. I know he had some idea of going to London. I expect that's what's happened."

"Did he say why?"

"No. I didn't pay any attention. It was only something he said casually. I was busy. There isn't time to talk when customers are waiting."

"I suppose not," agreed Bobby. "I heard you speaking about Mr Ned Bloom to one of your customers."

"I didn't know who you were till Miss Bates told me," she said resentfully. "I think you might have said. I thought you were just a customer."

"So I was then," Bobby said smilingly. "A customer who remembered the excellent teas he has had here before. I couldn't help hearing what you said. An army captain. He had his arm in a sling."

"You mean Captain Dunstan," she said, going rather red.

"You seemed to think there had been a quarrel between him and Ned Bloom. Can you tell me about it?"

"I think you ought to ask him, oughtn't you?" she retorted.

"Perhaps so," he agreed. "Can you give me his address?"

She looked as if she would like to refuse, but finally said he was staying with a Mrs Veale at Miles Bottom Farm not far away.

"I think Mrs Veale was his Nannie," she explained.

"Oh, yes—that's interesting," Bobby said.

"Why?" she snapped, but he did not attempt to explain.

Instead he remarked:

"You know, Miss Skinner, I find you rather an unusual young lady to be working as a waitress in a country tea-garden like this."

She stood still, drawing herself up to her full height—which really was not so very much below his own six feet though it looked much more. Icily, though icily is but a poor word, she said:

"Is that any business of yours?"

"I don't know," Bobby answered mildly. "In a case like this I never know what is my business and what isn't."

CHAPTER VII
'THE DEN'

BY NOW THEY had reached a small outbuilding, tucked away at the farthest end of the gardens and hidden by a trellis of climbing roses from that part where teas were served. Originally intended for a potting-shed or something of the sort, it had been smartened up, painted, provided with a small stove, with curtains for the windows, simple furniture, and so on. On the door was stencilled 'The Den'. Bobby stopped Kitty from going too near and began a close and careful examination of it and its surroundings. Somewhat impatiently Kitty said after a time:

"What are you looking for?"

"I wish I knew," Bobby answered.

With now not only an impatient but a scornful air as well, Kitty said next:

"Don't you think you ought to have a big magnifying-glass?"

"Well, big magnifying-glasses have their uses," Bobby admitted. "Indispensable sometimes. But we haven't got that far yet. Can't put a whole hut under a magnifying-glass. Looks like a professional job, though."

"Why?" demanded Kitty.

"Because there's nothing to show. Amateurs always leave traces. Professionals don't."

He pushed the door back and stood on the threshold, looking. The interior had been fitted up, not uncomfortably, as a small sitting-room or study, with a writing-table, chairs, shelves for books, and so on. There was a lamp hanging from the roof and a small stove for heating purposes. But there was something else that Bobby noticed as his intent glance travelled from one object to another. Everything had a disarranged air. The chairs had been pushed aside. The writing-table was a trifle out of place, several of the books were upside down, even the two or three rugs on the floor were crumpled as if they had been lifted and put back in a hurry. When he went farther into the room this impression became even stronger. Some one had been busy there, picking things up and looking at them and then putting them back again, hurriedly and not in quite the places they had occupied before. One could see from the marks on the floor how the writing-table had been moved several inches, and the ragged appearance of the book-shelves told the same story.

He began to look at the books on the shelves. There were several manuals of police work, including Sir Norman Kendal's edition of the monumental work by Hans Grosse. There were also a few books on puzzles and cyphers, others of travel and exploration, and some about boxing and prize-fighting. Fiction was represented by the tales of Edgar Allan Poe and the Sherlock Holmes stories. There were one or two box files as well, marked 'private and confidential'. When Bobby took one down, opened it, and began to examine the contents, Kitty was moved to protest.

"I don't think you ought to do that," she said. "Those are Ned's private papers. He wouldn't like it."

"I shall be only too pleased," Bobby told her, "if I get a chance to apologize to him."

"Did Mrs Bloom say you might?" she asked, still doubtful.

"No," he admitted, "but while I was talking to her, there was a word got itself spoken."

"A word?" she repeated, puzzled.

"Murder," he said, watching her closely.

She stared at him and then began to laugh. Yet he was not quite certain that that laughter was quite natural.

"Oh, that's silly," she declared.

"Let's hope so," he said amiably.

"Who on earth would want to murder Ned?" she demanded, still amused.

"I don't know," he answered, and went on glancing through the file he had opened. As Kitty continued to look doubtful, he added: "I don't think I'm the first."

"The first what?" she asked.

"The first to have a look at Mr Ned Bloom's den in his absence?"

"Why? What do you mean?"

"He was rather tidy and methodical, wasn't he?" Bobby asked. "Box files. That sort of thing. A place for everything and everything in its place idea. That's the first impression you get here, isn't it?"

"Ned's like that," she agreed.

"Well, if you look carefully, you will see that nothing is quite as it should be. Look at those books. Several of them upside down. He is right-handed. I know that, because I've seen him, you know. But the pen-tray on this writing-table is to the left. I think some one has picked it up and put it down in a different place. The rugs are crumpled. Been lifted, I imagine, and not replaced too carefully."

He showed her, too, the marks on the floor which suggested to him that the table had been moved slightly.

"That arm-chair, again," he added. "If you sat in it where it is now, your legs would be cramped. If you wanted to read, your book would be in the shadow. I think some one has been here before us."

"Yes, but," she said, with a somewhat bewildered air, "what . . . why . . . what for?"

"Searching for something, at a guess," Bobby said, "and not with a big magnifying-glass, either. Look at this, too."

He showed her the interior of the box file he had opened. It contained a number of newspaper cuttings, and here it was easy enough to see that they had been disturbed. They were all in an untidy heap now, and Kitty said:

"They do look upset. You do notice things, don't you?"

He went on glancing through the cuttings. They were all reports of criminal cases, of suicides, mysterious disappearances from home, or similar events. A few had pencilled comments. One or two of the cuttings dealt with cases in which Bobby himself had been concerned, and these were endorsed with severely critical comment. Bobby read them with interest.

"He spotted where I went off the tracks once or twice," Bobby remarked aloud, "but he missed a lot, and some of the worst bloomers, too, that I could have told him about."

"Are you going to be long?" asked Kitty, who was beginning to show signs of impatience.

"May be all night," Bobby informed her. "No telling. Police work is like that. My wife says that if you marry a policeman you never know anything about him, except that he's never where you think he is."

"Are you married?" Kitty asked, evidently surprised, as if she had not hitherto supposed any policeman ever had any but a strictly official background.

"It happens," Bobby told her, shaking his head gravely. "It happens to many of us. Why, some day it may even happen to you."

Kitty looked extremely haughty and indignant, and would certainly have said something crushing if only she had been able to think of it. Bobby, continuing to turn over the cuttings, came to one marked in blue pencil:

"Follow this up."

The cutting, from one of the more sensational Sunday newspapers, was headed 'The Strange Case of Admiral Sir Gervase Arlington', and was to the effect that among his service friends and in the circle of his private acquaintances there was much speculation and gossip over the whereabouts of the Admiral. He had a high reputation in service circles, and, before the outbreak of the war, though on the retired list, he had been thought of as likely to be entrusted with a responsible post. But he had been entirely lost sight of. None of his relatives or friends, private or service, knew what had become of him. It was known he had gone abroad in the spring of 1939, and that was all. The paragraph was worded very carefully, and had probably been passed as safe by the paper's legal advisers. But it was easy enough to see the underlying suggestion that possibly Admiral Arlington, like another British Admiral, had had Nazi sympathies and might be one of those potential Quislings of whom the Home Office has some knowledge.

"Just, but only just, on the windward side of criminal libel," Bobby commented. "Unless, of course, they've hit on the truth. But why did Ned Bloom find it interesting, and why did he want to follow it up? Was that what he wanted to tell me about?" Bobby whistled softly and discordantly to himself, a habit he had unconsciously adopted since domestic influence had been brought to bear to induce him to give up a previous habit of rubbing the tip of his nose which had begun to infect all his staff. To Kitty he said: "I think I must take possession of this, so if our young friend turns up unexpectedly, you can tell him I've got it."

He put the cutting down. Kitty picked it up to see what it was. Bobby closed the file and got up to replace it and to take down another. Kitty put the cutting back on the table and went to the door.

"I don't think I'll wait any longer," she said over her shoulder.

"Oh, are you going?" he said. "If you don't mind you might tell Mrs Bloom—"

He broke off abruptly, for Kitty had already gone, without waiting to hear what he had to say. An abrupt departure, Bobby thought, and not very polite. He went to the door, thinking perhaps that she had seen some one there. Nobody was in sight, nobody but Kitty herself hurrying away. Bobby went back, took down another file, and was sure that it also had recently been subjected to a hurried inspection. This time it was a collection of accounts of acts of courage displayed either in actual fighting in the war or else during the attacks on towns and villages by German bombers.

"Significant enough in its way," Bobby told himself, "but not much help to knowing what last night's visitors wanted."

He continued his search. There built itself up in his mind a picture of a young man, morbidly conscious of his physical disability, brooding over it, resenting it, trying to atone for it by an acquisition of knowledge, of knowledge to give power.

One box file was entirely empty, but had plainly been used. Then there was a steel deed-box, provided with lock and key. But this, too, was empty, and Bobby wondered if it had contained whatever had been the object of the previous night's search. He noticed that it had not been forced open, but had either been found unlocked or opened with the key.

He turned his attention to the drawers of the writing-table. There, too, he felt sure another searcher had been before him, but in one of them he found two receipts for registered letters, and both were addressed to Mr McRell Pink at the New Grand, Midwych. The letters had been posted at an interval of a week, and Bobby put both receipts carefully away in his pocket-book. It was getting late now; and, as he thought he had looked in every conceivable spot, he decided to go. One final glance round he gave, and noticed a letter-rack hanging on the wall. It held several old soiled envelopes and one or two circulars, apparently pushed there out of the way. A memory stirred in Bobby's mind, a memory of that story of Edgar Allan Poe's in which a man in possession of a highly compromising letter is supposed to baffle those searching for it by placing it in the most conspicuous position he can think of—in a letter-rack, in fact, hanging on the wall of his room.

CHAPTER VIII
SNAPSHOT SPECIAL

FOR SOME MOMENTS Bobby sat there, looking at the letter-rack and half ashamed of entertaining an idea so fantastic. But then he felt that Ned Bloom, driven in upon himself by a physical defect which his willpower had been insufficient to stand up against, which necessarily excluded him from many of the activities natural to youth, had sought compensation in fantasy. He had seen himself as the great detective; he had identified himself with the heroes of those exploits to the accounts of which one of his box-files had been devoted; he had imagined himself as the power in the background, contemptuously aloof from, but yet aware of, the secrets of others. Anyhow, it was easy to make sure, and Bobby went across to see what the letter-rack really held.

A postcard giving the date of the next meeting of the 'Green Dragon' darts club committee, an old bill or two, an empty envelope, an out-of-date local 'bus time-table, a scrap of paper bearing notes of various small expenses, another envelope that when Bobby opened it proved to hold an unmounted snapshot.

Bobby took it over to the light to see it more clearly. A strange photograph. It was blurred, indistinct, under-exposed probably in bad light and badly developed. But it showed a table, or rather a table-top, covered apparently with some such material as American cloth. On it lay in the foreground a triple row of beads—or were they pearls? Farther back lay, carelessly pushed together, what looked like a pile of jewellery—brooches, bracelets, rings, pendants. Above two hands hovered, one from each side; one hand, Bobby thought, that of a man, the other, smaller and of finer make, probably a woman's.

They made an odd impression, those two hands, held poised above what seemed as if it might be, if the things were genuine, jewellery of great value—of greater value than ever in days when some mistrust all forms of currency, mistrust even such tangible possessions as are not easily portable or as a bomb may destroy, but tell themselves, confident in human vanity, that women will always greatly desire jewels and men always be eager to win their favour by such gifts.

Was it this photograph, this evidence of such a hoard accumulated somewhere in the neighbourhood, for which the hut had been ransacked so thoroughly? Was this the secret at whose possession Ned Bloom had hinted during his visit to Bobby? Was it this, Bobby asked himself, gloomily, that had cost the boy his life?

No need as yet to take so extreme a view. Ned might well be in London, interviewing some private detective and showing a copy of this snapshot as proof that he must be taken seriously.

But, then, nothing to show, even if the photograph was all that it seemed to be, that this triple row of pearls—if pearls they were—or that pile of jewellery, however genuine or no matter of what monetary value, had been acquired dishonestly. It might all be the lawful property of the owners of those two hands held up above it. Bobby reflected that even if young Bloom had shown him this snapshot, there would have been nothing much he could do. No evidence, unless expert examination of the photograph showed some, of unlawful possession. None the less, Bobby knew very well that in London recently there had been two or three large-scale jewellery robberies. Lady Abbey, for instance, had lost her great pearl necklace, said to be worth, Bobby had forgotten how many thousands of pounds. Then Mrs Stokes, wife of the manufacturer of the famous Stokes breakfast food—'Stokes for stoking the fires of health'—had had her jewel-case stolen on one of those railway journeys which are no doubt really necessary. A country mansion or two had had nocturnal visits, with results distressing or gratifying, according to the point of view of burglar or occupant. Nor had so much as a ring or a pin been recovered nor the slightest clue to the culprit or culprits.

No good sitting there, though, staring at this enigmatic print that might mean so much or so little—anonymous photograph, so to speak. Bobby roused himself, fastened the hut door by a bit of broken board in such a way that removing it would upset with a clatter an empty tin behind, and returned to the house. When he knocked, Mrs Bloom came to the door. She stood there, waiting and silent, and once more he was aware of that impression she gave of one who walked in the darkness of past tragedies, of one who had endured so much that ill fate had now no longer power upon her.

A curious idea to have, Bobby reflected, about a woman who spent her days in the quiet, the commonplace, the homely task of providing cups of tea and toasted scones for casual holiday-makers. What does Melpomene in an atmosphere of currant buns and special teas at one and nine? None the less, Bobby could not shake off the sensation of unease and discomfort he experienced, as though it were unpardonable to intrude upon the deep and troubled thoughts of this waiting, silent woman.

He began to tell her what he had done and how he had fastened the door of the hut.

"Some one searched the place pretty thoroughly last night," he said. "Have you any idea who it could be or what they wanted?"

She made a slight negative gesture, and he went on:

"I shall put a man there to-night on watch. To-morrow I had better have another look and make some more inquiries. Of course, if Mr Bloom returns, that will be the end of the matter. At present I still feel uneasy."

She made no comment, standing there still and upright, absorbed, it seemed, in her own dark memories of evil things long past. It was almost as if she had not heard what he said, and yet he was certain that little escaped her attention. He had the idea that part of her mind lay shadowed in the past and that part of it was alert and vigorous to the present.

"Mr Bloom had a camera, I think, hadn't he?" Bobby went on. "Was he keen on photography?"

"He had a small kodak," she answered. "He took snapshots occasionally. I don't think he was very interested in it."

Bobby asked if he could see Ned's bedroom. She took him up to it—a small, tidy, impersonal room. Evidently everything private or intimate had been kept in the hut Ned had called his den. Bobby, before leaving, expressed some conventional hope that the morning would bring good news, and she thanked him in equally conventional terms. She added that if the constable he intended to put on watch would come to the house any time during the night, she would make him a cup of tea. Bobby said that was very kind of her, but he could not dream of allowing her to be disturbed like that. She answered that it would not be disturbing her in any way. She would be sitting up, waiting.

"Wouldn't it be better to try to rest?" Bobby asked. "No good breaking down for want of it. Nothing like a good sleep."

"Nothing so terrible as sleep," she answered, and he did not dare to ask her what she meant.

He went away then, and he had to admit to a feeling of considerable relief, once he was away from the house and her strange presence. He went on to the small local police station, where he arranged, over the 'phone, for a man to be sent out from headquarters to undertake the watch he proposed to set over 'The Den'.

"A plain-clothes man," he told Sergeant Young. "Of course, if Ned Bloom turns up safe and sound, as is quite likely, he will just report to you and go off duty. Oh, and tell him when he gets here that Mrs Bloom says she will be up all night and he can have a cup of tea any time he likes to go to the house and ask her for it. Tell him that will be all right so long as he isn't away more than a few minutes."

Sergeant Young did not look very enthusiastic.

"I'll tell him all right, sir," he said, "but if it was me I wouldn't go up there at night to take a cup of tea with Mrs Bloom, not if you paid me for it, I wouldn't."

"Why not?" Bobby asked.

"Lord, sir," Young answered, "I would as soon go to the churchyard at midnight to have a cup of tea with a corpse fresh out of its grave."

"Oh, nonsense," Bobby exclaimed, but Young shook his head.

"It's the way she takes you," he said.

"Well, her tea-garden seems to do pretty well," Bobby pointed out. "The people I saw there didn't seem to feel like that."

"Does well, and why not?" agreed Young. "Everything of the best. Tea always fresh. Cakes and buns like there wasn't any war at all. But those who drink her tea and eat her cakes and things don't ever see her. I tell you straight, Mr Owen, sir, if she came out and walked about that place of hers, all full of afternoon trippers taking tea, she would empty it same as the passing bell."

CHAPTER IX
DEAD ENDS

ALL NEXT DAY there continued to come in replies to the various inquiries Bobby had instituted. But all were of a negative nature. London reported that no private detective agency admitted having heard of any Mr Ned Bloom. Not entirely conclusive, of course, since, while the more reputable agencies could be trusted, reputable private detective agencies are in a minority. The others would not hesitate to keep to themselves any piece of information out of which they saw any chance of making profit—if they thought they could do so with safety. Nor did London art dealers appear to know anything of Mr Roman Wright. Again not conclusive. Picture-dealers are often inclined to secrecy while engaged in that mysterious process known as 'building up' an artist. There have been instances, too, of artists almost unknown in England and yet enjoying a good market abroad—America or elsewhere.

Nor could he find that there was any information available about Admiral Sir Gervase Arlington. No one seemed to know his present whereabouts. But, then, apparently there was no special reason why any one should know it. Bombed out, perhaps. And a good many people reported 'missing, no trace', during the autumn and winter of 1940. Nor is there any such lack of Admirals on the retired list, only too eager for any war employment in any capacity, as to make it necessary to try to trace one not in the queue. One fact did, however, emerge. Sir Gervase had connections with Germany through a sister of his who had married a German now holding an important post in the German Foreign Office. Sir Gervase had frequently visited the country, and was understood to be on friendly terms with several well-known personalities there. Also the Arlington family was a very old one, had at one time held large estates in Devon and owned the famous Arlington sapphires, of which so many romantic tales were told.

It was Sergeant Payne who had got together this information, though he was not inclined to attach to it any special significance. Nor did he quite understand why Bobby should seem inclined to take so much interest in Mr Roman Wright and his abilities as an artist.

"Well, sir, what's it matter," he asked, "if he was putting on side when he was talking to you? There's plenty like to swank. I've known chaps who hardly knew the difference between a popping crease and a popping ball, but quite ready to talk about the hints they gave Jack Hobbs and how grateful he was."

"Oh, I know," Bobby agreed. "Nothing in all that so very unusual. There are writers who will tell you how they gave Bernard Shaw his best lines and many artists more pally with Mr Augustus John than Mr Augustus John ever knew. All the same, one likes to be sure."

He did not say sure about what. But Sergeant Payne agreed. A safe principle certainly, though perhaps easier in speech than in fact. He went on to give such details as he had been able to gather about Mr McRell Pink. Not many. Results negative again. No one knew anything about him. No one had heard of him before he turned up at the New Grand, demanded an audition, so impressed the manager that he got an engagement on the spot, and had been appearing twice a night three nights a week ever since. His aloof attitude had not endeared him to his fellow artistes, among whom the favourite theory seemed to be that he was dodging the police.

"I suppose he can't be the missing Sir Gervase Arlington," asked Payne, chuckling at the joke.

Bobby smiled feebly, and said it didn't seem likely. He added that reports from Threepence were also negative, as still nothing had been heard of Ned Bloom, and the watch set on his 'Den' had also been without result.

Later in the day came in a report from the experts to whom Bobby had submitted the snapshot found in the letter-rack. Once more almost wholly negative. Too indistinct, too badly developed, for any trustworthy conclusions to be drawn. The objects shown might be genuine jewellery, or again might be imitation. One of the hovering hands was probably a man's. The other was almost certainly a woman's. Careful reasons were given for this conclusion which Bobby had reached at his first glance. It was added, however, that the man's hand showed on the first finger what seemed to be a signet ring, though this was not clearly enough shown for any useful description to be given. The feminine hand appeared to be ringless.

"What it all comes to," said Bobby gloomily, "is a classic example of the blind man looking at midnight in a dark cellar for something that isn't there."

"Yes, sir," agreed Payne, not quite catching this, "but if Ned Bloom isn't there, where is he?"

Bobby began to rub the tip of his nose, checked himself in time, said thoughtfully that that was just it, wasn't it? and proceeded to attend to the rest of his correspondence, which to-day had been a little less copious, less secret and confidential, less contradictory than usual. One communication held his attention. It was an almost apologetic note, dated from Theodores—pronounced Tedders—a country mansion near the southern boundary of the county of Wychshire. A Miss Thea Wood who described herself as secretary to Lady Vennery, wife of Lord Vennery, had written it. Lord Vennery was a well-known personage, who had recently crowned a highly successful business career by accepting a peerage in recognition of his many gifts for charitable and educational purposes—not to mention others, less widely known, to the party purse. Apparently Lady Vennery had thought it well the police should be informed of certain facts. But as Lord Vennery, Lady Vennery, and Miss Wood all alike believed that 'police' meant Scotland Yard, and Scotland Yard alone, it was there the letter had gone in the first place. Now it had reached Bobby, and the languid interest with which he had started to read it quickened to sudden excitement when he saw the name of Ned Bloom. It appeared that earlier in the week—on the morning, indeed, of the day on which Ned had appeared at county police headquarters—a 'phone message had been received at Theodores from some one giving that name and conveying a warning to keep a sharp look-out during the afternoon and evening of the forthcoming week-end. "Mischief is brewing", said the 'phone mysteriously, and then was silent. Miss Thea Wood's letter explained, still apologetically, that there was to be a house party at the time mentioned. Wealthy and important people would be present. Probably the whole thing was merely some form of silly joke. But Lady Vennery was nervous, and wished the warning passed on to the authorities, though Lord Vennery wanted to ignore the incident entirely.

Bobby felt very annoyed. He decided that if and when he met Ned again, he would tell that young man exactly and precisely what he thought of him. Apparently he had been scattering mysterious warnings wholesale, then had himself mysteriously vanished, and what was a worried, overworked C.I.D. inspector to do about it?

Had Ned really got hold of something serious, and, if so, what? Was this another thread in an unknown, uncompleted pattern slowly working itself out to its appointed end? Or was it all just a succession of mares' nests, their origin the fantasies of a morbidly imaginative, over-sensitive boy? This Theodores business sounded very much like a piece of mischief, a showing off, a fantasy from some sort of compensatory daydream, wherein the cripple from birth saw himself as the power in the background. Possibly he had even got what is called a 'kick' merely from ringing up so important a place as Theodores and talking to its occupants, just as the organisers of charitable appeals believe that it helps to ask for donations to be sent personally by name to some famous peer or politician, even though everybody knows perfectly well that the envelope will be opened by one girl typist and the receipt made out by another, using a rubber stamp for the great man's signature.

Once more Bobby rang up Sergeant Young, and once more received the monotonous reply that nothing had been heard of Ned. Next he rang up home, and astonished his wife by suggesting that she should accompany him that evening to the New Grand.

Olive sounded quite bewildered. The entertainment provided at the New Grand did not greatly attract her nor had Bobby hitherto shown any signs of such a preference. She reminded him that the Old Vic Company was paying Midwych a visit. Then there was a Priestley play running, attractive alike to the highbrow, the middle and the low. There were even films that might be worth a visit. So Bobby explained there was a Mr McRell Pink at the New Grand he had heard a lot about and whom he wanted to see. Slightly peeved, Olive said, oh, all right, but it did seem a waste of a perfectly good evening, and so Bobby rang up next the New Grand and secured two seats, for which he had to pay much more than he liked, since all the cheaper seats were already booked.

CHAPTER X
MUSIC-HALL

OLIVE'S INNER conviction that she had been condemned to a melancholy, boring evening was more than justified up to the moment when Mr McRell Pink appeared. Then, in spite of all prejudice, in spite of lingering regrets for her Priestley play, for her Old Vic company, she had to admit herself amused—if amusement is the right word to describe a condition of doubled-up mirth.

Mr Pink proved to be a fat little man with a head nearly as big as his body, and long legs and arms continually getting in his way and continually regarded by him with pained surprise when they did so. He was an expert ventriloquist, and he possessed the valuable knack of getting people to join in a chorus so heartily that they felt they were a part of the show and that therefore it was and must be a good show. He was an admirable raconteur, too. During the whole of his turn he was alone, depending in no way on the common trick of exchanging insults with a companion; and yet he was so active, he dodged with such agility about the stage, he changed his voice and manner so often and so completely that there was no effect of monotony. One advantage he possessed, the greatest any performer can possess, though one that has to be worked for—he had become so established a favourite with his audience that they were all ready to laugh before he opened his mouth. Indeed, if he had merely remarked that it was a fine day, he would have sent most of them into roars of laughter.

Humour at the New Grand had a certain tendency to be what is called broad—broad as the seven seas, indeed—but Mr McRell Pink's nearest approach to impropriety was his story of the A.T.S. girl who complained to her officer that a country march made her feet ache worse than ever they had done when she was a street-walker—and that tale owed much of its success to the perfect imitation of the girl's guileless voice and of the officer's cultured tones trying to conceal an appalling doubt. Then there was an equally exact rendering of the broad Wychshire accent, in which a Midwych lady on a Cook's tour before the war was supposed to tell how in Normandy they had shown her in an ancient abbey a window that went back to William the Conqueror, but she didn't know why it went back, probably didn't fit or something. Then she complained of her bad luck at Venice. Sunny enough when she arrived, but it had been raining that hard the whole place was flooded. She went to Pisa, too, and when she got back their Annie wanted to know if she had found out what made the tower lean. Silly, because if she had, she would have taken one herself. Finally he brought down the house by asking if any one there had heard the story about the Scotsman who treated an Englishman to a drink. The house answered No and waited expectantly, whereupon he said he hadn't either and skipped away.

Olive, whose chief appreciation had been given to the brief sketch of the man in the kitchen after listening to Mr Freddie Grisewood of the B.B.C. kitchen front, told Bobby she thought it one of the cleverest performances she had ever seen, and Bobby said he thought so, too, and she wouldn't mind, would she, if he went behind for a few minutes to make Mr McRell Pink's further acquaintance? Therewith he departed; and Olive could not help wondering if he were really the husband she had once thought, when he could leave her thus, alone and unprotected, to meet the full blast of the jazz band which was the next item.

Behind the scenes Bobby's request for an interview was met with a flat refusal, and, on his insisting, he was referred to the manager, whose refusal was even more flat—flat as the Platonic flatness idea, indeed. It didn't matter who it was, explained the manager. Even an emissary from the B.B.C. wanting him for a broadcast had been refused, just like any ordinary common mortal. As for newspaper men—Mr Pink had a positive phobia about newspaper men. Hadn't Bobby seen his sketch 'Newspaper man interviewing newspaper man'? The only really spiteful, vicious thing in his whole repertoire. So Bobby explained he was neither B.B.C. emissary nor yet a newspaper man, and produced his official card.

"Just a little information we think he may be able to give," he explained hastily. "Nothing, of course, to do with Mr Pink personally."

The manager still hesitated. He said there was no contract with Mr Pink. Mr Pink would never sign anything. An engagement for one night only, and paid for cash down each night. Nothing to prevent Mr Pink clearing out for good any time he chose. Most unsatisfactory arrangement, but there it was; and if

Mr Pink took offence, he, the manager, might lose at any moment the biggest draw on the New Grand programme.

But Bobby still insisted; and as the New Grand licence had more than once been in danger and probably would be again, so that the good-will of the police was important, the manager sighed and surrendered. Fortunately he was not very clear about the distinction between the County and the City police and their respective spheres, and Bobby made no great effort to enlighten him.

So off the manager went to ask Mr Pink to make an exception to his draconian rule of 'no visitors', and returned presently to say that Mr Pink had no idea what it was all about, but if the police insisted, he supposed they must have their way. Bobby said that was very kind of Mr Pink, very kind indeed, and would save a lot of trouble. Introduced into the performer's dressing-room, Bobby found him busy renovating his make-up for the second house. He abandoned this task when Bobby appeared, his countenance thus half made up looking more grotesque than ever. Indeed, in what was apparently nervousness at Bobby's intrusion, he began dabbing at it with a towel, and so reduced it to just one vast smear.

"I don't know," he said in an irritable, high-pitched voice as he peered at Bobby over the towel, "what right you have to force your way in here in this manner?"

"No right at all," Bobby answered, "except the right every police officer has to call upon every citizen for aid and assistance in the performance of his duty."

"I don't know what you mean," grumbled the other. "Nothing I can do that I know of."

"Of course not," Bobby agreed, "but police would soon be at a standstill but for the help they get from the public, and often from those who have the least idea they can give it. What I wish to ask is what you can tell me about Mr Ned Bloom, of the Pleezeu Tea Gardens at Threepence."

"Never heard of him or the what do you call it either," retorted Mr Pink.

Bobby looked at him steadily. Still more nervously the other dabbed at his face, making it still more one vast, grotesque smear.

"Are you quite sure?" Bobby asked gently. "If you tried to re-member—tried hard. So easy for a name to slip one's mind."

"Can't remember something you've never known," Mr Pink grumbled sullenly. "I tell you I've never heard of the chap."

"Well, it's a little odd," Bobby said, "because, you see, I have here the receipt for a registered letter sent you by him."

Mr Pink was certainly taken aback, would probably have looked it had his countenance showed anything but a confused mess of greasepaint. After a time he mumbled:

"I never read letters. I never do. I get a lot, but I just throw them into the waste-paper basket. I never even open them."

"Even registered letters?"

"Registered letters, too," declared Mr Pink firmly. "I don't suppose I should even notice they were registered—just chuck 'em in with the rest."

"An unusual proceeding," Bobby remarked. "May I ask the reason?"

"Because I choose, that's all," retorted Mr Pink. "Can't a man do what he likes with his own letters? Any business of yours?"

"Well, I don't know; it may be or may not," Bobby answered. "You see, Mr Ned Bloom has disappeared, and it is part of police duty to try to trace missing people if their relatives are uneasy or if there is any reason to suspect something may be wrong."

"Why should there be?" demanded Mr Pink. "What do you mean—disappeared? Gone off for a day or two on his own, most likely. Nothing for Mrs Bloom to worry about. Is she worrying?"

"Well, naturally. Most mothers worry when an only son vanishes without a word of explanation. Besides, he came to see me just before."

"To see you? What about? What did he say?" demanded Mr Pink, and Bobby was certain that in his voice as he asked this question there was deep anxiety.

"He didn't make himself very clear," Bobby answered, and was sure again that now anxiety was replaced by relief.

But that was about all Bobby, in spite of further questioning, could extract from Mr McRell Pink. The last glimpse Bobby had as he closed the door of the dressing-room behind him, showed the performer turning with relief to his mirror and his grease-paints to reconstruct his ravaged face.

All the same, Bobby had the conviction clear in his mind that all this clearly meant something, though exactly what was anything but clear.

CHAPTER XI

LITERARY REMUNERATION

CONVINCED, TOO, WAS Bobby by now that he must do all he possibly could to find out what, reality or mare's nest, lay behind all these activities of young Ned Bloom, and what consequences for Ned himself they had produced, if any.

Because it was still possible that next morning the young man might turn up, smiling and complacent, to explain he had just been having a day or two's holiday, and what was all the fuss about? In which case Bobby himself would look a bit of a fool, and that was a prospect that did not appeal.

Next morning, when he again rang up the Threepence police-station, it was to be told that still there was no news. Fortunately the lull in the daily barrage of official documents continued; and after a comparatively early lunch he found himself free to cycle out once more to Threepence, a preliminary 'phone call having warned Sergeant Young to expect him.

"It's got about as young Ned's missing," Young reported on Bobby's arrival, "and most seem to think it's a good riddance. He wasn't liked, sir—that touchy and quarrelsome and always trying to ferret out what was no concern of his. It's only his being like he is, with that foot of his, as saved him from a good thrashing more than once. And now it's going about that old Mr Skinner threatened to put a bullet in him not so long ago, if he caught him again peeping and prying."

"Who is Mr Skinner?" Bobby asked. "Any relation to the Miss Skinner at Mrs Bloom's?"

"Her father. A very superior old gentleman, Mr Skinner, but lost all his money, seemingly, and now he and his lady have to depend mostly on what Miss Skinner earns, him being unable to work through being tied to his chair with rheumatics in the legs and Mrs Skinner not much better at her age, though a pleasure to pass the time of day with. Miss Skinner is a real lady; but she works just the same as if she wasn't—looks after the old people, does most of the garden, and as smart as you like at Mrs Bloom's place, and always pleasant and friendly like."

"Couldn't she get a better job?" Bobby asked. "Plenty going, you would think, for a capable, educated girl."

"I reckon," explained the sergeant, "she doesn't feel she can leave the old people for long. It's only two minutes from Mrs Bloom's by the back, and any time things is slack she can pop in on them. Old Mrs Skinner is getting a bit tottery, and the old gentleman tied fast to his chair, though you wouldn't think it, to look at him, and not the sort of gent to take liberties with, either."

"Doesn't the doctor think he'll get better?" Bobby asked carelessly.

Sergeant Young looked a bit puzzled.

"I don't think he has a doctor, sir," he said finally. "Says he don't believe in them and they've never done him any good from the start."

"I see," said Bobby. "What about this talk of putting a bullet into Ned? Has he a gun of any sort? I don't remember any Skinner in the firearms register."

"Well, sir, I took it that was just talk."

"Very likely," agreed Bobby; "only a pity it was talk to a man who has since disappeared. Have they been here long?"

"No, sir. They came just after the war began. Been living in France, but got out in time."

"Where do they live now?" Bobby asked, and added that perhaps he would try to have a chat with Mr Skinner before he went back to Midwych. He went on to ask what Young knew of Mrs Bloom. Not much, apparently; though that seemed to be chiefly because there was not much to know, and perhaps also because she was not a person it was easy to know. "She puts the wind up you without you knowing why," declared Young. She had lived in Threepence ten years or so, arriving there as the new proprietor of the Pleezeu Tea Garden, then in anything but a flourishing condition. She had turned it into a very successful little concern, and she had also built up a very good business in cakes. Her cakes, it seemed, were famous, and probably this line could have been much further developed had she been willing to employ more labour. But apparently she preferred to do everything herself with the sole aid of Miss Bates, Ned, and a waitress or two—four, in actual fact, before the war; but now only two—Kitty Skinner and the Liza child. She lived an entirely secluded, hard-working life, so seldom stirring beyond the confines of her own domain that many of her neighbours did not even know her by sight. Young seemed to think it wasn't a bad idea for her to stay so much in the background. Apparently he considered that people might have relished her cakes less had they seen her more.

"Makes you think," said Sergeant Young, "that that's the way Lazarus looked when he came out of the tomb."

Bobby listened to all this in silence; merely encouraging Young to chatter on by the occasional gift of a cigarette, accepted by Young without gratitude and solely to oblige a senior officer, since he himself was firmly of opinion that only a pipe, an old pipe and very foul, made tobacco worth while. Still, as all sergeants know, inspectors have to be humoured.

Probably Bobby would have been inclined to dismiss most of what he was told as imaginative nonsense had he not himself retained so strong a memory of the strange impression she had made on him, as of one who stood apart from all the common hopes and friendliness of everyday life. Now that he had seen and talked to her, that comparison Sergeant Young had made with one risen from the dead did not seem so fanciful, or so far-fetched, as it might otherwise have done.

"Did Ned get on well with his mother?" Bobby asked.

"Well, sir, there was some said," Young answered hesitatingly, "that when the beer was in at the 'Green Dragon', which he used pretty regular like, he often got very sorry for himself. Blamed his mother for that foot of his, and why had she let him live? Why hadn't she smothered him in his cradle? Hadn't she ever heard of mercy killings?"

Bobby said it was all very worrying, and especially worrying to think there might be no reason to worry. Was there any one else likely to be able to give any information—any one with whom Ned might still be in communication? Or any one with whom he had been specially friendly—or on specially bad terms, for that matter? There was a Captain Dunstan, for instance, staying in the neighbourhood, and Bobby had heard there had been a quarrel between him and Ned. Did Sergeant Young know anything about that?

The sergeant shook his head. He knew there was an Army gentleman at Miles Bottom Farm, recovering from an accident. He knew also that the Army gentleman seemed much attracted by Mrs Bloom's cakes and teas. He knew again that the Army gentleman had been seen calling at the Skinner cottage, where, however, his reception had not been cordial. Miss Skinner was an extremely attractive girl, and he wasn't the first by any means who had tried to start a flirtation with her. But Miss Skinner wasn't that sort—no one got any change out of her. Nor had any boy as yet been permitted to cross the threshold of the paternal cottage.

"Freezes 'em out, so she does," explained Young, with a faint chuckle. "Scares 'em as bad as does Mrs Bloom her own self, only different like, if you see what I mean. She'll give you a smile when she's serving you because you're a customer, and that's thrown in as a makeweight, and all the same, whether you're a boy or the oldest old lady in Threepence. Only difference: the smile for the boy is professional and he had best remember it, or be squashed same as a cream bun under a tank, while the old-lady smile would be more than meant."

All the same, Bobby had to remember that in fact there had been a quarrel between Captain Dunstan and Ned, accompanied apparently by a threat, or at least a hint, of violence. And when a quarrel centres round an attractive girl and two young men, the cause is not difficult to guess, as Bobby told himself, and there is always the possibility that the consequences may be grave. Sex rivalry and sex excitement can produce strange results.

An interview with Captain Dunstan seemed indicated, and Bobby asked the way to Miles Bottom Farm. Young told him the best route to follow, and that it would take him past the Skinner cottage, too, so Bobby decided to call there on his way. He asked again if Young could not think of any one in the village or vicinity likely to be able to give useful information.

"I did hear young Bloom had been talking about a visit to London," he added. "Know anything about that?"

Young shook his head. There was the parson, certainly—Mr Martin Pyne. A hard-working clergyman like Mr Pyne naturally gets to know a good deal about his parishioners, though Ned had never been a regular member of the congregation. Recently, he had attended church sometimes, but chiefly, it seemed, for the purpose of criticising Mr Pyne's sermons, which, indeed, were of no more than average merit. Possibly he bestowed on them even too much preparation, and that made them seem a trifle laboured and aloof in tone. Both Friday and Saturday afternoons and evenings he gave so entirely to their preparation as to be invisible—'unget-at-able', the parish said—during those times. Besides, Mr Pyne was a much-occupied man. Since his widowed sister and her boys had come to live with him, he had undertaken a good deal of literary work. Ned, indeed, in his usual sneering way, had suggested that the afternoons and evenings ostensibly given to sermons were really devoted to this extra work. By it at any rate he appeared to earn enough to pay for the education of his sister's three boys, since she herself had been left penniless on her husband's death. There was, however, or so it was understood, some claim against the Government for scientific work he had been engaged in. Probably, Sergeant Young opined, a claim that would come to nothing, Government departments being notoriously unwilling to part with money. Odd that men, as officials, could be guilty of meannesses they would never consent to as private individuals.

Bobby agreed with this point of view, having experience, having more than once endeavoured to obtain for his men or their dependants payments that he was promptly informed were forbidden under section XX/365,642, clause 37, or by Regulation 27B 198. He was interested, though, by the remark about literary work.

"What sort of literary work?" he asked.

Sergeant Young had no idea. Literary work to him was just literary work, just as digging was digging or carpentry carpentry. Mr Pyne was a very learned gentleman. Probably that was why his sermons seemed a little—well, productive of somnolence.

"Bring him in a deal of money, though, does his writing work," declared Young, plainly much impressed by learning that was not only rare, but remunerative. "Living's a poor one, but with what he makes writing like, he keeps them three boys at Eton."

Bobby was indeed impressed. Few country clergymen earn enough by literary work—especially not by 'learned' literary work—to keep three boys at Eton. Six or seven hundred a year at the least, he supposed. Bobby began to think that Mr Martin Pyne must be some one like Mr J. B. Priestley or the late Edgar Wallace in disguise.

CHAPTER XII
IDENTITY CARDS

THE SKINNER COTTAGE stood alone, a small and humble dwelling in a small and humble garden, a garden devoted more to flowers, it seemed, than were most of those nearby, where cabbages and carrots seemed your only wear. When Bobby knocked there came to the door a fraillooking old lady, dressed as simply as any cottager, but showing plainly in every gesture, in her manner and in her speech, to what good use she had put the privileges that ease of circumstance can confer.

Bobby offered his apologies for troubling her and asked if he could see Mr Skinner. He explained who he was and said he was making inquiries about Mr Bloom. Mr Bloom had disappeared from his usual surroundings, and it had been suggested that possibly Mr Skinner might be able to suggest an explanation.

"My daughter told us Mrs Bloom was feeling very worried," the old lady said in her gentle voice. "But I don't think my husband can help in any way. Will you come in?"

She drew back to admit him. The door opened directly into the kitchen, the cottage being of that type known as 'two up and two down', kitchen and scullery on the ground floor, two bedrooms above, this being considered ample accommodation for even the largest family—if, that is, of the labouring class. The kitchen was dark, looked damp, and yet had a pleasant and comfortable appearance. It showed at once both great poverty and a cultured appreciation of what the use of line and colour can do, with the simplest means, to make a pleasing whole. In an invalid chair sat an elderly man, his legs covered by a thick rug. He had large, well-shaped features and in his youth must have been a handsome and striking personality. Now his hair was white, his skin too pale, about his mouth lines of pain and suffering. But his gaze was still strong and direct, and there was still something grim and daunting in that strong gaze of his, in his whole expression, indeed. One had the impression of a ruin, perhaps, but of a ruin which yet held fierce hidden fires. Bobby noticed specially his hands—large, well-shaped, firm. There was about him, too, an air as of one more used to command than to obey. As ill suited he seemed to his present surroundings as was his daughter to her present rôle of tea-room waitress.

"What's all this?" he demanded when Bobby entered, in his strong voice that note of authority which went so well with his personality, if not with his humble environment. "Police inspector, are you? You've got your warrant card, then?"

Bobby produced it. Mr Skinner examined it and handed it back.

"Well, what is it you want?" he said then, with a tone and manner that made Bobby feel less like a responsible officer of police conducting a serious inquiry than like a subordinate presenting a report he had little reason to suppose higher authority would receive with any great favour.

"I'm making inquiries about Mr Ned Bloom," Bobby explained again. "He came to see me the other day, and since then nothing seems to have been heard of him. Naturally his mother is anxious. So am I, for that matter."

"Came to see you, did he?" growled the old man, and once again Bobby thought he detected the note of uneasiness, even of alarm, that reference to the young man's visit was so apt to produce. "What about?"

"That, of course, I am not prepared to say," Bobby answered.

"Oh, you aren't, aren't you?" thundered Mr Skinner—'thundered' is hardly an exaggeration, it sounded like thunder in that small kitchen. "Why not?"

"Oh, well," said Bobby smilingly.

Mr Skinner glared more formidably than ever. Bobby remained unaffected. Mr Skinner rested two great gnarled hands on the arms of his invalid chair and seemed as if, had he had the power to move, he would have launched himself upon Bobby. Old, helpless in his chair, surrounded by every sign of great poverty, he managed still to give the impression of a seated Jove, preparing to launch his thunderbolts upon all who opposed his will. Mrs Skinner said in her mild old voice: "Now, Jerry". He turned at that the full force of his whole fierce, dominating personality upon her. She said again, more mildly than ever: "Now, Jerry, dear". The seated Jove collapsed. In quite a chastened voice he said to Bobby:

"Well, why come to me?"

"Because," explained Bobby, "it has been reported to me that you have used threats towards him."

"Who told you that?" demanded Mr Skinner.

"There you see, Jerry," said Mrs Skinner, so exactly in the voice of a nurse rebuking a naughty small boy that Bobby had to smile.

"What sort of threats?" asked Mr Skinner next, and Bobby noted that Mr Skinner seemed a good deal more accustomed to asking questions than to answering them.

"I'm told the actual expression used," Bobby answered, "was that you would put a bullet in him."

Mrs Skinner remained silent, but she might just as well have said out loud: "There, you see, Jerry, and serves you right, too"; so plainly did her whole attitude express it.

Mr Skinner, still pursuing his role of questioner rather than questioned, said:

"Suppose I did, does that mean you think he is missing because I shot him?"

"That would be rather jumping to conclusions, wouldn't it?" observed Bobby mildly. "I gather you agree it's what you did say?"

"I caught him sneaking about the garden, trying to peep and eavesdrop. He made off when he saw me. I couldn't follow. You can't chase any one when you're laid up in dry dock like this. I shouted after him. That's all. It would have served the little—" Here a warning cough came from Mrs Skinner—"the young fool right if I had, and I hope I scared him. And," he added, "I told my girl to warn him I meant it."

"Our daughter is engaged at Mrs Bloom's tea-garden," explained Mrs Skinner gently. "She is a waitress there."

"I think I had the pleasure of seeing her the other day," Bobby said. "May I ask you a rather personal question? Miss Skinner is an extremely attractive young lady. Is it possible Ned Bloom was trying to pay her attentions that possibly neither you nor the young lady much appreciated?"

Mrs Skinner smiled faintly, very faintly, very tolerantly. Evidently such a suggestion did not strike her as one to be taken seriously. Mr Skinner looked at first utterly bewildered, seemed to be gathering all his wrath for one stupendous outbreak, and then unexpectedly collapsed into a chuckle.

"Bless my soul," he said, "Kitty and that little twerp . . . ."

"Now, dear," said Mrs Skinner, inclined to be severe again, "you mustn't forget the poor boy's misfortune."

"Poor boy indeed," snorted Mr Skinner. "Upon my word, Nell, I believe you would make excuses for the devil himself."

"Well, you know, I've often thought," mused Mrs Skinner, "he must be dreadfully unhappy."

"Pah," said her husband, looking very disgusted. He turned to Bobby. "Kitty is quite able to deal with that sort of thing," he said. "Anyhow, why should that make him come prowling about my garden late at night peeping and listening?"

"You don't know that was what he was doing," said Mrs Skinner.

"Looked like it," said Mr Skinner.

"That is when you threatened to shoot him?" Bobby asked.

"Being unable to give him what he wanted, a good kick on his behind."

"Jerry," said Mrs Skinner, shocked.

"Well, that's where it would have done most good," said Mr Skinner, unabashed.

"I see," said Bobby thoughtfully. "By the way, have you firearms in your possession?"

For once Mr Skinner was thoroughly taken aback. Finally he said:

"I think I've answered enough questions. I've told you what I said and why. I wanted to give him a fright. That's all. I don't think you need take it seriously. If you choose to, you must. I don't think it necessary to continue this conversation, and I decline to answer any more questions."

"You are, of course, within your rights," agreed Bobby pleasantly. "Every one has a right to refuse to answer questions, but it is a right it is not always wise to exercise. I am afraid there is one thing more. May I see your identity card? I am sure you know a police officer has a right to ask that."

Mr Skinner did not answer, though he gave the impression of wishing to say much. He glanced at his wife. She went upstairs and came back with them.

"Miss Skinner has hers with her," she said.

"Quite right," agreed Bobby. He looked at them. They seemed in order. He read out the names: "'Harold Maurice Skinner, Agnes Alice Skinner.' Thank you. They were issued when you returned from France, weren't they?"

"After the outbreak of the war," Mr Skinner answered. "We had been living in France till then." He added moodily: "I hope you are satisfied?"

"I shall not be able to call myself satisfied," Bobby answered gravely, "till I know what has become of Mr Ned Bloom." After a pause he added, still more gravely: "Perhaps not then."

CHAPTER XIII
FRUITFUL VISIT

BOBBY LEFT THE Skinner cottage—as befitted its humble condition it had neither number nor name—and went on towards Miles Bottom Farm. He had to pass not far from the Threepence parish church, and near it he noticed a monstrous barracks of a building that he guessed was probably the vicarage. It struck him that this might be a good time to find the vicar at home and that he might be able to provide some helpful information. Bobby turned aside, therefore, taking a convenient path that led direct to vicarage and church. The church was comparatively modern, having been largely rebuilt towards the end of the eighteenth century after a disastrous fire. The vicarage was older, dating probably from the beginning of the same century, when parsonic families always ran to double figures, when accommodation was required for tithes paid in kind, when servants cost little more than their keep, and their keep cost almost nothing. But now we have changed all that, and it is no longer by any means the same. Bobby, as he drew near, surveyed it with something like awe, and told himself that with a living listed in Crockford at under £200 a year, it was no wonder Mr Pyne had tried to find ways and means of increasing his income—even apart from providing for three nephews at Eton. Most of the windows on the upper floor were boarded up, he noticed, and he thought he saw the curtains of the window of a room on the right of the front door move slightly, as though some one there were watching his approach.

When he knocked, a not too tidy, middle-aged woman—presumably a daily help—came to the door. She said Mr Pyne was in, and took Bobby into a small room at the back, evidently the study, very plainly furnished. Indeed, there was hardly anything in the room that did not look as though long since it had won the right to an old-age pension. Bobby surveyed it with renewed awe. Wonderful to think that this rickety writing-table, this old kitchen chair with one leg recently repaired, produced the wherewithal for the education of three boys at the most expensive school in England, probably in the world. And sure enough there on the mantelpiece was a photograph of three boys. Bobby picked it up to look at it more closely. He noticed at the same time that though the writing-table was covered with books and papers, all of them seemed to deal with the ordinary business of a country parish. Nothing to show the nature of the vicar's remunerative literary work. It struck him, too, that there was something missing he would have expected to find prominent in the room of any working journalist or author. He heard the door open. He replaced the photograph on the mantelpiece and turned. A middle-aged, prim-looking lady was there, simply dressed in black, and appearing embarrassed and nervous. The widowed sister, Bobby supposed, who had recently come to live with Mr Pyne and who was the mother of the three boys in the photograph.

"I am so sorry," she said, "Mr Pyne is not at home. I mean he has been sent for—at least, I mean he had to go out unexpectedly."

"Oh, I'm sorry," Bobby said, a little surprised. "I understood he was in."

"Yes, he was, but he had to go out unexpectedly," the new-comer repeated in the same nervous and embarrassed manner. "He was so sorry—I mean he will be. I'm Mrs Billings—Mr Pyne's sister. Is there any message? It happens quite often—I mean it often happens that Mr Pyne is wanted in a great hurry. Like a doctor. In the middle of the night even, or quite late."

"I'm sure," agreed Bobby politely, "a country clergyman is kept very much on the go—at the beck and call of the whole parish."

Mrs Billings agreed. Not a moment to himself. Never sure from one moment to another where he would be wanted next. Bobby said he must call again, and Mrs Billings looked both relieved and disturbed, and opened the door very wide. Bobby lingered to apologize for his intrusion and for having looked at the photograph of the three boys.

"Three fine lads," he said. "Your own, I think. At Eton, aren't they?"

Mrs Billings looked surprised and a trifle vexed. Not Eton, she said. Such a silly story. She named another school, not one of the magic nine. Probably, indeed, its name had never penetrated the sacred Eton precincts, but nevertheless a school of good standing, and one where the fees and expenses would not be small. Bobby apologized for the mistake, and Mrs Billings said crossly she had told Sergeant Young before her boys were not at Eton, but he seemed unable to grasp that fact. He seemed to think that the only schools in the country were the village school, the Midwych High school, and Eton. Then she opened the study door more widely still, and Bobby, still murmuring apologies, passed into the hall. As he neared the front door he saw through an open door on his left into another small room, where was a table laid for tea—two cups, two plates, on each plate pieces of half-eaten toast. The call for Mr Pyne's services had evidently been so sudden and so urgent that he had not had time to finish what was on his plate.

Bobby went away thoughtfully, telling himself his visit had been a success. Another important item of information gained, though what it all signified he had not at present so much as the ghost of a glimmer of an idea.

The sight of the plates and cups had, however, served to remind him that he wanted his own tea, and it also struck him that if he went to the Pleezeu Tea Garden he would probably have as good a chance of finding Captain Dunstan as at Miles Bottom Farm. Thither therefore he decided to go now, and on the way he met Mr Roman Wright, who greeted him with smiling recognition.

"I had no idea," he said, "when we were having our little chat together, that I was talking to the famous Inspector Bobby Owen."

Bobby, suspecting that this was sarcasm, looked closely at the speaker, Mr Roman Wright continued to smile.

"Excusable, I think," he said. "Somehow one doesn't associate our admirable police force with being so knowledgeable about matters of art. 'A brother of the brush and palette,' I told my niece, I remember. Down at the 'Green Dragon' they say it's about young Ned Bloom you've come. Any news?"

Bobby said none at all, either one way or the other.

"Well, I hope nothing has happened to the young man," said Mr Wright. "Gone off on his own affairs, probably. Any girl missing as well, by any chance?" He paused to chuckle and went on: "At the 'Green Dragon' the most lurid theories are in favour. Suicide, some of them think. The boy never struck me as the suicide type—much too full of his own importance. Though he did sometimes talk a bit wildly, too, when he had had an extra pint."

"In what way?" Bobby asked.

"Oh, a lot of nonsense about why hadn't he been put out of the way when he was born? What was the use of letting a crippled baby live? Hitler had more sense, and he had told his mother so.

Mercy killings they called it in Germany. Not that he meant one word. All that extra pint."

"What did Mrs Bloom think of it, I wonder?"

"No idea. Probably told him to go to bed and not be so silly. I've never seen the woman myself—keeps very much to her kitchen, I'm told. At the 'Green Dragon' they all seem rather afraid of her. I could never make out why; they didn't seem to know themselves. I'm afraid Ned will be more missed than regretted." With an apologetic smile, Mr Wright added, "I hear all the local gossip, playing darts at the 'Green Dragon'."

"I've gathered already Ned Bloom wasn't popular," Bobby remarked.

"Too fond of trying to find out things about you. No idea of minding his own business. I remember he asked me some rather cheeky questions. After all, there are limits. A queer lad. He would boast sometimes about how much he knew and how if he sent letters round to some people about here, just saying 'All is known. Fly,' half of them would. I told him I hoped he wasn't going to send me one. I should hate to have to move in such a hurry."

"Did he try it on with anyone?" Bobby asked.

Mr Wright laughed and shook his head.

"I don't suppose so," he said. "Showing off, that's all. Anyhow, he didn't favour me."

He laughed again, nodded, and went his way, and Bobby continued to the Pleezeu Tea Garden, which was as busy as ever. In spite of the press of customers, Kitty came to his table almost at once. But looking very angry and indignant.

"Why have you been bothering father?" she demanded.

"Well, you know," Bobby answered mildly, "I told him. I've heard he once threatened to shoot Ned Bloom."

Kitty became transformed from a merely normally indignant young woman into a veritable goddess of scorn.

"You don't mean to say—?" she began, and then she asked, and how she asked it: "Are you really silly enough to suppose my father . . . ?"

When she left the sentence unfinished, Bobby answered:

"Oh, well, in the police we often get silly ideas—and sometimes some not so silly."

Kitty gave him a long look and walked away. Bobby watched her go with some disquiet, a trifle afraid he was not going to be allowed to have any tea. But she soon came back, now the calm, efficient waitress with no thought in her mind beyond serving the needs of her customers.

Bobby gave his order, and while he was waiting saw a youngish woman go to one of the more distant tables, and seat herself. He thought he recognized her, and when Liza—not Kitty— brought him his tea, he said to her:

"Isn't that Miss Jane Wright over there? Mr Roman Wright's niece."

"That's right," agreed Liza. "Gomes every afternoon now, and like as not goes away without bite or sup of what she's ordered."

CHAPTER XIV

S.I.W.

BOBBY LINGERED OVER his tea. It was pleasant there in the garden, and he watched with some interest Miss Roman Wright sitting apart and silent at her solitary table. When she got up abruptly and went away, he strolled across. She had poured herself out a cup of tea, but did not seem to have tasted it. The scone on her plate had been crumbled, but little, if any, appeared to have been eaten. Whatever had brought Miss Roman Wright here, it could hardly have been a desire for refreshment. Thoughtfully Bobby went back to his own table, and as he did so saw that Captain Dunstan had arrived and was sitting not far away.

So Bobby went across to him, too. Captain Dunstan greeted him with that stare of outraged indignation reserved by the true Britisher for any intrusion on that privacy wherewith he tries to hedge himself about, even in such public places as restaurants or railway trains. Bobby said:

"Captain Dunstan, isn't it?"

Captain Dunstan said "Well?" and said it in a tone calculated to freeze an iceberg. Bobby once more produced his official card and explained he had been on his way to call on Captain Dunstan.

Possibly the captain could spare time for a few minutes' chat now. It would save time later on. Suspiciously and ungraciously, Captain Dunstan said "All right" and what was it all about?

Bobby seated himself. Kitty came up and regarded Bobby with disfavour.

"The inspector has been asking father and mother questions," she said to Dunstan. "He thinks perhaps father shot Ned—and buried him in the front garden."

"What's that?" asked Dunstan, staring.

"Miss Skinner," explained Bobby gravely, "wants you to know I am a policeman. To warn you against being trapped by the cunning, disguised detective."

"I never," said Kitty, very red and angry.

"Are you quite sure?" asked Bobby mildly.

Kitty turned him a shoulder that only respect for the language saves from being described as 'literally' bristling. It certainly got as near 'bristling' as a shoulder well can.

"What can I get you?" she asked Dunstan in her most ultra-waitressy voice.

"What on earth is it all about?" demanded Dunstan, looking thoroughly bewildered.

"I am making inquiries about Mr Ned Bloom," Bobby explained.

"Well, why come to me?" demanded Dunstan. "I don't know anything about the little bounder, and don't want to. Gone off on his own, I suppose."

"It's all a lot of nonsense," declared Kitty.

"Does Mrs Bloom think so?" Bobby asked.

Kitty looked at him and walked away.

"There," Bobby said to Dunstan, "you've never given any order. Now you won't get any tea."

"Look," said Dunstan, "what's the idea? I don't know anything about Bloom. Why should I? I haven't spoken to the young bounder more than half a dozen times."

"But I understand," Bobby retorted, "that on one of those half-dozen occasions you threatened to knock his head off."

"Well, suppose I did?" growled Dunstan. "Besides, I didn't. All I said was that was what he wanted, only he knew he was safe, or he would be more careful what he said. You can't give a cripple a thrashing, even if he asks for it."

"Do you mind telling me what the trouble was about?"

"Yes, I do."

"I am afraid I must press you."

"Press away."

"Perhaps not necessary," observed Bobby thoughtfully. "A very attractive young lady and two young men. A familiar situation, of course."

Captain Dunstan first looked very amused, then very surprised, and finally very angry.

"Rot," he said briefly, and added the curt order: "Leave Miss Skinner's name out of it."

"Can't be done," said Bobby. "She's in it."

"Look," began Dunstan, "you can't seriously suppose that a little—little . . ." Dunstan searched for a word adequately expressing his opinion of Ned Bloom, and found none. Giving up the quest, he continued: "For that matter, I don't think he ever tried to bother Miss Skinner. A nasty little mischief-making tale-bearer, and wanted to be tarred and feathered. But that's all."

"Had he been trying to make mischief between you and Miss Skinner?" Bobby persisted.

Captain Dunstan tried to control himself. He did not succeed very well. Speaking slowly and with care, as if afraid he might let slip words better not spoken, he said:

"I consider your questions insolent."

"You know, captain," observed Bobby, meditatively contemplating the horizon, "I shouldn't wonder if some of your men didn't consider some of your questions insolent when you want to know why they overstayed their leave or something like that."

"That's entirely different," pronounced Dunstan. "You are not my superior officer, and I have not overstayed leave."

"Perhaps the question is more serious than an overstayed leave," Bobby pointed out gravely. "Nothing has been heard of Mr Ned Bloom for some days. There are disturbing features. It is necessary to be sure. A responsible officer of police making such inquiries has a right to expect, to demand, the help of every citizen. And a soldier is still a citizen. You know a policeman has been defined as a man who is paid for doing what it is the duty of every citizen to do without pay."

Captain Dunstan looked sulkier than ever.

"It's all such nonsense," he complained. "Why should you suppose anything of the sort? What disturbing features, anyhow?"

"Well, for one thing, one person—Mr Skinner—is reported to have threatened to shoot him. Another—yourself—is also said to have used threats. There's a story that he talked of sending letters to people, saying 'All is known. Fly.' I know he sent two registered letters recently to a man who denies knowing anything about them. All in all, I'm getting quite a lot of disturbing information. And I'm also meeting with a good deal of reluctance to answering my questions. People tend to be called away when they see me coming. Unfortunate. Do you still refuse to tell me what was wrong between you and him?"

"Oh, I don't know," Dunstan said. "I suppose it doesn't matter really." He indicated his injured arm in its sling. "The young blighter was putting it about that I did it myself to dodge going abroad with the battalion. We've been told we may be going soon, though of course we've no idea where. Might even be only to the coast. They don't tell us much. I was pretty mad," he ended abruptly.

"Well, yes, I can understand that," agreed Bobby. "Enough to annoy any one. How did you hear, and what made you think Ned was responsible?"

"Mrs Veale told me. She heard a story was going about that it was an S. I. W. She didn't know what it meant, and she asked me. I didn't get it at first. 'S. I. W.' is an old expression from the last war. 'Self-inflicted wound.' Men did sometimes, they got so fed up in the trenches. Mrs Veale's where I'm staying. Miles Bottom Farm. She's my old nurse. She said she thought young Ned Bloom started the talk. She said he was like that. So I asked him. The young fool wanted to fight. That's all."

"I see," said Bobby thoughtfully. "Thank you for telling me. I can understand a story like that would annoy any one. All the same, wasn't it a bit too silly to be taken seriously?"

"It's easy to throw mud, and mud sticks," Dunstan answered. "No one would believe it. But there might remain a sort of vague notion that I wasn't so awfully keen, and that might be enough to turn the scale over an appointment I've applied for. What happened was this. You know live ammo. is used a lot in training. Some ass of an airman muddled his targets and put a burst of machine-gun bullets into a post I was holding against a tank advance. He says he was told the post was only held in dummy and he was to make a token attack to indicate the post was wiped out and the tanks could advance. Luckily for us it was only token, or we should have been wiped out good and proper. Several of my chaps were hit—two or three seriously. My share was a bullet or two through my forearm and wrist. Messed them up a bit. Now I'm on leave. The hospital said I must be careful for a time till the sinews knit up, or something. That's why I have to keep it like this, in a sling." He added, half defiantly: "You can check up on that, too, if you want to."

"Oh, we shall," Bobby assured him. "Routine. Of course, I accept it really, and I'm glad you've told me. May save me from going off on a wrong trail. An investigation can be badly fogged like that, just as minor false information can mess up military operations, I suppose."

"Look," Dunstan said, "you can't believe anything serious has happened to young Bloom? Why should it? You can't really think it has?"

"I always try," Bobby explained, "never to think till I know something to think about. At present all I know is that since he came to see me Ned Bloom seems to have vanished."

"I take it," Dunstan said after a long pause, "you are wondering if I was so mad with Bloom I did him in after he got back from Midwych?"

"Well, naturally," Bobby admitted, "there is the possibility that the quarrel started again—and with unfortunate results."

"Jolly for me," Dunstan observed unhappily.

"Nothing at present," Bobby told him, "to suggest that that is what happened. If it didn't, and if you've told me all you know, you've nothing to worry about."

Dunstan shrugged his shoulders. He did not look much consoled. Bobby said he must take himself off, but he might have to bother Captain Dunstan again, though he hoped not. Captain Dunstan said he hoped not too. Then he asked if Bobby hadn't heard anything else that might help? If he himself heard anything and rang up, would he be able to get in touch with Bobby at his office this week-end? Bobby said "No, he didn't think so", to the first question, and "Yes, certainly", to the second, and Captain Dunstan remarked rather viciously that he had seen so much red tape and officialdom in the Army that he was a trifle pleased to find it in civil life as well.

"If soldiers are citizens still, I suppose police remain civilians," he added as a parting shot.

Bobby wondered vaguely what this cryptic remark meant, supposed that perhaps the captain was merely trying to be rude; and, since he felt there was no more he could do in Threepence for the time, went back to the police station to give Sergeant Young a few final instructions.

"Oh, by the way," he said as he was going, "have you heard any gossip in the neighbourhood to the effect that the Army officer at Miles Bottom Farm—Captain Dunstan his name is—had inflicted his own wound on himself in order to avoid being sent abroad?"

Sergeant Young looked very surprised.

"Good lord, no, sir," he said. "People will say almost anything, so long as it's spiteful, but that's a bit too silly, even for the worst of them. Can't very well machine-gun yourself. Anyhow, there's no such talk going on that we've heard of, and we hear most all."

CHAPTER XV
POSSIBLE PATTERN

OLIVE WAS HARDLY disappointed, merely resigned, when she learned that Sunday, too, was to be a duty day. Long ago she had discovered that while in peace time any day may at short notice become a duty day, in times of war 'duty day' is merely a euphemism for every day and all day.

"Though what you expect to happen at this Theodores place," she complained, her tone showing but small respect or liking for the place referred to, "and why you can't let some one else go instead, I'm sure I don't know."

"It's not so much what I expect," Bobby explained, "because I don't think I expect anything. What I do hope is that there may be a chance of finding out what Ned Bloom expected."

"Why suppose he really expected anything?" Olive demanded. "It all seems so vague and silly. I don't see that there's any need to take it so awfully seriously. I mean sending letters to people about 'all is known. Fly.' It's all so like a rather hysterical boy trying to make up for his lameness by making himself important. What the psychologists call 'compensatory reaction'."

"Yes, I know," Bobby agreed. "But suppose one of those 'All is known' letters happened to be sent to some one who had jolly good reason to 'fly' if 'all was known'? He might try to make sure the 'all' wasn't known to any one else. I'm sure Ned thought he was on something important—something of a criminal nature, or why come to me? He knew something about police work, too. He knew enough to know that whatever it was would be a County police job. Most people think all police are one, and that one Scotland Yard. I expect I shall get into trouble for letting him go so easily."

"But he said he would only tell you if you took him into the force, and you couldn't, could you? Not a boy with a club foot."

"That won't go for anything," Bobby told her. "Only results count, and you are supposed to know by instinct how things will turn out. I daresay the real swells do. The rest, like me, have to wait and see. Even now I don't know. It may all turn out a mare's nest. Ned Bloom may just be spending a pleasant week-end somewhere."

"At Theodores—pronounced Tedders?" suggested Olive teasingly, but to her surprise Bobby took the suggestion seriously.

"I had thought of that," he agreed. "Not actually at the place itself, but hanging around, trying to nose out some tit-bit or another, trying to find material for another of his 'All is known' letters. That's why I want to be on the spot myself. I think it possible he does try to get to know things other people don't want known. If I didn't take him seriously enough, possibly some one else took him very seriously indeed. You remember—there were three 'phone calls that afternoon, asking about him?"

"One was from his mother, wasn't it?"

"Yes. One. But all three claimed to be from her—from his mother, that is—and you can't very well have three mothers. So two were fakes, and why? Again, that shed at the back of the tea-gardens he called his 'Den' had been gone through pretty thoroughly. So some one wanted badly to find something there, and was that something the photograph snap hidden in the letter-rack—à la Edgar Allen Poe? It seems to show what looks like a pile of jewellery, and there have been some big jewel robberies lately. The Stokes jewel-case some one walked off with at Euston, wasn't it? All the Stokesian jewellery in it. Quite a lot, too, the reward for stoking up the fires of health. The great Abbey pearl necklace, too, from the Park Lane flat in London. Others as well. Well, suppose Ned had managed to find out where all that loot is hidden? None of it come on the market yet, as far as we know. Suppose that snap of his shows it?"

"Good gracious me!" said Olive.

"Rather a breath-taking idea," Bobby agreed. "All that stuff hidden somewhere round here, waiting disposal, and Ned Bloom knew it. If he did know it, he knew too much for good health."

"Yes, but—" began Olive, and then paused, looking worried.

"Another thing," Bobby went on. "There is actually a Sir Gervase Arlington, an Admiral in the British Navy—retired, but an Admiral all the same. Once an Admiral, always an Admiral, I suppose. And it is a fact that no one seems to know where he is. His pension is being paid to his solicitors. They say they have instructions how to deal with the money, but have had no communication with their client since before the war. What did Ned Bloom know that made him cut out that newspaper paragraph and mark it 'Follow this up'? Did he follow it up, and, if he did, where did he get to?"

"Why should he have got anywhere?" asked Olive. "You can't suppose—suspect—?"

"Why not?" asked Bobby.

"Oh, well," said Olive, looking resigned.

"I suspect everything and every one," said Bobby. "Take every one I've talked to. Mr Roman Wright, for instance."

"But he's an artist."

"That's not a reason," said Bobby.

"Yes, but there's no connection," protested Olive.

"I know there isn't—very suspicious fact, that," Bobby declared. "Besides, don't you remember what I told you?"

"About the way he talked?" asked Olive. "Nothing in it," she pronounced firmly. "Just showing off. People do. He wants to be thought a great artist, so he has to pretend he makes a lot of money. Proves you're a great artist if you earn big money."

"More likely to prove you aren't," observed Bobby. "But I didn't mean only that. Remember what I told you about Prospect Cottage, where he lives?"

"Oh, well, yes, I see what you mean," admitted Olive, but still doubtfully. "Same thing. He wants to be thought an artist, even if he isn't."

"If he isn't, what is he?" asked Bobby, and went on: "Other things, too. And his niece, Miss Jane Roman Wright. Why does she go to Mrs Bloom's tea-garden and order tea and never touch it?"

"Can't she be worried about Ned?" Olive asked. "Perhaps they're friendly or she's sorry for him or something. Only she doesn't want her uncle to know or any one. So she goes there for tea, though she doesn't want any, just to see if he has got back yet."

"It might be that," agreed Bobby thoughtfully. "You mean she's in love with Ned? I suppose it's possible—goodness knows, women are like that. Fall in love with anything."

"Yes, don't they?" agreed Olive, dangerously meek, "even with policemen, little knowing they'll never see anything of him any more except his coat tails vanishing round the corner."

"I," Bobby pointed out with dignity, "I wear a lounge suit."

"Don't quibble," said Olive severely.

"Then there's Mr McRell Pink," Bobby continued.

Olive smiled. Her smile became broader, it ended in her low, rich laugh.

"Such a funny little man," she said.

"Isn't he?" agreed Bobby. "Only why did Ned send him registered letters? It may be true he destroyed them without opening them. Takes a certain amount of strength of mind to tear up a registered letter unopened, though. Would you?"

"Goodness, no," said Olive in a hurry. "But a man might. Men," said Olive thoughtfully, "will do practically anything—if it's silly," she added as an after-thought.

"You remember he appears only three nights a week—Mondays, Fridays, Saturdays?"

"Gives him scarcity value," suggested Olive. "Makes people queue up, the way they will for almost anything if they think they can't get it."

"Well, there's that," conceded Bobby. "But why does he refuse to see prominent agents or the B.B.C. people?"

"I suppose he's satisfied where he is with what he gets," Olive suggested again. "Unusual, of course, but it's possible. There's Miss Skinner. She stops on working as a waitress where she is, when she could get better-paid work somewhere else, because she has an old father and mother to look after. Perhaps Mr McRell Pink has an invalid wife he won't leave." Olive paused, looked quite sentimental, and then added, less sentimentally: "I've even heard of men who put their wives before their work, though I don't much believe it."

Bobby winced. He went cm hurriedly:

"There's her father—Mr Skinner."

"Invalids tied to an invalid chair," pronounced Olive dogmatically, "are out of it."

"How do we know he's so much of an invalid as all that?" demanded Bobby. "No doctor, apparently. I don't like that identity-card business. Is it genuine?"

"It has to be, hasn't it?" Olive asked. "You can check up, can't you? Why should there be anything wrong with it?"

"I told you," said Bobby reproachfully.

"You didn't," said Olive firmly.

"You'll see I did if you think it over," Bobby told her. "Let's go back to Miss Skinner."

"A girl like her," said Olive, looking disdainful. "There's no need to be ridiculous."

"The man who is afraid to be ridiculous," said Bobby sententiously, "will never be anything else. Besides, you've often told me that now-a-days women can do anything, just like men."

"So they can," said Olive loyally, "except when it's too silly, like seeing whether you can hit some one else harder than they can hit you. Boxing," she explained, in case Bobby failed to get it.

"Well, then, crime is included," Bobby said. "So she's in. Then Captain Dunstan."

"Bobby," Olive cried indignantly, "why, you said yourself you think he's in love with Miss Skinner."

"Again, not a reason," Bobby said. "The Army would be the perfect camouflage for a wrong 'un, wouldn't it? And wrong 'uns make good soldiers sometimes. The hero in war may be the burglar or worse in peace. Bit of a family resemblance between war and crime. Drop him and go on. To the Rev. Martin Pyne."

"Now it's the vicar of the parish," sighed Olive resignedly. "Really, Bobby."

"Why did he clear out when he saw me coming?"

"How do you know he did?"

"Well, anyhow, he wasn't there after I knocked," Bobby pointed out. "Isn't there something else strikes you as a bit queer?"

Olive shook her head. Bobby told her to think hard. She pointed out she wouldn't have to if he told her. He said not likely. It would do her good to work it out for herself, and then she exclaimed suddenly when all at once she saw what he meant.

"But, Bobby," she protested, "I don't see that that need mean much."

"Very likely not, but it's there all the same," he answered, "to remember. Well, leave it at that and go on. Mrs Bloom."

"Oh, Bobby," cried Olive, really outraged this time. "His own mother!"

"I know," Bobby said, "but all the same there is something about her I don't understand. I can't describe it. She is like some one who died long ago, only she still goes on living."

"I don't know what you mean," Olive protested, puzzled.

"I don't either. No one has a word to say against her, but if you mention her they all talk of something else as soon as they can. The authorities wanted to close down her place. Superfluous. Well run and all that, but superfluous. Wouldn't it be better if she would agree to take a job they were sure they could find her—running a British restaurant or a factory canteen—that sort of thing? Better money and less worry, they said. She didn't take much notice. They started to hint they might cut off her supplies. I don't know if they had the right. Do anything under the Defence Regulations, I suppose. No doubt they could have made things awkward for her, if they had tried. She went to see them. They told Payne about it. She didn't say much. Just sat there. Apparently they went all cold and shivery. Finally they were so glad to get rid of her, they told her it was all right, she could carry on. Payne says the man who saw her sent out for a tot of brandy as soon as she had gone."

"What a lot of silly nonsense!" said Olive contemptuously. "I'll go and see the poor woman. I can get the Threepence 'bus at the 'Yeoman Inn' crossing, can't I? Besides, what's all that got to do with her son being away?"

Bobby hesitated, and when he answered it was with some reluctance.

"There's talk going on," he said at last. "About what they call mercy killings. Mr Roman Wright mentioned it, for one. Ned himself seems to have talked about it. When he had had a little too much at the 'Green Dragon'. You know the old saying: 'In Vino veritas'. In beer, 'veritas', too."

"Nonsense," said Olive again, even more contemptuously, more firmly. "Not a mother, his own mother."

Bobby said nothing. Olive found his silence disconcerting. She said:

"I'll never, never, never believe it."

But she had become a little pale.

Bobby said with an air of cheerfulness:

"I expect very likely it'll all end in smoke. If it doesn't, nice lot of suspects I'll have on my hands. His mother. The vicar of the parish. A most superior waitress in a local tea-garden. Her invalid father. A highly successful music-hall comedian. An artist with a steady market in water-colours of Wych Forest. The artist's niece with a fancy for ordering teas she never touches. An Army captain on leave with a wounded arm."

"A scratch lot," pronounced Olive. But she still looked pale and uneasy. "A scratch lot," she repeated.

"Yes, I know," Bobby agreed. "If it's one of them, it's a case of take a pin and spot the loser." Then he said thoughtfully: "All the same, if you put all that together, one thing with another, I do almost think I see—"

"What—?"

"A possible pattern of things that were."

CHAPTER XVI
DISCUSSION

THEODORES was situated in the extreme south of the county of Wychshire, in the rich farmland that was so great a contrast to the lonely forest district and the bare high moors that lay west and north of Midwych city.

From Sergeant Payne, who knew a good deal about the history of the county, Bobby learned that Theodores was a comparatively modern building, dating only from towards the end of the eighteenth century. The former home of the Labois family had been abandoned at that time and this new mansion erected on a new and more convenient—and drier—site some two or three miles away. Probably too much money had been spent on its erection. Probably, too, its upkeep had proved too heavy a burden. At any rate, since then the fortunes of the Labois family had steadily declined. The final blow had been the upheaval consequent on the first German war, and the house and grounds had had to be sold when the last owner and seventeenth Baron Stern of Eddington was killed at Loos. The title then became extinct, and the heirs to the estate, a junior and collateral branch of the family, had found their inheritance only sufficient to pay off debts and mortgages. After that there had vanished from the district all trace of a family whose name had been prominent in local talk and tale for nearly a thousand years.

The present owner was Lord Vennery, an extremely rich and important person, chairman and director of probably he himself could not have said offhand how many companies, and reputed an expert in that odd profession or occupation, sport, nightmare or game, usually known as high finance. His political views were said to be advanced, his many gifts to charities and public objects had made him popular it was generally believed that the Government took no important step without consulting him, as a private in the local Home Guard he derived much innocent pleasure from telling how he served under his own butler as platoon sergeant.

"And a damn good one, too," he used to say. "Much better than I should ever be. You ought to see us jump to it when he yells 'shun'. I remember when I was green—greener than I am now, I mean—I dropped my rifle on parade. He nearly wept. He just looked at me and said, 'Private Lord Vennery, that's as bad as if a butler dropped the entrée when he was handing it round'. I tell you that cut deep."

Lady Vennery, though very much the great lady—and why not? since she came from the chorus and there had learned to quell the presumptuous with a single glance—was very popular, too, and very busy from morning to night with social and welfare work she admitted quite frankly she would never have been able to cope with but for the help of her super-efficient secretary, Miss Thea Wood.

The distance from Midwych to Theodores was too great to be covered conveniently by cycle, so Bobby took the police car, driven by an elderly constable named Cox who had retired on pension before the war, and, to his great though concealed delight, been recalled to service exactly at the moment when pensioned leisure had begun to bore. This Sunday afternoon was warm and pleasant, the country charming, the roads clear, and in the ordinary way Bobby would have found the drive agreeable enough. But now he was feeling worried, puzzled and uneasy. Was he, he asked himself gloomily, wasting on a wild-goose chase both time, so precious in the mass of detail needing attention, and petrol, equally precious with every drop brought here at the risk of men's lives? So very likely, he knew well, that it was all no more than the fantasy of a mischievous or imaginative boy, trying, in the old phrase, 'to make himself important', in the new, to relieve an inferiority complex. But also Bobby knew there were other possibilities, grim possibilities. The boy might well have stumbled on some secret, and there are secrets that can be dangerous—deadly.

At any rate there was the solid fact that Ned Bloom had vanished from his accustomed surroundings without a word of explanation or of warning. And Bobby promised himself that if Ned turned up again to-night, nosing round Theodores, if that was what his 'phone message indicated, then Mr Ned would get such a talking to as would give him good reason for a much-increased inferiority complex.

"I'll run him in for a public mischief if he doesn't look out," Bobby promised himself, and composed various biting phrases calculated to cut and pierce and destroy the most complacent.

They passed through Eddington village, whence the old Labois had taken their title, past the ancient church where so many of them lay in marble effigy. Soon they came to where once great iron gates—now sacrificed to the exigencies of war—had guarded the entrance to the Theodores grounds. A long, straight drive provided a fine vista, with the house itself at the end of the avenue of magnificent old elms. An imposing place it looked, in the late Georgian style, the façade framed in tall doric columns and a really fine front entrance approached by a great flight of polished stone steps flanked by marble balustrades ending in the wyvern that was the Labois crest. Altogether a stately, indeed magnificent whole, a reminder of the days when a lord was still a lord and not merely an interesting historic memory.

The car stopped before the imposing entrance. Bobby descended, feeling that he ought to have arrived in a post chaise and four with a couple of postillions or so. An old man in dingy overalls appeared and called:

"Round to the right if you want the door."

"Isn't this it?" Bobby asked, surprised.

"We don't use that no more," said the ancient, "not now. Haven't the staff for it. It's round to the right."

He vanished. Bobby obeyed, relinquishing regretfully the prospect of a magnificent approach up that imposing flight of steps and through those great doors to a waiting butler and, no doubt, as he had once read in a most amiable American poem, "row upon row of tall young footmen". On the right, as instructed, he found another and a smaller door, a sort of poor relation of a door, almost a plebeian door, indeed. When he knocked there appeared a maid, to whom he gave his official card, explaining that he wished to see Lord Vennery on business. He was asked to wait, and then was conducted to a larger room, the modern boudoir, with feminine knick-knacks on the top of a card-index cabinet, a telephone concealed under a fascinating doll in crinoline, a table covered with neatly arranged piles of papers and documents kept in place by little goblin paper-weights, two or three shelves of reference books half hidden by dainty curtains, a typewriter in colour to match the general scheme. Altogether a satisfying and slightly alarming presentation of mingled femininity and efficiency. In front of the fireplace stood an elderly, rather carelessly dressed woman, smoking a cigarette in a long holder. At the typewriter sat the perfect picture of the confidential secretary, punctuality, reliability and no nonsense radiating from every inch of her small person, from her cropped head to her stockingless legs and her sandals with wooden soles.

Bobby guessed these must be Lady Vennery and her secretary, the Miss Thea Wood who had written the note sent on to him from Scotland Yard. It also struck him that the atmosphere seemed a trifle frigid. Lady Vennery announced her name, explained that her husband was occupied at the moment, and managed to convey that she was faintly surprised by Bobby's appearance, which was quite unexpected. Bobby asked if there was any misunderstanding? He had received a letter sent on to him from London. He had acknowledged it, he said, and Miss Thea Wood interposed to say they had heard nothing beyond a formal printed note saying that the matter would have attention.

"Well, that's why I'm here," Bobby said, slightly annoyed. "To give the matter attention."

"It didn't sound as if you were bothering yourselves much," said Lady Vennery. "Lord Vennery said it was more bureaucracy. Passing the buck from Scotland Yard to Midwych and back again, most likely. Dodging responsibility. He said we had better forget it."

Bobby understood now. The Vennerys were so important and so used to being so regarded that they had considered a mere printed acknowledgement as insufficient. Gross negligence it had seemed to them. He ought to have come in person at once; or, at the very least, have written a long letter, expressing concern and giving full details of what was intended. A mere promise to "give the matter attention" had displeased. Very likely they had taken precautions themselves. Very likely there had been a decision to lodge a complaint if anything did happen. Possibly even there was a touch of disappointment that a senior police officer had in fact arrived on the scene. No one likes to be deprived of a grievance.

"Well, we didn't forget it," Bobby said tartly. "Perhaps just as well you did, though. The less said the better if there is mischief on foot. Nothing to do with Scotland Yard, though. Scotland Yard is County of London. This is Wychshire."

He asked one or two questions about the 'phone call, and learned no more than Miss Wood's original letter had conveyed. The call had been taken by one of the maids. At first it had been supposed that some one was trying to be funny. But it was the fact that the date given was one when several important people would be assembled at Theodores, and so Lord Vennery had said that it might be just as well to let Scotland Yard know. Lady Vennery's tone made it clear that in her opinion Scotland Yard, no matter what Bobby might think or say, was the proper department to concern itself about the affairs of the Right Hon. Lord Vennery.

"Very probably," Bobby agreed, "it was only some one trying to be funny, but you never know, and it is also a fact that some specially cheeky—and successful—jewel robberies have taken place recently. We are very anxious to clear them up. A new operator, we think. Certainly some one who has never been through our hands."

"Lord Vennery mentioned that," said Lady Vennery, still severe. "It's why he thought we had better do something. He said no arrests had been made, none of the jewellery recovered. I don't think he seemed much impressed by the efficiency of the police."

"People seldom are," Bobby admitted. "Impressed by their own efficiency all right, but not by other people's. About your house-party this week-end. Is it a big one?"

"Hardly a house-party," Lady Vennery corrected him. "Lord Vennery has asked some of his business associates for the week-end to talk over post-war business problems. Preparing for the return to normalcy."

Bobby winced. 'Normalcy' was a word that hurt. Privately, too, he thought that to wish to return to the pre-war normal was like an adult wishing to return to childhood. However, that was no affair of his, nor did he suppose that the course of events would be very much affected by the chatter of elderly rich men. He said:

"I take it that even if it's to be chiefly a business discussion, some of Lord Vennery's friends will have brought their wives? And some of the ladies will have brought their jewellery?"

Lady Vennery looked at Miss Wood. That young lady said briskly:

"One is a bachelor, one is divorced—at present. Two have brought their wives. One has brought her husband. One is a widow. She is Mrs Carlyle. Mrs Armitage has brought her diamonds as well as her husband. Lady Vere had the bed covered with jewels when I was in her room just now. It looked like a pre-war Bond Street jeweller's. Mrs Carlyle was wearing the Arlington sapphires. I don't wonder they are famous."

CHAPTER XVII
HISTORICAL RETROSPECT

"THE ARLINGTON SAPPHIRES," Bobby repeated, suddenly excited, for was it possible that thus unexpectedly, almost casually, he had stumbled on the clue he needed whereby to link together these recent happenings?

"Are they real?" Lady Vennery was asking. "I didn't think they could be, not that size."

"Why are they famous?" Bobby asked.

"Oh, they are real," Miss Wood said, answering her employer first. "Overpowering. Nature must have been in her most vulgar mood when she produced them. They are famous, partly for their size, partly for their history. A Portuguese captain brought them from Burma in the sixteenth century. He was burned alive for heresy—or else for refusing to give them up. From the Inquisition, who had arranged the burning, they passed to an Italian Cardinal. Moors—pirates from Algiers—burnt the Cardinal alive in his church and went off with the sapphires. One of the captives in Algiers was an Englishman, Sir Gervase Arlington, a slave in the house of the captain of the Moors. He and some others captured with him rose suddenly, burnt the Moorish captain alive in his house, and escaped with the sapphires. Sir Gervase was the only one of the party who reached England. The others died on the way, with or without assistance from Sir Gervase. Anyhow, no one was left to dispute his ownership, and the sapphires remained in the Arlington family until recently—heirlooms under entail, so they couldn't be sold. At least, every one thought so, till somebody discovered that through some slip of a lawyer's clerk, a hundred years ago, only the necklace was specified as an heirloom. So the earrings and the pendant could be sold. There's a story that an Argentine millionaire offered some enormous sum for the full set—earrings, pendant, necklace. When he couldn't have the necklace he sulked and said he wouldn't have any. So Mr Carlyle stepped in and bought the earrings and pendant over the Argentine's head. Made him furious, and he tried to buy from the Carlyles, but they wouldn't part. The story is he still wants to buy, and now Mr Carlyle is dead he is waiting for Mrs Carlyle to go bankrupt or something. They are rather a responsibility to have in the house."

Lady Vennery looked at Bobby with a proud air. She had exactly the manner of the mother showing off a precocious child, or of a schoolmaster exhibiting a prize pupil.

"Miss Wood always knows all about things," she said.

Miss Wood contrived to look both modest and intolerably efficient. Bobby regarded her with disapproval, and mentally thanked Heaven there were so many things of which his Olive knew absolutely nothing. Mere masculine jealousy, of course.

He asked a few more questions, and then explained that he would like permission to remain in the grounds near the house for a time, so as to keep watch until dark.

"Dinner-time is generally the zero hour for burglaries, you know," he said. "Every one at table and the servants all fussed. If the 'phone message you had means something, and wasn't merely an attempt to be funny, whatever it is will probably come off then."

He also asked if he could be shown over the first floor, so as to make himself acquainted with the lay-out of the rooms and passages.

"Just in case," he explained, "any one manages to get indoors without our seeing him. Unlikely, because the first thing any professional does is to make sure of his retreat by trip lines on the lawn or some dodge of that sort, and that ought to give him away."

"You seem to know all about it," remarked Lady Vennery in rather a dissatisfied tone, and she looked across at her secretary in a way and with an expression Bobby did not at all understand.

Perhaps almost disappointed, she and her secretary both, that the police authorities they had made up their minds were inefficient were proving attentive and competent. Unreasonable, of course, but, then, people did on the whole tend to be slightly unreasonable.

However, no objection was raised to granting his request, and the efficient Miss Wood undertook to act as guide. As she led the way upstairs he asked about the domestic staff, and learned that the butler was now the only inside man servant. There were also two aged gardeners, long since pensioned off, but now returned to grow tomatoes in the erstwhile orchid house, potatoes in the former rose-garden. The butler, too, was well over sixty, explained Miss Wood, with that touch of pitying contempt for age which has replaced the reverence youth was once expected to show, though probably never feeling it.

"Not much good for tackling burglars, if that's what you're hoping," pronounced Miss Wood.

Apparently lest this might discourage him too much, she added a promise that she would have a poker hidden ready so that she herself could come to his help if any "bust up"—her expression—did take place.

Bobby thanked her gravely, and under her guidance got a good idea of the geography of the first floor. He learned also that there were three stairways: the great central stairs, ornate and magnificent, not much used for the moment, as it debouched on the great closed front entrance; the backstairs used by the staff; the garden stairs, so called because they led directly to the door by which Bobby had entered. At present these stairs were the most convenient and nearest communicating link between the bedrooms and the rooms now in use on the ground floor, where most of the larger ceremonial apartments had been shut up "for the duration". He asked Miss Wood which was the room occupied by Mrs Carlyle, and after she had shown it him and they were walking back along a passage he noticed a smell of tobacco.

"Some one in there smoking a cigarette," he remarked, indicating a door. "Will that be one of the guests?"

"That's my room," she told him abruptly. "No one's there," and she hurried on along the passage towards the stairs.

Bobby had to follow her. None of his business, he supposed, if she did not wish him to know who it was. It couldn't be the hypothetical housebreaker, he supposed. She had run downstairs already, and was waiting for him in the passage below. He thanked her for her guidance, declined politely an offer of refreshment, and, returning to the waiting Cox in the car outside, drove back to Eddington police station, where he had some arrangements to make, as the village constable, a youngish man named Adams, had received his call-up papers and would have to be replaced—by whom Bobby had no idea, as the force was already combed out to the limit. He supposed gloomily that he was expected to call a substitute from the vasty deep, and if none came then he would be held responsible.

However, that was merely a normal war-time headache. Adams had been warned by 'phone to keep a sharp look-out for any stranger seen in the neighbourhood. But Bobby was much inclined to suspect that in the bustle and excitement of preparations for departure these instructions had not been carried out with any marked zeal. A weeping wife, three awestruck children and many solemn farewell visits from neighbours had probably pushed police duty into the background.

No good saying anything to a man who in a few hours would care nothing for inspectors or superintendents, however much he might be learning to tremble before corporals and sergeants. So Bobby went to the village public-house, where he dined on bread and cheese. There he learned that shortly before his own arrival a motor-cyclist had passed through the village and had inquired the way to Theodores, which apparently he knew had to be asked for as Tedders. Unfortunately Bobby could get only the vaguest, most general personal description of this stranger, as neither of the two men to whom he had spoken could be found at the moment.

Bobby wondered to himself if this meant that Ned Bloom had put in an appearance at last. Nothing to show it was actually Ned, of course, but the possibility remained.

His bread and cheese finished, Bobby went back to the cottage that served both as police station and as residence, tore a reluctant Adams from a justly indignant wife and solemn children wondering more than ever what all the fuss was about, placed him and Cox at what seemed the most suitable strategic points to cover all approaches to Theodores, hired a small boy to act as liaison officer, parked the car near the entrance to the drive, where once those great iron gates had stood, so that it might be ready for instant pursuit if necessary.

For his own share he had given himself a roving commission, and as he kept watch, he found himself wondering again whether the sudden appearance of the Arlington sapphires in all this tangle of events and possibilities was pure coincidence, or whether there was some connection with Ned Bloom's 'phone call or with that note "Follow this up" made by him on the newspaper cutting about the disappearance of Sir Gervase Arlington. And was it the disappearance of the Admiral or the whereabouts of the sapphires that Ned's note referred to? He wondered, too, whether that super-efficient secretary, Miss Thea Wood, had the history of all famous jewels by heart, or whether there was some special reason why she knew so much about these sapphires?

Then he saw Miss Wood herself coming briskly towards the house. She had changed her attire, and was wearing now a close-fitting dinner-gown, which somehow seemed to suit her less, as if she had fallen in significance from the necessary secretary to the mere superfluous dinner guest. She had thrown a light-coloured scarf or wrap of some sort over her shoulders, and as Bobby watched she took it off, held it up for a moment, as if wondering how to readjust it—or was it possible she was making a signal?—and then draped it to cover not only her shoulders, but her Eton-cropped head.

She went on towards the house and, watching her go, Bobby told himself that it might be as well to take up her references. He drew a little nearer to the house, stepping from shadow to shadow as the twilight deepened. On the ground floor the black-out curtains were being drawn in good time. Bobby watched a stout, elderly man—no doubt the butler mentioned once or twice—moving from window to window, and then he saw quite clearly the head and shoulders of a younger man showing for a moment above, at the window of what Bobby was certain was the room occupied by Mrs Carlyle, the owner of the Arlington sapphire earrings and pendant.

CHAPTER XVIII
HIDE AND SEEK

BOBBY'S FIRST ACT was to call to his small liaison officer to warn his two assistants, Cox and Adams. Then he raced for the house. Fortunately the garden door was not kept locked. He threw it open and ran down the corridor towards the foot of the stairs. From behind one door he passed there came a babel of voices. The dining-room, he supposed. A maid appeared, and stopped, open-mouthed and staring, on seeing him.

"Police. A man upstairs. Tell Lord Vennery," he called to her, and flew on up the stairs, three at a time, to the floor above.

He made at once for the door of Mrs Carlyle's room. He flung it open. The room was empty. But to one side was another door, that of a dressing-room, probably. He leaped across to it. It opened outwards, and it resisted when he tried to throw it back. Blocked; probably by the old and simple plan of placing against it a chair, the back of the chair under the handle of the door. He did not waste time trying to force it. He ran back and out again into the corridor, just in time to get a glimpse of a coat tail vanishing round the corner into the other, the main, corridor that bisected this part of the house. But when he got there the corridor stretched emptily on either hand. No sign of any fugitive, who seemed to have the faculty of vanishing like the coin a conjurer palms. Bobby ran down the corridor, flinging open each door that he came to. No one to be seen, but he thought he heard from somewhere behind a low chuckle; and, as he dashed back, he saw the stub of a cigarette lying half-way up the stairs that led from this floor to that above.

A trick, perhaps, he thought, a false scent laid to send him searching the second floor, while whoever was hiding here on the first could effect an escape. But any one who had taken refuge on this upper floor would be safe for the time, and Bobby ran back along the corridor he had already traversed. Coming up the stairs from below was now a stout, elderly gentleman in a lounge suit—Lord Vennery, who sternly and patriotically had forbidden even dinner-jackets for the duration.

"What's all this?" he demanded. "Who are you?"

"Police," Bobby answered briefly. "I think there's a burglar up here. Probably after the ladies' jewellery. Please see all exits are watched downstairs."

"Burglar?" repeated Lord Vennery, looking very bewildered. "Where? Why?"

"I saw a man at one of these windows," Bobby explained. "I want to find him. I'll look in all these rooms. He must be hiding somewhere. I don't think he had time to get away. Please see to downstairs. I have two men outside."

"Yes, but—" began Lord Vennery, looking more bewildered still.

He was well known for the rapidity and firmness of the decisions he arrived at, but he liked to arrive at them in a comfortable board room, over a cigar, with attentive and deferential colleagues sitting round. This violence, this shouting, this running to and fro, he found prohibitive of all calm thought. Bobby was already dashing at doors, opening them, giving the room within a swift and competent examination, darting out again to renew the process elsewhere. Lord Vennery wished to stop him, but did not know how. He got as far as framing the words "young man" in his mind, though without actually pronouncing them. Bobby came to a door that would not open.

"Locked inside," he said to Lord Vennery. "Whose room is it?"

"I don't know," said Lord Vennery helplessly.

"It's Miss Wood's," said Lady Vennery, who, with others of the party, had now arrived on the scene.

"What's all this about?" demanded Lord Vennery, beginning to recover slightly. "Are you a policeman?" he asked doubtfully, for his vision of a policeman included helmet, blue uniform, the air of deference the well-to-do expect to receive from the law they have made. And this young man showed none of these things, neither helmet nor blue uniform, nor, especially, any deference whatever. "Are you a policeman?" he repeated.

"I called before," Bobby explained. "You were engaged. I saw Lady Vennery. We had warning there might be an attempt at robbery. Some of your guests are rich people with valuable jewels. Jewellery is in demand to-day. Portable property in case of invasion. Keeps its value if currency flops. So I had the place watched. I saw a man at a window here. What man? One of your party? All at dinner, weren't they? One of your staff? I'm told your only man servant is the butler I saw downstairs doing the black-out. Who was it I saw?"

"Are you sure you saw any one?" Lord Vennery asked, still finding it very hard to grasp what it all meant. Then, with renewed suspicion: "How do I know who you are?" and he very nearly said and certainly thought: "If you're a real policeman, where's your helmet?"

From the midst of the little group of guests and staff now arrived, Miss Wood said:

"He showed Lady Vennery what he called his warrant card. Of course, it may have been forged," she added warningly.

"May I break this door open?" Bobby asked Lord Vennery.

"Here, that's my room. What for?" demanded Miss Wood.

"The door's locked," Bobby said. "I take it you don't generally lock your door?"

"Not as a rule," she agreed.

"It's locked now," Bobby said. "On the inside. There must be some one there. Have you a spare key?" To Lord Vennery he said again: "May I force it?"

"I said, 'not as a rule'," interposed Miss Wood. "But I did this evening."

"Why?" snapped Bobby.

"No clothing coupons," said Miss Wood sadly, and, as Bobby glared: "Don't look so cross," she said. "If you've no coupons left you have to try to make do. I've got the bed simply covered with sewing, so I locked the door and put the key in my bag before I went downstairs. I didn't mean to have the maid going in to turn down the bed and upsetting everything. I've got to the most awfully critical part you can imagine."

"Well, then," said Bobby, though thinking to himself that this explanation seemed just a little too glib, "may I have the key to make sure?"

"What for?" demanded Miss Wood. "No one can possibly be there. The door's been locked all the time and the key's in my bag."

"All the same, I'll make sure, please," Bobby said firmly. "Some men boast they can open a lock by blowing on it. It's nearly true. Kindly let me have the key."

Their eyes met in challenge. Bobby was certain Miss Wood wished to refuse, was inclined to refuse. But she read the determination in his look. She hesitated and seemed to make up her mind. She said:

"If you don't mind, I'll go in first." She cast down her eyes. She positively simpered. She exchanged up-to date efficiency for Victoria demureness. She explained modestly: "I know I'm most awfully old-fashioned and it's very silly, but I would like to tidy one or two things away first. One doesn't want men going giggling at one's private things."

"I don't giggle," said Bobby furiously.

"I quite understand, Thea dear," said Lady Vennery, approval for her secretary, rebuke to Bobby in every tone of her voice, and from the other women-folk behind came a further murmur of feminine approval. "You go in, and call out when you're ready."

"I shan't be a minute," said Miss Wood, skipping gaily in front of Bobby.

She opened the door the merest crack. She slipped through. Almost at once she was back, opening the door wide.

"Now you can all come in," she said.

Bobby was gloomily certain that now there was nothing there, but he entered all the same.

"You will look under the bed, won't you?" said Miss Wood earnestly. "I was too frightened myself."

Bobby took no notice. He would have dearly loved to put Miss Wood across his knee and administer correction with a slipper. Happy, happy dream; but, alas, a dream only. The bed did not seem unduly ruffled, he noticed. Indeed, the whole room was extremely tidy, considering that Miss Wood said she had left it in the throes of dressmaking. The window was wide open. He went across and looked out. There was a gutter pipe that ran close by. Bobby leaned farther out. There were small signs, scratches on pipe and brickwork and so on, that seemed to show some one had climbed down to earth thereby quite recently. He looked down. In the gathering gloom he saw lying there, inert and prone, the body of a man.

He said over his shoulder:

"Some one there—knocked out. Or worse. I'm going down."

CHAPTER XIX
DEMURE SECRETARY

ALMOST AS SWIFTLY as he had spoken Bobby was through the window and clambering to earth by aid of a gutter-pipe that swayed, but held. His feet touched ground. He was conscious of astonished heads crowded at the window above, watching his descent. He ran to the side of the still and prostrate man he had seen. It was Adams, the local constable. He opened his eyes as Bobby turned him gently on his back. He tried to sit up. He said feebly:

"There was a man. He laid me out."

"What was he like?" Bobby asked.

"I don't know," said Adams and closed his eyes again. "It's all going round," he complained.

Bobby shouted to the window above.

"He's been knocked out. Please see to him."

To himself he thought that at any rate it could not be Ned Bloom who had been here. Ned wasn't capable of knocking out a hefty youngish man like Constable Adams. Who was it, then? And what had become of him? Not much chance of successful pursuit with darkness falling and a good start gained. He heard some one shouting. It was Cox calling at the top of his voice:

"There he is. Hi. Stop, you. Stop."

There came the report of a pistol shot—or was it an engine back-firing? Bobby set off running. He caught up Cox, who was pounding down the avenue.

"I saw him, sir. Chap had one arm in sling," he panted. "Our car—he'll get it."

Bobby increased his speed. The car had been duly immobilized according to regulations; so if the fugitive, knowing where it was, hoped to use it, he was heading for disappointment. Not so, however, for now as Bobby raced along he heard the chug-chug of a motor-cycle. Not the car, then, but this motor-cycle was to provide for the fugitive's escape. Well, some police cars are fairly ancient, and this was no new model, but it had a fair turn of speed, and should be a match for any motor-cycle. A good race, Bobby thought. Now the car was there before him, waiting and ready. Only it refused to start. Bobby sat bewildered in the driver's seat, into which he had hurled himself with such *élan*. The car that should have leaped to life beneath his eager hands remained dead, inert. He tried to discover why, and could not. All seemed in perfect order. Nothing wrong, except that nothing happened. He experienced a touch of that feeling of frustration one has sometimes in bad dreams. Then it occurred to him to look in the tank. It was bone dry, drained to the last drop.

Disconsolate and defeated, he sat there, listening to the sound of the motor-cycle dying away in the distance. Arm in sling, Cox had said. What did that mean? Captain Dunstan? How did he come into it? Or some one else? There came to Bobby a clear memory of Miss Thea Wood, suave, smug, demure, returning from the evening stroll that had taken her in this direction.

There arrived Cox, running and gasping. He seemed to think Bobby was waiting for him. He tumbled into the car. He panted unnecessarily:

"It's me, sir . . . get going, sir."

"No petrol," said Bobby.

"What?" said Cox.

"No petrol, no juice, no gas, no chance," said Bobby gloomily.

"Where?" said Cox.

"Take a look," said Bobby.

"There must be," said Cox. "I filled up before starting."

"Take a look," repeated Bobby.

Cox did so. He had some difficulty in believing it, even though he touched and felt. Finally he said:

"Somebody's gone and been and pinched the lot."

"Yes," said Bobby. "Are you sure the man you saw had one arm in a sling?"

Cox, it seemed, was sure, or as sure as his present bewilderment over the vanished petrol would permit him to be sure of anything. Bobby alighted. They walked back to the house together. Bobby told Cox to try to borrow there enough petrol to take them home. A promise could be made to return it, since rationed petrol has a value beyond that of rubies. Bobby said:

"I told you to keep an eye on the car. Did you see any one near it?"

"No, sir," said Cox emphatically. "I had one eye on it steady like, and I'll take my oath not a living soul came near it the whole time, nor could without me seeing."

"No one," Bobby repeated. "Quite sure? Think again. That petrol went somehow. When you say no one, are you sure?"

"Why, yes, sir, of course I am," answered Cox, slightly offended. "Not a living soul, nor could have without me seeing. Quite close I was all the time, till Adams started shouting, and then I run, but there wasn't time between then and now. There was one of the ladies from the house went along by there and stopped to have a look, too. You ask her. No one didn't pass, no living soul, and to that I'll take my oath."

"Wasn't she a living soul?" asked Bobby bitterly. "You say she stopped to have a look?"

"Yes, sir, so she did," Cox replied. "Ladies often take an interest in cars—quite knowledgeable like, too, some of 'em. You can't think, sir, as she—not her, an' she a lady and all."

"In these days," Bobby told him, "ladies resemble Voltaire's Habakkuk."

Cox blinked, never having heard of Voltaire's expressed opinion that that prophet was capable of all. They had reached the house now, and found Adams sitting up and taking nourishment in the shape of a fairly stiff brandy and soda provided by a reluctant butler on the express orders of a compassionate Lady Vennery.

Bobby, not too sympathetically, suggested that the patient might now be regarded as convalescent, asked Adams one or two questions, from which he learned only that Adams had seen a man climbing down the gutter-pipe, had run across to ask what he was doing, had seen for answer a large fist shoot out, and had known no more for the time. Feeling tenderly a rapidly swelling jaw, he said:

"Hit me a whack he did before I knew a thing, and me all unready like and not suspecting."

"Served you right," said Bobby crossly. "A policeman who isn't all ready and suspecting deserves all he gets and more."

"What a horrid shame," said a clear whisper from behind, "to go bullying the poor man just now, and only look at that awful bruise."

Bobby swung round. As he had guessed, that clear whisper came from Miss Thea Wood, gazing at him now from large, reproachful eyes.

"I should like a word with you in private," Bobby said to her. He turned to Lady Vennery. "I've a few questions to ask Miss Wood," he said. "Perhaps you or Lord Vennery could arrange to be present?"

Lady Vennery looked very surprised. Lord Vennery asked what was the idea. He added that nothing seemed to be missing. Bobby said he was glad to hear it, but apparently unlawful entry had been effected, and he would like further information on some points. So the four of them adjourned to another room, where Bobby began the interview by asking for Miss Wood's identity card.

"What on earth for?" asked Lord Vennery.

"What's it got to do with it?" asked Lady Vennery.

"Oh, I'm sure I don't mind; it's here," said Miss Wood, and promptly produced it. "I keep it in my bag," she explained. "I sewed in a special place for it."

Bobby examined it and made a note or two. In order, as far as he could tell. Not that identity cards tell very much. Some day, Bobby hoped, there would be thumb-prints on them or something like that.

"May I ask," said Lady Vennery, "the reason for this? I admit I am—surprised," and when she said "surprised" she made it sound like thunder rumbling in the distance.

"Madam," said Bobby, "there has been what I can only suppose was an attempt at robbery here this evening. One of my men has been assaulted in the execution of his duty." ('And served the silly ass jolly well right, too,' Bobby paused to add mentally.) He resumed: "When Miss Wood was so kind as to show me over your first floor, I thought I smelt tobacco. Miss Wood said that the room I thought it came from was hers, and that no one could possibly be there. I had no reason—or power—to insist. Later on, when I was hunting round for the man I had seen at the window of Mrs Carlyle's room, the only locked door was that of Miss Wood's room. Miss Wood made some difficulty about opening it. When she did finally consent, she insisted on going in first. There is plain evidence a man had been hiding there, and that he escaped by the window, either just before or just after Miss Wood's entrance."

"Preposterous," said Lady Vennery.

"Ridiculous," said Lord Vennery.

"Why?" asked Bobby.

"I never heard such nonsense in my life," said Lady Vennery.

"I shall make a point," said Lord Vennery, "of mentioning all this to the Home Secretary next time I see him."

"Furthermore," continued Bobby, quite unmoved, "the petrol has been removed from the tank of my car. That prevented me from following a man we saw escaping on a motor-cycle. The only person seen near the car was Miss Wood."

"I did go for a stroll just before dinner," agreed Miss Wood. "You remember," she said to Lady Vennery, "I said I would take that letter to Conrads to the post-box. Does the inspector think I pocketed his petrol and brought it back with me?"

"I think there's been enough of this," said Lord Vennery.

"I think the facts I have mentioned, facts within your own knowledge," Bobby told him, "justify me in asking for an explanation."

"If you mean," said Lady Vennery, "that you are trying to accuse Miss Wood of having anything to do with what's happened to-night, I can only say she has had no more to do with it than I myself. Please understand I guarantee that. Or do you want to accuse me, too?"

"Lady Vennery and myself," said Lord Vennery, "have the most complete confidence in Miss Wood—as complete as in ourselves. I am sure," he added more graciously, "we all appreciate, inspector, that you have shown great energy and zeal, and I fully understand your position. But I think the matter must now drop. Nothing is missing. We have lost nothing, no complaint to make about anything. We are much obliged to you, inspector, for your efforts, and that ends it."

Bobby hardly heard. From behind the protective forms of Lord Vennery, of Lady Vennery, Miss Thea Wood looked at Bobby, and then slowly and quite deliberately put out her tongue at him.

"What's the matter?" asked Lady Vennery, seeing how Bobby gasped and stared, and she turned to see what he was staring at, as if Medusa had suddenly appeared.

All she saw was her demure, efficient secretary standing meekly there, butter certainly quite unable to melt in her small, made-up mouth.

CHAPTER XX
JITTERS

OVER LATE—VERY late—supper that Sunday evening Olive listened with interest while Bobby recounted the events of the day. At the story of the behaviour of Miss Thea Wood she shook a sympathetic head and said severely that she really didn't know what girls were coming to now-a-days.

"I do wish I had been there," she added dreamily. "I always seem to miss the best bits."

"What best bits?" asked Bobby suspiciously.

"Oh," said Olive in a hurry, "just—well, you know. That's all."

"If," said Bobby with dignity, "you see anything to laugh at . . ."

"Oh, I don't," Olive declared. "Certainly not. Why, I was as grave and solemn as if—as if I had been thinking about points."

"Outwardly perhaps," conceded Bobby, "but inwardly you were—amused. In fact, inwardly you were nothing but one vast grin. There, it's coming out now," he added, as Olive's solemnity showed signs of giving way.

"Well, you know," Olive admitted, "it must have been rather funny—your face, I mean, dear. All the same, Miss Wood is a horrid little wretch, and I suspect her of the worst; but I don't think you do, do you?"

"I don't know what to think," Bobby said. "There was certainly something going on behind the scenes, and she was in it up to the neck, but I don't know what, and nothing I could do with the Vennerys sticking up for her the way they were."

"Do you think it was Captain Dunstan who got away?"

"There again," said Bobby, "I simply don't know what to think. The one thing quite certain is that it wasn't Ned Bloom. He isn't physically capable of climbing down gutter-pipes and knocking out Adams."

"Is Captain Dunstan? Mightn't the arm-in-sling be a mistake of Cox's—or even a put off, camouflage?"

"Might be. Even so, it still suggests a link—some connection somewhere. Dunstan is all right physically, except for his arm, and that wouldn't prevent him from climbing down a gutter-pipe—I daresay Army training includes doing things with one arm out of action. And he could have knocked out Adams all right. Or fired a pistol, for that matter. An army officer is sure to have a revolver, I suppose."

"Poor Mr Adams," said Olive sympathetically.

"Poor Mr Nothing," snorted Bobby. "He simply walked into the other fellow's fist—asked for it, and got it, and I'm only sorry it wasn't more."

"Oh, Bobby," said Olive, and looked quite shocked.

"Got treated with a brandy and soda," added Bobby disgustedly, "when better men than Adams have forgotten what brandy tastes like." He went on: "First thing to-morrow morning I'll have a talk with Dunstan. No good. He'll bluff it out all right. No evidence. There is one clue, though, one scrap of evidence. May be a help. Tyre-marks on a soft patch of ground. Quite distinctive marks. If we can find the cycle, we can identify it. Got to find it first, though, and that's a bit of a forlorn hope. But we'll have a try."

"Suppose," said Olive, "suppose it's known the tyres leave distinctive marks and they're changed?"

"Then we're sunk," admitted Bobby. "Quite likely, too. Or the machine may turn out stolen for the occasion. Common trick. I suppose it's possible Ned Bloom was mixed up in it somehow. He is the sort to like working in the background."

Olive shook her head.

"I don't think he is alive," she said.

Bobby looked up quickly. Somehow the quiet words had fallen across the homely, comfortable supper-table with an unexpected accent of doom. He put down the cup of coffee he had been raising to his lips.

"Why do you say that?" he asked.

"Well, do you?" she asked.

"No," he said; and was surprised himself to feel with what strong inner conviction he said this. Then he asked again: "Why did you say that?"

"I went to Threepence to-day," Olive said. "I thought I would like to see Mrs Bloom's tea-garden. They were very busy there. I wanted to see Miss Skinner, too. She is awfully handsome—sort of daughter-of-the-gods type. She looks—well, formidable somehow. As little like a tea-shop waitress as any girl could. First class at the job, all the same. Never hurried, never made a mistake, eyes everywhere, no one kept waiting. And I believe she knew who I was."

"How could she?"

"I don't know. Perhaps not. But I am sure she knew very well I wasn't there simply for tea?"

"Why? Why do you think that?"

"Well, I do. Miss Roman Wright was there."

"Are you sure?"

"Yes. Mrs Bloom came to sit with her."

"What?" cried Bobby, astonished.

"Mrs Bloom came to sit with her," Olive repeated. "Miss Wright was there when I got there. Sitting alone. I knew her at once from what you said, and I got a seat quite near. She had tea and a scone, but she never tasted her tea or touched her scone. She just sat. I was watching. Mrs Bloom came out from the house. Bobby, she made me afraid."

"Mrs Bloom? Yes, I know. She does. Why?"

"I think she has known dreadful things, and I think perhaps she lives with them still, so that the memory of them is about her like a garment."

"Oh, well," Bobby said uncomfortably.

Olive went on after a pause:

"You could see people look up in a startled way as she passed and look at each other, and some of them who had only been sitting got up and went away. She sat down at Miss Wright's table, and they never said a word to each other. At least, I don't think they did. They sat there together, and somehow it was rather awful to watch them, but I don't know why."

Bobby didn't say anything. Had he never seen Mrs Bloom or known that dreadful stillness which lay about her, he might have smiled. As it was, he had no such inclination. It was Olive who laughed, or tried to.

"It's sounds silly, doesn't it?" she said. "Just a lot of people having tea out of doors, just a pleasant Sunday afternoon, everyone trying to forget the war for half an hour, and why should that give you the jitters?"

"If they never spoke to each other," Bobby said, "what was the idea?"

"I think there is something they both know, and they each know the other knows it, and I think what they know is that Ned Bloom is dead."

"Does that mean—?" Bobby began and paused. "Do you think that means," he resumed, "that one of them killed him?"

"I don't know. It doesn't follow," Olive said. "You can know about things you haven't done yourself."

"Mrs Bloom's his mother," Bobby said.

"Yes," Olive answered, and after a pause she said again: "Yes."

"If they know, why don't they tell?" Bobby asked, speaking more to himself than to Olive.

"I daresay it's all my fancy," Olive said abruptly. "Perhaps I was only imagining things. It was just as if he were sitting there between them—Ned Bloom, I mean—and they knew, both of them. At least, I mean that's what I thought, but I don't know why. I expect I was letting my imagination run away with me. Only I shall always remember seeing them, sitting there together, never speaking, not even looking at each other. Then Miss Roman Wright got up and went away, and Mrs Bloom returned to the house. I saw Miss Skinner watch them both as they went, and then I saw her look at me, and I knew that she was afraid—just like me."

"Look at the time," Bobby said. "I'm going to bed. I hope I shan't have bad dreams."

CHAPTER XXI
A WATER-COLOUR

THOUGH HIS NIGHT's sleep was disturbed by no bad dreams, yet when Bobby awoke his mind returned at once to that picture of the two women in the tea-garden sitting side by side before untasted scone, untouched cup, and yet exchanging no word. He came down to breakfast in no cheerful mood.

"There's so little to go on," he complained, "and at the same time so much. A young man missing from his home—but perhaps off on his own private affairs. A man hiding in a girl's bedroom—and that may be immoral, but isn't necessarily illegal. Another woman with a sudden fancy for ordering teas she never tastes, and if she likes it that way, why not? A shot fired in the dark, unknown by whom at whom, and that's a bit vague. A music-hall performer who tears up registered letters, and a country vicar who clears out in a hurry when he sees a policeman coming, and country vicars do sometimes get urgent calls, and sometimes music-hall performers get writs served in registered letters. And there's a tea-shop waitress who doesn't look like one, and an old boy who sits about in an invalid chair and yet threatens to shoot people, and what about it? Invalids have tempers still, and almost anybody can be anything these days—even waitresses in tea-shops. Oh, and I had forgotten an artist who can't draw for nuts, but boasts of giving tips to Mr Augustus John, and I've met quite respectable citizens who liked to swank about how they are pals with the great. So there you are; and if a junior came to me with a lot of chat and gossip like that, I should tell him to lay off and get on with the day's work."

"Well, why don't you?" asked Olive.

"Because," said Bobby, and lapsed into such gloomy and absorbed thought that he helped himself to Olive's rasher as well as his own.

"And that," said Olive, as firmly though kindly she retrieved her share, "is the last of the ration—porridge tomorrow, and not much milk."

But even this announcement did not stir Bobby from his inner abstraction, and so Olive added:

"Here are two more facts. The missing boy said he knew things when he came to see you, and three people were so anxious to know what it was he knew that they rang you up—all three of them claiming to be his mother, which does not seem probable. But it shows two of them at least thought it worth a lie to try to find out. And it shows that they all three knew—something."

"Oh, a lot of people know a lot," said Bobby; "it's only me that doesn't."

Therewith he asked for another cup of tea, and, having drunk it, went to ring up head-quarters to explain he would be late, as he intended to go round first by Threepence. Not, he told himself privately, that there was much chance of getting anything out of Captain Dunstan, even if Captain Dunstan were in fact the man involved. He came back from the 'phone looking more worried than ever.

"Sergeant Young," he told Olive, "has just rung them up to report a complaint by Mr Roman Wright that his motor-cycle has been stolen. Any connection, or just another coincidence?"

"Coincidence—aw, nuts," said Olive; yet another victim to the American film language so rapidly replacing Esperanto, Volapuk, Latin, pidgin, basic and all the other tongues that have ever striven to become universal.

But all the same Bobby knew how often a foolish coincidence has tangled and confused a problem already sufficiently confused and tangled. Part of a detective's business, no doubt, to be able to distinguish the unnecessary coincidence from the relevant fact.

"I'll call at Mr Roman Wright's on the way to see Captain Dunstan at Miles Bottom," he said. "Prospect Cottage is near the 'bus stop. I'll have to run," he added, glancing in alarm at the clock.

In fact, he only just managed to catch the 'bus, and when he alighted at Threepence and went to Prospect Cottage the door was opened to his knock by a profusely apologetic Mr Roman Wright.

"Brought you on a fool's errand, I'm afraid," he said. "The thing's turned up."

"Oh, how's that?" Bobby asked.

"We've just found it inside the front garden gate. Some one must have put it there during the night. But come inside and I'll tell you all about it."

He led the way into a small, bleak sitting-room with conventional furniture; on the walls, one or two Landseer engravings—'Dignity and Impudence', 'The Monarch of the Glen'—another entitled 'His Majesty's Progress', showing a small child toddling through a press of traffic all stopped to permit his passage, and two or three water-colours, all so bad Bobby felt convinced they must be Mr Roman Wright's own work.

Mr Roman Wright fussed about a little, offered Bobby a drink, but agreed it was still early, produced cigarettes, and seemed disappointed when Bobby explained that in the interests of discipline he had to keep the 'No smoking on duty' regulation much more strictly than did, he feared, most of his subordinates, and finally was persuaded to resume his story.

None of them, he explained, had had occasion to go into the front garden that morning, and they had known nothing of the return of the motor-cycle till the daily woman arrived and told them it was there. It had evidently been used, for there were still a few drops of petrol in the tank.

"Hasn't been a smell of the stuff here," declared Mr Roman Wright ruefully, "since they shut down on the supply. I asked for an allowance. I need it for my work. How can I study a sunrise effect out there in the forest, miles out perhaps, if I can't use my motor-cycle to get there and carry my materials? Am I supposed to carry my stuff, my easel, all the rest of it, a few odd miles before dawn? No good, though. I might as well have talked to a blank wall. I was simply told right out that art was not a work of national importance. Typical British outlook."

Bobby sympathised politely, asked a few more questions, learned little more. The motor-cycle was kept in a shed at the back of the house. During most of Sunday there had been no one at home. Mrs Roman Wright and their niece, Jane, had gone into

Midwych by an early 'bus—the only convenient one—to attend service at Midwych cathedral. Mr Roman Wright himself had been away for the week-end on business. To see his dealer about a new commission he had been offered. It was to make a new version of one of his forest pictures.

"The idea is to put in kiddies playing with rabbits or squirrels," he explained, "and call it 'Babes in the Wood' or 'Folk of the Forest', or something like that. For reproduction as an engraving. One of my things did well in the States a year or two ago, and my dealer wants me to try again."

Bobby, sacrificing truth, said he thought it an excellent idea. Still offering up truth on the altar of politeness, he made one or two complimentary remarks about the water-colours on the wall, remarking, this time with perfect truth, that he remembered Mr Roman Wright's brushwork and his command of line so well that at the first glance he had recognized them for Mr Roman Wright's own work.

Mr Roman Wright smirked and purred, and yet, or so Bobby fancied, there was behind the smirking and the purring a curious sly, excited triumph, as though in some odd way these somewhat vapid compliments had for him their own significance. He was voluble enough, all the same, in explaining how much he valued Inspector Owen's appreciation. The very first time they met he had seen at once that the inspector "understood". He emphasized the word "understood", and again as he said this there was in his voice, in his eyes, that same expression of a sly, a hidden, almost a leering triumph very hard to understand. Then it vanished again, as if on command, and Mr Roman Wright ventured to draw the inspector's attention to one water-colour in particular. His own favourite. His wife's favourite, too. He wondered if the inspector, in whom he recognized a brother art lover, a kindred soul, could tell why? Bobby, to whom the thing seemed neither better nor worse than the rest of Mr Roman Wright's very tenth-rate efforts, made a few vague remarks. The picture showed a desolate bit of boulder-strewn woodland, a tangle of undergrowth of bramble and rock and bracken it would not be easy to penetrate. To Bobby's eyes the scene showed nothing to indicate why any one should want to paint it, and nothing in the execution of the work to explain the somewhat odd excitement with which the artist seemed to regard it, seemed also to expect his visitor to regard it. He interrupted Bobby's somewhat embarrassed examination of the picture by saying with a high, affected laugh:

"Now, Mr Owen, you might as well confess you see nothing much in it. Now, do you?"

"Well, I must admit," agreed Bobby, "I don't think—"

"—You would have picked it out," interrupted Mr Roman Wright, completing the sentence. "Yet I think it my most remarkable bit of work—sometimes I think it the most remarkable picture ever painted. That'll make you laugh." He laughed himself, again in the same odd, sly, excited manner. He went on: "Sometimes I bring my wife in to look at it again. It never fails to have its effect."

Bobby gave it another polite look or two. Roman Wright asked him to notice how the stunted pine in the centre of the picture served to tie the whole composition together. Bobby said, untruthfully, that certainly that was a clever device. Mr Roman Wright said he wished there had been an oak growing there, on one side of that stunted and ill-shaped pine. Perhaps there would be some day. You couldn't tell. For the sake of saying something, Bobby remarked that he thought that would throw the composition out of balance. Still trying to give the thing the attention he felt it did not deserve, he noticed that it was dated 1941, and certainly it had been completed a year or two. The time must have been the early spring, he supposed, to judge from the appearance of the trees and undergrowth. Having by now had enough of this chatter about a highly uninteresting water-colour—one that from its date, he supposed, could not possibly have any connection with recent events—Bobby asked if he could see the returned cycle and the shed whence it had been taken. Mr Roman Wright said certainly, he would show him them at once; and as they went Bobby was still aware of a kind of inner heat of excitement and of exultation in the other's bearing, as though he had just accomplished with success something full of danger and of risk and wherein success had brought him a new conviction of power and security.

"Curious," Bobby thought, "a puzzle," and it interested him and worried him, because all puzzles interested him and worried him till they were solved.

He told himself the incident was one he must remember, must try to think about. He made a clear image in his mind of every detail of the water-colour. Perhaps if he went over it again and again in his memory he would be able to discover what hidden significance, if there were one, it enshrined for Mr Roman Wright.

But then perhaps the whole thing meant no more than that Mr Roman Wright was so unused to compliments, or to any show of appreciation, that even the purely polite remarks made by Bobby had gone to his head. Praise is heady stuff at times, especially for those not used to it, more especially if they themselves doubt if it be truly merited.

CHAPTER XXII

EX DEAN

THE EXAMINATION OF the shed and of the returned motor-cycle brought Bobby no further information, except, indeed, that a glance at the back tyre showed this was undoubtedly the machine on which escape the previous night from Theodores had been effected.

This fact, however, Bobby did not mention. For one thing, identification of the machine in no way helped to identification of the rider, which would have been so much more interesting and important. In the second place, what is not known cannot be told; and Mr Roman Wright seemed too chatty and talkative to be trusted with a detail Bobby had no desire should be spread abroad.

So he said no more than that every effort would be made to clear up the matter—one of those nice official phrases Bobby always found so useful as camouflage—but that even if the culprit were discovered it was not easy to say what could be done.

"Generally," he explained, "there can be a prosecution for theft of petrol, but this chap seems to have provided his own."

Bobby departed then, as there seemed no more to be seen or learned or done at Prospect Cottage; and as he walked away he found that just as he had wakened that morning still obsessed by Olive's tale of the Pleezeu Tea Garden and two silent women sitting there side by side before an untasted tea, so now his tormented thoughts returned perpetually to that incompetent effort in water-colour to which Mr Roman Wright had drawn his attention so pointedly, and of which he seemed so curiously proud.

"Most remarkable picture ever painted, indeed," Bobby repeated indignantly and aloud. "Talk about conceit—incredible," and the last word he muttered twice over to himself. "Never fails of its effect on his wife, doesn't it?" he said again, and wished he had a chance to ask Mrs Roman Wright for her own opinion of the thing.

Abruptly he discovered that he had in his abstraction taken the wrong path and was now almost opposite the vicarage. On a sudden impulse he turned in by the garden gate. Monday is the parson's holiday, and so he might have a chance to catch Mr Martin Pyne at home and disengaged. But when he knocked, Mrs Billings, Mr Pyne's widowed sister and housekeeper, came to the door to tell him that the vicar had gone away for a few days' change and holiday. Nor had he left any address. His holiday was to be a walking tour, and he had no settled plans.

"Dr Reynolds—the dean, you know—is most kindly taking duty for him while he's away," she explained.

"Not most kindly," corrected a voice from behind, "not most kindly, dear lady, but most gladly." There came towards the door a pleasant-looking, silver-haired clergyman, a man of probably about seventy years of age, but still strong and vigorous in appearance. He went on smilingly: "And not a dean. An ex-dean. Once a bishop always a bishop, but an ex-dean is a dean no longer." He chuckled at his little joke and to Bobby he said: "Is there anything I can do in the vicar's absence?"

"It's the police inspector," explained Mrs Billings. "There's one of the young men in the parish gone away, and his mother's worried about it, so the police are trying to find him for her."

"Oh, yes, I remember," said Dr Reynolds, "Martin said something about it." To Bobby he said: "Did you think the vicar could help in any way? I understood the boy wasn't one of his congregation and he didn't know much about him."

"I did think perhaps there were one or two things," Bobby answered vaguely. "Sometimes any scrap of information is helpful. There are complications."

"I trust no harm has come to the young man," said Dr Reynolds. "I'm sure the vicar would have been only too glad to give any help in his power. One of my oldest friends. I've known him since he was a student at the theological college where I was lecturing, and we've kept in touch ever since. Did you know he won a decoration in the first German war? Probably not. One of his little secrets. He won it when he was serving with the Dublin Fusiliers in the days when Ireland's name was still one to be proud of, still blazed in battle. One of the finest examples of our country clergy— the backbone of the Church. But don't tell him I said so," he added with another smile to Mrs Billings. "If you give him any praise he worries because he knows he doesn't deserve it, but he'll try to, and so he works harder still, when he is working too hard already."

"Indeed he is," said Mrs Billings, and sniffled and dabbed at her eyes. "I feel it's all my fault."

Dr Reynolds patted her on the shoulder and told her she must not say or think that, and she snivelled again and said she couldn't help it, and Bobby said how sorry he was to miss the vicar and retired, feeling almost as puzzled as when leaving Prospect Cottage.

Did Dr Reynolds, he wondered, and he remembered the name as that of a former and popular dean of Midwych, usually indulge on the doorstep in such paeans of praise of his friends? Not very dignified and very forthcoming, and yet the former dean was as dignified in manner and appearance as one should be who had held high office in the Church. Nor did he give the impression of being much in the habit of growing confidential to strangers. Nor yet of often using the somewhat flamboyant and excited language he had just indulged in. Was it possible all that had been deliberate, planned, and intended to prove to Bobby that the vicar was above all suspicion? Yet if his friends had to go to such lengths to show him beyond suspicion, then they must feel that grounds for suspicion existed? Suspicion of what? An ugly question. Had they any knowledge about which they preferred to keep silent? A still uglier thought: was such suspicion better founded than they knew?

Impossible, of course, to suppose that a man of Dr Reynolds's character and standing was concerned knowingly in any wrong-doing. But was it possible that that character and standing were being used as a cover for things of which he had no knowledge? Again a disturbing thought. And there was still the question of where the money came from that allowed Mr Pyne to pay for the education of three nephews? And was this sudden departure on a holiday, no address left, merely a coincidence?

Bobby seemed to hear again Olive saying so deplorably: "Co-incidence? Aw—nuts," and he was much inclined to agree. He gave himself an angry shake as these and other such thoughts buzzed to and fro in his brain, like bees preparing to swarm. He wished his thoughts would swarm like them on a central point, and so find refuge in the hive of truth. Yet how likely it was that all this was mere irrelevant detail, with no place whatever in the pattern he was trying to construct—a pattern that must neces-sarily remain incomplete till he knew where was the key piece, Ned Bloom.

He told himself it was as inconceivable that a man like Dr Reynolds could be playing any part in this doubtful and sinister drama as that, for instance, a water-colour painted some two years back could throw any conceivable light on recent happenings.

By now, worried and irritable at finding himself faced by so many irreconcilable contradictions, Bobby had reached Miles Bottom Farm. He was not surprised, late as had become the hour, to find Captain Dunstan only now finishing his breakfast, nor in any way surprised to be greeted with no great show of cordiality.

"Still snooping round, inspector?" Dunstan asked. "You know, if I had lost any one like Ned Bloom I should let him stay lost and glad of it. Why not call your men together and thank God you're rid of a meddling young bounder?"

"Bounder or not," Bobby said with some sternness, "he has a right to the protection of the law. If it is too late for that, then he has another right and the law another duty."

"Oh, well," Dunstan said, a little uncomfortably. "Oh, well," he repeated. He pushed back his chair. He began to fill his pipe. "I don't see why you need take it like that," he said. "Poking his nose into other people's business somewhere else, I expect. That's all. If you ask me, I can't see any reason to take it seriously."

"I shall continue to take it seriously," Bobby said, "till I know what has become of Ned Bloom."

"Well, I can't help you," Dunstan grumbled. "I don't know anything."

"Where were you last night?" Bobby asked.

"In bed."

"All night?"

"Depends on what you call all night. I sat up a bit late. Why?"

"Last night there were some curious happenings at a house called Theodores. You know it?"

"I've heard of it. They call it Tedders, don't they? Typical British joke. Well, what about Tedders and what did happen there?"

"Don't you know?"

"No."

"We had warning that an attempt at burglary might take place there. My men were on the watch. One of them saw a man climbing down a gutter-pipe from the first floor of the house. He tried to arrest him, but was knocked out. His assailant was followed, but got away safely. He was seen by another of my men and was described as tall and having one arm in a sling. There is further evidence that he came from this neighbourhood. Was it you?"

"Well, I must say that's putting it straight," Captain Dunstan exclaimed. He smiled as he spoke, but Bobby noticed that though he had filled his pipe, he left it lying by his plate as though he had forgotten it, and was now fumbling for a cigarette. "I thought detectives were more subtle than that. I thought you led your suspects on by clever, cunning questions till at last you got them cornered."

"I generally prefer to ask a direct question," Bobby said. "It is simpler, for one thing. Simplicity is sometimes more effective than clever cunning. Only when I ask a direct question I like a direct answer."

"Well, you know," Dunstan answered slowly, "I'm not so sure in your case whether it is simplicity or—or something else. Anyhow, I am not the only tall man in the world, or even in Threepence, and any one can put an arm in a sling. It comes to this; you suspect me of assault, attempted burglary, and I'm not sure you don't suspect me of attempted murder, too, for good measure. Well, that's quite a lot, and I don't like it one little bit. So I'm going to refer you to my solicitors, and I'm going to refuse to answer any more questions till I've consulted them."

"That is your right," Bobby answered quietly.

He took a note of the name and address of the firm and agreed that any further inquiry he had to make would be either direct to them or in their presence. "But you will forgive me for pointing out," he added gravely, "that your attitude is not that generally adopted by entirely innocent men."

"If it were," retorted Dunstan, flushing a little, "innocent men might save themselves quite a lot. I don't know what right you have to ask people questions like you are doing, or popping off pistols at them either, or hinting accusations of all sorts of crimes, but I tell you straight I don't like it, and I don't mean to put up with it any more than I can help."

"Well, then, I'll get on," Bobby said, rising, "with apologies for having disturbed your breakfast—and I hope you won't mind if I say that I was rather wondering if this morning I should find you had got up a bit late."

With this parting shot, which he felt Dunstan deserved, Bobby retired, having learned no more than that once again he was face to face with contradiction; for if he felt this talk had given him proof that Captain Dunstan was in fact the man seen at Theodores, there still remained the question of who fired that pistol shot, at whom, and why? Miss Wood, perhaps, he told himself; as capable, he believed, of firing pistols with intent as of sticking out her tongue.

CHAPTER XXIII

BOY SCOUTS

FROM MILES BOTTOM Farm, after an interview as unsatisfactory as he had fully expected it to be, Bobby went on to the small Threepence police station, where he found Sergeant Young waiting for him and already informed of the return of the missing motor-cycle.

"Some one pinched it just to use it," declared the sergeant, puckering his brows. "Leastways, that's what it looks like to me."

"Looks like that to me, too," agreed Bobby gravely. "I suppose you haven't any report of any motor-cyclist behaving suspiciously or attracting attention in any way?"

"Well, you see, sir," explained Young, "Mr Roman Wright's place is right on the main Midwych road, and even in black-out there's a deal of traffic up and down—Army dispatch riders and what not. No notice would be taken in a general way."

"I suppose not," Bobby said. "No reason why a motor-cyclist should be noticed. No report of any one seen near Prospect Cottage early this morning?"

"Now you mention it, sir," admitted Young, looking a trifle worried, "Constable Jones did say as he saw Miss Kitty Skinner there round about daybreak, and he wondered why she was there so early. He didn't report it, sir, there being nothing to report; just mentioned it, like."

"Well, give him a pat on the back for having kept his eyes open," Bobby said, and Sergeant Young looked very puzzled.

"You don't think, sir," he ventured, "as a nice young lady like her, always a smile for you and good to her pa and ma—"

"No, I don't," declared Bobby as Young came to a pause. "Only you never know, do you?"

This being incontrovertible, Young was reduced to silence; and Bobby decided that instead of returning at once to Midwych to try to catch up with all the other matters there needing attention, he would have a meal first at the Pleezeu Tea Rooms. He knew light lunches were served there, though the main profits of the business came from teas and, more especially, from the cake trade Mrs Bloom had built up.

First, however, he asked for a sheet of paper. Thereon he tried as best he could, and not without success—for he had a good visual memory and had taken very special notice of the thing—to reproduce an outline of the water-colour to which Mr Roman Wright had drawn his attention, which also had seemed to inspire in him so queer a kind of sly and leering triumph Bobby found more and more unpleasant the more he thought of it.

With the aid of the rough reproduction in outline, he thus produced, and by verbal description, he tried to convey to Young as clear an idea as possible of the scene painted by Mr Roman Wright.

"What I want to know," he said, "is it, as I think it must be, an actual sketch of an actual spot in the forest, and, if so, can it be identified?"

Sergeant Young thought it very doubtful. Wychwood Forest was a big place. There were spots in it that no human being visited from year's end to year's end—spots, indeed, that perhaps no human foot had trodden since the creation. This apparently was just such a wild and desolate spot for ever unvisited. A rummy sort of spot to go and paint, in Sergeant Young's opinion, but, then, artist gentlemen often were a rummy lot. For his own part, he wasn't very familiar with the forest, and didn't want to be. Threepence kept him busy. Growing potatoes in his garden was as near as he ever wanted to get to what some called Nature. If he ever had a day off, which happened once in a blue moon, as goodness and the inspector both knew—this with a glance and accent of sad reproach—he didn't spend it traipsing about the forest, and hadn't since he was a boy with no more sense than any other kid.

"What about the Boy Scouts to help?" asked Bobby, taking up the unconscious suggestion thus made.

Sergeant Young admitted reluctantly that there wasn't much those youngsters didn't know. If he had known half as much at their age, his old dad would have up-ended him, so he would, just for the cheek of it. If the inspector so wished, he would show the outline sketch to Mr Fletcher, the local Scout-master, repeat the inspector's description, and they could be sure the forest would be alive the next few days with the kids, poking about everywhere and thoroughly enjoying such a fine chance to get into every kind of mischief.

Bobby said he thought it was a jolly good idea of the sergeant's, and would he see it was put into action as soon as possible? He wondered he hadn't thought himself of asking the help of the Boy Scouts. Much pleased, Sergeant Young undertook that every Boy Scout in the neighbourhood would be on the job that very day; and Bobby was well pleased himself that by a few words of quite undeserved praise he had transformed Sergeant Young into an enthusiastic supporter of a project of which at first he had not seemed much inclined to approve. Now, Bobby felt, the Boy Scouts would be given every help and encouragement. If it were possible to identify that forest scene, of which the presentation never failed in its effect on Mrs Roman Wright, he told himself they would succeed.

"By the way, sergeant," he added, "do you know anything about Mr Roman Wright's niece, Jane, I think she's called—the one who lives with him and his wife? She is always hanging about Mrs Bloom's place as if she were worrying about Ned Bloom? Did you ever hear there was anything between them?"

The sergeant shook his head. He had never heard even a hint of such a thing. Young Ned Bloom had been different in that from most young lads. He kept away from girls. If they were nice to him he thought it was out of pity, and he took offence; and if they weren't nice to him, then the offence was deeper still. So far as he knew, Miss Wright and Ned Bloom had never even spoken to each other, unless it were to say "good morning". Not that he knew much about Miss Wright. She had been living with her uncle and aunt about eighteen months; looked after the house for them, did the shopping that, especially in a small village—and Three-pence was not much more—had become in war-time very nearly a full-time job. The Wrights seemed quiet, inoffensive people. Occasionally Mr Roman Wright, on one of his periodical trips to London, took her with him to see her parents, who were, it was vaguely understood, in poor circumstances, and glad to have her provided for. Certainly she was young enough to do war work, the sergeant agreed, but presumably she had been excused for some reason. Bad health, she said, though she looked strong enough, or else on the grounds that she was taking care of two old people.

"Mr Roman Wright looks strong enough and not so old as all that," Bobby remarked. "Quite capable of looking after himself and his wife, too. They have a daily woman, haven't they?"

"Three mornings a week, and not much help," said the sergeant, "seeing as it's Mrs Harris, deaf as a post and half blind, but very like the best they can get. Mrs Wright isn't up to much. Sort of worn-out, faded like. 'Non est', as the Frenchies say," and Sergeant Young could not forbear a glance at Bobby to see how this bit of culture had gone down. Satisfied, for Bobby looked so startled it was plain he had been impressed, Young added: "Mrs Harris did tell me once as everything was going to rack and ruin there after Mr Roman Wright's other niece left to join the A.T.S., and before Miss Jane came."

"When was that?" Bobby asked.

Sergeant Young scratched his head and tried to remember. About two years ago, he thought. He went off to consult his wife, and came back with confirmation. Almost exactly two years ago. Mrs Young was sure of that because it was at the same time that Miss Carrie Veale's disappearance had provided a nine days' sensation.

"Went off without a word to her mother or any one," Mrs Young said, "and no rhyme or reason to it. At first everyone thought she had joined the A.T.S., too, and then there was scandalous talk that she had run away to join Captain Dunstan—lieutenant he was then. Not a word of truth in it. Captain Dunstan was with his battalion the whole time, training in Scotland. Not that that had prevented tongues from wagging, though. But then the captain came back to spend a leave with Mrs Veale. That had put an end to the talk. Mrs Veale would hardly have had him lodging with her if he had run away with her daughter."

Bobby said that certainly seemed conclusive, and, not much interested in Miss Carrie Veale's fate, asked a few more questions about Mr Roman Wright's other niece. Quite different from this one, Sergeant Young informed him. Rather a noisy, on-coming young woman, in fact. Visited the 'Green Dragon' at times, and didn't at all keep herself to herself, as did the Roman Wrights. No one had been much surprised when she disappeared in a hurry into the A.T.S. No doubt the discipline had been good for her. Mr Roman Wright had only heard from her once or twice, and both he and his wife were a little hurt by her neglect. In Sergeant Young's considered opinion—and he spoke as the father of two—what most girls wanted today was discipline and lots of it.

"Only," he added moodily, "in our house, it's me that gets it."

Bobby sympathised, said he had found their talk most interesting and suggestive, and would the sergeant get the Boy Scouts on the job as soon as possible? Then, as he was going, he paused to ask if Young's inquiries had resulted in finding anything to show that old Mr Skinner did in fact possess firearms and therefore the means to implement his threat to put a bullet into the missing Ned Bloom.

"Well, sir," answered the sergeant, "there's some do say as he's been seen firing blanks to scare off the birds from his cherry tree. But I asked him, and he said he had neither gun nor blanks either. Even if it's true, he might have borrowed the gun, like. I couldn't find any one who had seen it themselves—just talk, seemingly. And then there's often shots fired and no one takes much notice—rabbits, rooks, pigeons, and suchlike vermin."

Bobby thought that was interesting, too, and then, as it was now getting late, he went on to the Pleezeu Tea Rooms for lunch; though those served there well deserved their saving description of 'light'—repasts, in fact, more calculated to satisfy a young woman intent on slimming than twelve stone, six feet of hungry masculinity.

Kitty came to attend to him when he took his seat, and came, he fancied, with a certain air of wariness and anticipation in her manner. He made his choice, repressing a greedy desire to order three lunches instead of one, and then said:

"May I ask you a question or two?"

"I suppose you will whatever I say," she answered.

"Well, yes," he admitted. "You see, I am still worried about what has become of Ned Bloom."

"He has not written or anything," she said slowly.

"What does Mrs Bloom think?"

"I don't know," she answered. "I haven't asked her. Why don't you?"

He wondered if it was only fancy that made him think she said this as if she did not much suppose either he or any one else would dare any such thing.

"Do you know Miss Jane Wright?" he asked. "A niece of Mr Roman Wright's?"

"She comes here sometimes," Kitty answered, and she had grown a little pale. "Why?"

"Do you know if there was anything between her and Ned Bloom? Any sort of flirtation, I mean?"

Kitty looked less startled now, almost amused.

"No," she said, "I'm sure there wasn't. Ned never had much to do with girls."

"You tell me Miss Wright comes here for tea sometimes. Does 'sometimes' mean fairly regularly?"

Kitty did not speak, but she nodded. Presently she said:
"Why shouldn't she?"

Without answering this, Bobby said:

"One more question, and more personal. You were out near Mr Roman Wright's house early this morning?"

"Yes," she said.

"Early this morning Mr Roman Wright's motor-cycle, which had been stolen the afternoon before, was brought back?"

"Yes," she said again.

"You will notice a certain coincidence?" he said, slightly irritated by this repeated "Yes".

"Yes," she said once more, and his irritation did not diminish.

"Do you wish to say anything?" he asked sharply.

"What about?"

"You don't care to explain why you were taking a walk so early in that particular spot?"

"Is it necessary to explain why one takes a walk in any one spot?" she asked. "If you mean: did I take the motor-cycle away or return it or know anything about it—I didn't and I don't. I knew Mr Wright had a motor-cycle, because he used to go off on it into

the forest, making his sketches. But I thought he had had to give
it up now there's no petrol."

With that she went away to attend to another customer, and
Bobby wondered if in this talk he had gained one more bit of in
formation to fit into the jigsaw puzzle of which he felt the pattern
was slowly becoming evident—unless, of course, the true pattern
was some other quite different from that of which he thought he
saw the outline.

CHAPTER XXIV

MUSIC-HALL AGAIN

BOBBY, EATING HIS lunch—his semi-demi lunch, he called it to
himself—and meditating how best to frame the questions he
wished to put to Mrs Bloom, was interrupted by word from Ser
geant Young to say he was urgently wanted on the 'phone.

The message proved in fact to be of some importance, not so
much, perhaps, in itself as because of its origin.

At any rate, Bobby felt obliged to return at once to Midwych
His talk with Mrs Bloom had therefore to be postponed, nor on
the whole was he much inclined to regret the delay. There would
be time to see if any of the lines of inquiry he had put in motion
seemed likely to be successful. Then, after his return, there came
another 'phone call, this time from Olive, asking urgently if he
could possibly find time to accompany her that evening on anoth
er visit to the New Grand Music Hall.

"Fell for it, did you?" asked Bobby, considerably surprised. "I
you want an evening out, hasn't your pal Priestley something on
somewhere? Generally has, hasn't he?"

"Mr Priestley," returned Olive severely, "is an Eminent Au
thor, and would be a knight at the least by now, not a pal, if only
he knew enough to keep in with the right people, and I did fall
for that funny little man we saw there, and what's more I've go
two tickets for the second house, and if you don't come I shall ask
Some One Else—never you mind who."

"Oh, all right," Bobby said. "I'll try to make it, only—second
house? What about the black-out and getting home?"

"In war, as war is," retorted Olive and rang off; and accordingly in due course Bobby found himself once more in the New Grand, and not best pleased to be there, either.

"I don't see—" he began grumblingly; and Olive told him to be quiet, he would see soon enough. So he said "O. K." and dropped off into a quiet and pleasant doze till aroused by Olive's elbow, diligently applied.

"Wake up and listen," she said. "I didn't bring you here just to turn a perfectly good fauteuil into a sit-up bed."

Bobby rubbed his eyes and tried to remember where he was and why. He discovered that Mr McRell Pink was on the stage. He was already well on with his first sketch—one of his most popular, 'The Man in the Kitchen'—and after it had ended and after one or two smaller items, including a funny story or two, he announced that he was now going to give 'A Slice of Life: The Detective Investigates the Missing Spring Cabbage'.

Bobby smiled and prepared to listen. At first he thought it was clever, amusing—rather too much of a burlesque, no doubt, but he heard with tolerance the shouts of laughter from a rocking audience. He found himself chuckling once or twice, then he laughed heartily, then grew grave, puzzled.

"What's the fellow think he's doing, anyhow?" he asked Olive in a whisper.

"I've no idea," whispered Olive back again.

"He might anyhow try to make it something like," Bobby grumbled.

"So he might, mightn't he?" agreed Olive.

After a pause, Bobby whispered again:

"I say, you don't think he's having the infernal cheek—"

"Certainly not," said Olive hastily. "Hush."

"—to be trying to make a skit on—"

"Oh, no," said Olive, "of course not."

"—Me."

"Hush," said Olive. "Why? What makes you think that?"

"It isn't a bit like, anyhow," declared Bobby heatedly.

"Well, then," said Olive soothingly.

Mr McRell Pink came to the front of the stage, and the laughter evoked by a last wisecrack—one that sounded as funny from him on the stage as it seemed feeble in memory—died away into a silence of anticipation.

"And there, ladies and gentlemen," he said in his high-pitched, far-carrying voice, "there we leave the lost spring cabbage, last seen on the way to Miles Bottom Farm in the company of a tall and attractive young lady."

The audience laughed and cheered because Mr McRell Pink had them in that mood—the mood all great comics can evoke—in which they were prepared to laugh at anything or nothing. Bobby jumped to his feet with a muttered exclamation and made himself extremely unpopular by the way in which he pushed and hurried and scrambled his way from his seat into the gangway. Mr McRell Pink skipped off the stage. By the time Bobby managed to get behind the scenes it was only to be told by a worried and bewildered staff that Mr McRell Pink had not gone to his dressing-room, but had walked straight out of the theatre in his make-up, just as he was. There the black-out had swallowed him up, and no one knew which way he had gone or what had become of him. Nor had he left a single article of personal belongings behind him—nothing but a note an/angry and dismayed manager was engaged in tearing furiously into the smallest fragments possible.

"Just says he's given his farewell performance for the time being, and perhaps for ever," the manager told Bobby, lifting despairing arms into the air. "Is that the sort of thing you expect between gentlemen? Walked out on me at a moment's notice—without a moment's notice."

"Can he do that? Haven't you a contract?" asked Bobby.

"No, I told you," answered the manager. "Fresh engagement every evening, so to say. Terms—cash before appearing and no guarantee. I could sack him any time I wanted to, he said, and he could quit as and when, and so he has," wailed the manager, and looked as if he were inclined to lay his head on Bobby's shoulder and there sob out his sorrows.

"Unusual sort of arrangement," Bobby suggested. "What's behind it?"

"Unusual?" snorted the manager. "Positively uniquely unparalleled—I mean to say, nothing like it that I ever heard of. But there it was. Talk you might. Take it or leave it, was all you got. So you took it." He sighed. "Like the strawberry-and-cream season— too good to last. Anyhow, he was worth ten times what I paid, and he got people into the way of coming regularly. That's to the good, anyhow, and while the entertainment boom lasts like now, possibly they'll go on coming. Thank God, people will pay anything for anything at present, and I believe I could put up some one to read Bradshaw aloud and still have the 'standing room only' boards out." So he spoke, seeking consolation, and then he paused and looked at Bobby. A new idea had come to him. "Is it you?" he asked. "Is it you he's dodging?"

"I don't know," said Bobby and in an injured voice: "Was he trying to take me off in that new thing of his to-night?"

"Oh, no," declared the manager hurriedly. "I told him myself. No personalities, I said. Besides, there was no resemblance."

"I know there wasn't," agreed Bobby heartily.

"Not a scrap," said the manager, equally heartily, for who wants to get on the wrong side of the police when any opposition they offer to the renewal of a licence receives such absurd attention?

"Not a scrap," echoed Bobby.

"No, indeed," said the manager.

"Which explains, I suppose, why my wife laughed so much," said Bobby, and went off to rejoin Olive, whom he found waiting for him in the foyer, no longer amused, looking very grave.

"Bobby," she said, "what did he mean?"

"He's done a bunk so I shouldn't get a chance to ask," Bobby said. "Let's go."

On the way home Olive told him what had happened. The two tickets had arrived by post. There had been nothing to show who had sent them. She had rung up the box office to inquire, and had been told that the purchase had been effected some days earlier. There was, of course, nothing to show by whom. Tickets were often purchased well in advance when Mr McRell Pink was billed. He had made Mondays and Fridays as popular as any other night.

Olive had further inquired about the programme, and then had learned that Mr McRell Pink was introducing a new item—'The Detective and the Lost Spring Cabbage'.

"I thought just possibly," confessed Olive demurely, "it might turn out to be a skit on you, and I thought it might be rather fun. I never dreamed—Bobby, he meant you to be there, and he meant you to hear what he said."

"Looks like it," agreed Bobby, "and now he's vanished into the blue. And was he trying to help, or was he merely trying to be funny, or did he want to put us off on a wrong trail, and if it's that—why? I tell you, my girl, I don't like it a bit."

CHAPTER XXV
CHILD SIGHT

THOUGH THERE WAS much needing his attention, Bobby was so far impressed by the music-hall incident that he put all else aside in order to return to Threepence the next afternoon. He had also put in train all the accustomed routine of search by which it might be possible to trace Mr McRell Pink. But there he knew he might receive less help than usual. Some of his confrères and colleagues in the police forces of the country would be sure to suspect what they would call "a publicity stunt", and put it down as no more than the attempt of a music-hall performer to get his name before the public.

"Some of these artist blokes will do anything to make themselves known," complained one Chief Constable's office over the 'phone. "Remember how many actresses have had their pearl necklaces stolen? Blown on a bit now-a-days, but used to be common form. When there's been fuss enough, ten to one your man will turn up smiling and say he never meant a thing—just being funny."

Bobby said he didn't think it was like that. Anyhow, there were other things about which he wanted to talk to Mr McRell Pink. The Chief Constable's office grunted and rang off. Bobby reflected that very likely that was the general belief, and it didn't look as if he were going to get very enthusiastic co-operation. For the one thing that annoys the Law more than any other, is the faintest hint of a suspicion that it is being made use of for advertising purposes. Then he fortified himself with a meal more substantial than the dream-like repast of the previous day and took the 'bus for Threepence.

When he alighted, his way into the village took him past Prospect Cottage. At a first glance he thought there was no one in the garden, and then he noticed in it the same small elderly woman he had seen on the occasion of his first visit and took to be Mrs Roman Wright. As before, she seemed somehow to be there only to be overlooked, so insignificant did she seem, so like something left over and forgotten. He had an impulse to speak to her on some excuse or another, but when he looked again she was no longer visible—"non est", Bobby remembered the sergeant had described her, and the quaint expression now seemed to him appropriate. Odd, too, how she had slipped away, as if she had by practice acquired a special skill in disappearance.

He went on to the Pleezeu Tea Gardens, and there met, hovering undecidedly near the entrance, Captain Sidney Dunstan. He greeted Bobby without enthusiasm. Bobby asked if he were having tea here. Captain Dunstan said, no, he wasn't. Why should he? Plenty of places where a bloke could have his tea if he wanted it, weren't there? Washy sort of stuff anyhow. Then he scowled more dreadfully even than before, though the scowl seemed intended more for the universe in general than for Bobby in particular, and therewith marched away, very much as if he were on a forlorn hope from which he never expected to return.

"Now, what's up?" Bobby asked himself. "General bad temper? Had a row? Who with? Well, well."

Therewith he entered the tea gardens and found himself a convenient seat. It was early still, and he apparently the first customer; though almost immediately he was followed by a youngish woman, burdened with packages and accompanied by a curly-headed, solemn-eyed little boy some three or four years old. She chose a table not far from Bobby's. The child pointed a finger at Bobby and said firmly "Man". Kitty appeared, took first the new-comer's order, produced a tall chair for the small boy, and then came over to Bobby, but very much as though she would have greatly preferred to do nothing of the sort.

"I thought you would be back," she said.

"I always shall," Bobby told her quietly, "till all this is cleared up."

"Will it ever be?" she asked.

"I hope so," he answered. "Will you ask Mrs Bloom if I can have a word with her—later on will do if she is busy now?"

"What for?" Kitty asked, and then said: "I will tell her."

"Thank you," Bobby said. "I saw Captain Dunstan outside here as I came in," he added.

Kitty managed to convey without speaking that nothing in all the world interested her less than anything concerning Captain Sidney Dunstan and that it was totally incomprehensible why Bobby should even mention his name to her.

"I have some fresh information now," Bobby continued. "Till now I've not been able to find that any one had seen Ned after he left my office. Now I'm told he was seen later that day on the road to Miles Bottom Farm."

Kitty could hardly turn more pale than the strain of these last few days had left her. But the quick glance she gave him and away again was full of fear and trouble. Profoundly disturbed she seemed. She said:

"That's a road that goes to many places."

"He was in company, I'm told," Bobby went on, "with a tall young lady. Was it you?"

But she went away without answering, and when his tea came it was brought to him not by Kitty, but by Liza, the same zealous if not overexpert child he had seen before.

Kitty had to appear presently, however, as more customers arrived and the tea garden grew busy. Bobby made no effort to attract her attention. Further questioning could wait. The question might work upon her, as such questions sometimes did work on people, and produce spontaneously an answer more significant than any pressure could have drawn. So he was content to sit and watch and to notice how often she looked in his direction, to see perhaps, if he were still there. A war of nerves, he supposed, and it is not only in politics and war that that can be effective. He fancied he saw Captain Dunstan once more hovering and scowling at the entrance. But he was not sure, for he had had no more than a glimpse, and the captain did not come in. Later on, Miss Jane Wright appeared and took her place at a table away from the others. Bobby watched with interest. She gave an order to the zealous Liza. When it arrived she poured herself out a cup of tea, but he did not see that she drank. Something attracted his attention—another glimpse of a hesitant young man at the entrance, who, however, was not Captain Dunstan, but probably some one waiting for a friend. When Bobby looked again, Mrs Bloom was sitting at Miss Wright's table. She had not come from the house, of that Bobby was sure. She must have made her way round by the back somehow and then by the side of the hedge. He could not see that either of the two women spoke, or indeed were so much as aware of each other's presence. Nor did he know why, as he watched them sitting there so quietly, he found himself experiencing a strange sense of unease and wonder—even of fear—so that he felt a pricking of the skin, an odd dryness of the tongue. He beckoned with authority to Kitty, whom he saw close by, but when she came he did not know what to say. She seemed to understand, though. She said to him:

"It is often like that. Not every day, but often."

"What does it mean?" he asked.

She did not answer, and went away. Bobby got to his feet, intending to go and speak to them. He did not do so, though he did not know why. He told himself it might be better to wait rather than to interrupt them, but he knew that was an excuse. He began to move towards the gate, since now that he was on his feet he had to go somewhere. He passed by the table where the woman with the child was still sitting. The child had been running about and playing while his mother rested after finishing her tea. Now he had run back to her, and she was telling him placidly not to be so silly. She was saying:

"But, darling, there isn't any man there. There never was, only two ladies."

The child insisted.

"Funny man," he said, "and now he isn't any more. Where did he go, mummy?"

"Darling," said his mother, not taking much notice, "I don't know what you are talking about."

Bobby stopped and said to her:

"Does your little boy think he saw a man sitting there at the table where those two ladies are?"

The mother looked surprised. The child, overcome with sudden shyness, did not speak, but nodded vigorously, then buried his face in his mother's lap. She said:

"It's only his fancy. There hasn't been any one there."

"Funny man," said the child, looking up. "Where did he go, mummy?"

"Never mind, darling," said his mother, beginning to collect her parcels. To Bobby she said smilingly: "Children have such quaint fancies. I'm afraid my Tommy's worse than others. Imagining things. It's not telling lies," she explained, "it's only that they can't quite tell the difference between what's real and what isn't."

"Or perhaps we can't," Bobby said.

"The bear under the table is quite real to Tommy," she assured him. "He'll grow out of it."

"I expect so," agreed Bobby.

"Anyhow," she concluded, "there certainly wasn't any man at that table. If there had been I should have seen."

"I saw no one, either," Bobby said, "and they were sitting just in front of me."

The mother smiled again, finished collecting her parcels, took the child's hand, and went off with a "Good afternoon" to Bobby. He went back to the table where now Mrs Bloom was sitting alone, for Miss Wright had just got up and had gone away. Still with that air as though she watched from an immeasurably remote distance, Mrs Bloom sat waiting for him. He said to her without preliminary:

"You haven't had any news of your son yet, have you?"

She replied only by a slight negative gesture of the head.

"What do you think has happened?" he asked.

"I do not know," she answered slowly. "But I do not think he can be still alive, or I should have had some word by now, or else he would have come back to me."

"Is that all you can tell me? You know no more?"

"No."

"Why does Jane Wright come here so often for her tea she never seems to want when she gets here?"

"I do not know, but I think it may be there is something she would tell me if she dared."

"Has she ever said anything?"

"She has never spoken a word, that I know of, to me or to any one else."

Bobby stood looking down at her gloomily and doubtfully. He had made no attempt to seat himself, nor had she asked him to, nor had she risen herself. Yet his feeling was that she looked down on him from above, rather than he on her, as was in fact the case. But it did not seem so. She made no effort to speak again, nor did she seem to expect him to say more. He told himself she was like an iceberg, as easy to question as an iceberg would have been. He said:

"One would think you did not much wish to help."

She did not answer in words, but when she looked at him and he saw the remote, deep glow in those strange greenish-hued eyes of hers he was no longer sure whether it was an iceberg he spoke to or a volcano. He said presently:

"You say you do not think your son is still alive. But you will not tell me why. Surely you have some reason, something more than merely that he has gone away. Do you think there may have been foul play?"

"Yes."

"Why?"

"He was strong and healthy except for being lame. If he had been taken ill, I should have heard. If there had been an accident, I should have heard. If he were safe and well, he would have written. What else is there?"

"Yes, I know," Bobby agreed. "That's how I've worked it out, too. But I don't get any farther. In a way I feel responsible. I feel if I had been more tactful, more sympathetic, when he came to see me that day, he might have told me what he knew, and then it would never have happened."

She considered this for a long time and in silence. Presently she said:

"He had a secret. He would not have parted with it so easily. He loved a secret more than anything else. Whatever you had said or done he would still have kept his secret, for a time at least."

"All the same, it makes me feel the more strongly," Bobby said, "that I've got to know, that if there's been foul play, then I've got to see it doesn't go unpunished. You, too, you suspect foul play?"

"I said so."

"By whom?"

"I do not know. I only—guess."

"Will you not tell me your guess?"

When again she shook her head with that slow, solemn negative movement she had used before, he said in an exasperated tone:

"Well, why not? I don't understand you. Why not?"

Hitherto she had spoken with that same strange manner, far distant and remote, she had always shown, as of one who spoke from another world. But now on a sudden she blazed into an intensity of emotion that seemed somehow both more understandable and more human than her former icy detachment from all earthly things.

"I only guess; a guess may be wrong," she said with a fierce intensity of emotion in her voice. "I'll say nothing to put doubt, suspicion on any one when she may be innocent, or when it may be what she did she did against her will. I'll not help you send any one else to go through it all, to stand and wait and watch and listen, while those you've never seen before decide what they'll do with you, and all the time questions, questions, questions go on and never end." She stopped, and the heat of her emotion died down as suddenly, as swiftly as it had arisen. Once more she was her own emotionless, unutterably remote self. She said: "What was I saying? I'm so sorry."

"Questions must be asked if truth's to be known," Bobby said. Murderers must be found and dealt with, or else they murder again and none are safe."

She seemed to ponder this, and it was as though for the first time into her distant and aloof detachment there broke an element of doubt.

"No," she said at last. "If you have killed once, you never kill again. That would be too dreadful. Not again. No." She got to her feet and now stood facing him. She said in a voice less calm, more broken: "I can't talk any more. I must go. There's nothing I know, nothing I can tell you."

"Could Miss Wright, do you think?" he asked gravely.

She did not answer that. Instead she said:

"When Ned was a baby, it was told me what would happen, but what is the good of remembering that now? I must go," she repeated.

She turned and went away gropingly by the hedge, and Bobby watched, more troubled than he cared to think by what she had said.

CHAPTER XXVI
PETROL DUMP

ALL THIS HAD taken so much time that by now it had grown late, teas were over, customers had departed, Kitty and her zealous little helper were busy at the task of clearing up. A humble task enough, and yet once more, as he glanced in her direction, Bobby was struck by a certain stately grace in all her movements; as though in gathering up cups and saucers, and shaking and folding cloths, none the less she remained still the great lady. He told himself she could have scrubbed a scullery floor in the same grand manner. He fancied, too, that she was well aware of his presence and his actions, but he decided not to speak to her. He left the tea gardens and went on to the Threepence police station where he found Sergeant Young in the company of the scout-master, Mr Fletcher, who had just arrived there with unexpected information.

"Mr Fletcher's boys have made a find he wants to tell us about," the sergeant explained to Bobby.

Mr Fletcher, a tall thin man with an M.C. and an artificial arm from the first German war, explained that his boys had been putting in a busy time roaming through the forest.

"I don't know that we've got what you want," he said, "but two of the lads have found a petrol dump."

"A petrol dump," repeated Bobby, astonished.

"Yes, not a very large one," Mr Fletcher said. "A dozen two-gallon tins, very carefully hidden underground in a kind of enlarged rabbit burrow. I've left two boys on watch."

Bobby thought they had better be relieved at once. Not at all a pleasant idea, two boys in that lonely forest on guard over what might well prove an essential link in the chain of evidence needed to bring a murderer to justice.

Considerably disturbed by this view of the situation, a perturbed Mr Fletcher undertook to conduct a constable to the spot forthwith, and it was with some relief that Bobby saw him start off again, this time in the company of a bewildered and resentful Sergeant Young, snatched literally at a moment's notice from his comfortable official desk, without even so much as a sandwich or a thermos flask, to spend what might prove to be a whole long night out in the forest. Certainly Bobby had promised that he in turn would be relieved as soon as it could be managed, but the promise had been made so hurriedly, and both the inspector and the Scout-master seemed so upset, that Sergeant Young had his doubts—but no supper. In his view, a desperate lot of fuss to make about a couple of kids.

Besides, even if a relief were duly dispatched, would the relief ever find him? Sergeant Young gloomily contemplated a relief lost in the forest wastes and himself wearily waiting all the long night through.

Alas! his fears proved to be but too well justified; his relief did get lost, and the sergeant still remembers resentfully that long chill vigil, all on account of a couple of kids. Nor has he yet overcome a consequent tendency to take but a jaundiced view of Boy Scout activities.

This settled, unheedful of the martyrdom to which he had condemned his unhappy sergeant, Bobby left the little cottage police station and found, to his surprise, Kitty waiting for him.

"When I went home," she said, "I told my father you were here. He would like a few words with you."

"Oh, yes, certainly," Bobby said, slightly surprised, for it was seldom when he was engaged on an investigation of this sort that any one ever showed any keen desire to talk to him. As they started to walk along together, he said: "I asked you a question just now. You didn't answer it. Are you the young lady who, I am told, was seen with Ned walking towards Miles Bottom Farm on the afternoon of the day on which he disappeared?"

"Father said," she replied cautiously, "that I was not to say anything till he had spoken to you."

"Well, that's prudent," Bobby agreed, "but perhaps there arc one or two things you would rather I asked you first. To begin with, I take it you know that suppressing evidence—that is, not telling all you know—may become quite a serious offence? It might even in some cases amount to what is called being an accessory, after or before the fact." She looked at him, her eyes nearly level with his own, and she had that air of haughty self-possession and control that went so ill with her assumed position of waitress at the beck and call of all.

"I am ready to answer for what I do," she said briefly.

"Well, yes," he agreed, "I think you would be. A self-reliant young lady, if I may say so. Yet I wonder if that answer of yours would be always fully satisfactory. However, to leave that. The question I want to ask is this: why have you quarrelled with Captain Dunstan?"

"I haven't," she told him with cold indignation. "There has been no quarrel. How do you know?"

For all her dignity of mien and manner, as little logical as any other woman, Bobby thought. He said with a faint smile:

"Well, you see, when a young man hangs about a tea-garden and then says, very bad-temperedly, that anyhow tea is washy stuff and he doesn't want any, and when a young woman in that tea-garden shows a complete and utter indifference at the men-

tion of that same young man's name, even a mere dull-witted policeman like myself can put two and two together."

She gave him another stare of haughty indignation and
surprise.

"The conclusions policemen come to do not interest me,"
she said.

"You know, I'm afraid this time they've got to," Bobby told her
quietly. "I will tell you how I see things, and you can correct me
if I'm wrong. It is true you were on the road leading to Miles Bottom Farm in the company of Ned Bloom. I am inclined to think it
was an accidental meeting, due to your both wishing to see Captain Dunstan and expecting to find him at the farm. I don't know
what Ned Bloom wanted—"

"You are quite wrong," she interrupted; "he was going away
from Miles Bottom Farm, not towards it, when I met him."

"You stopped to talk to him. Then you went on, and so did he,
the other way?"

"Were you watching us?" she asked with angry suspicion.

"Dear me, no," he said. "Merely putting two and two together
to see what they make. For instance, I don't think you would be
walking out to Miles Bottom Farm to see Captain Dunstan except for some very good reason, and as I know there had been a
quarrel between him and Ned, and threats had passed, I suggest
you wanted to make Captain Dunstan promise to take no notice
of Ned."

"Well, what's there in that?" she asked when he paused.

"Only this," Bobby continued. "I suggest that when you
found Ned had disappeared, and the time passed, and nothing
was heard of him, you began to grow uneasy, and the longer Ned
was away the more uneasy you grew, especially when you knew
that Mrs Bloom believed the boy was dead. So finally you asked
Captain Dunstan if anything had happened, and he thought you
were accusing him of being a murderer and—well, he was extremely angry, and you were angrier still at his being angry, and
that was that."

All Kitty's former self-possession had vanished. It was, in fact, a very subdued and even frightened young woman who was looking at him now.

"I don't know how you know all that," she faltered. "How do you? You can't have put it all together. It's just guessing."

"What matters," Bobby said, "is not how I know, or if I've guessed, or even if I've guessed right, but whether your suspicions are correct."

"Besides, you're all wrong," she told him eagerly. "It wasn't like that at all. I never called him a murderer. He had no right to say I did. I thought perhaps it was a duel."

"A duel?" repeated Bobby, considerably taken aback, for this was an idea that had never occurred to him.

"When I met Ned that day," Kitty continued, "he said Captain Dunstan had been trying to bully him. He was angry because he thought I was going to Miles Bottom Farm to see Mr Dunstan, and I wasn't at all—I was going for some eggs Mrs Jenks promised to let me have for mother. Mrs Jenks lives a long way past Miles Bottom Farm. Ned wouldn't believe me. He said Captain Dunstan thought he could say what he liked because of Ned's lameness. Ned was always awfully sensitive about it. He hated you to notice it, and at the same time was always making sure you couldn't help. He said he might be lame, but he could use a pistol as well as any one, and he would challenge Mr Dunstan to a duel. I told him not to be so silly, but when Ned didn't come home and it was so long I—I did wonder a little. I don't see that it was anything for Captain Dunstan to get so angry about."

"You say you met Ned," Bobby remarked. "You mean he was coming away from the Miles Bottom Farm direction. Had he been there?"

"No. He said he hadn't, and it was true, because I asked afterwards."

"I am wondering," Bobby explained, "how he managed to get to where you met him. I had all possible inquiries made. No one saw him on the Threepence 'bus, no one saw him about here except you. He leaves my office in Midwych, and the next that's heard of him he is on the road on the farther side of Threepence on the road leading back to Midwych."

"I think he came away from Midwych by the Barsley 'bus," Kitty explained. "There's a stop on the road where it turns away from Wychwood forest. I think Ned got off the 'bus there and walked across to the Threepence road. It's a very lonely part of the forest, all scrub and rock, and there isn't any path, but you can get through if you don't mind scrambling and climbing and getting your clothes torn."

"That explains a good deal," Bobby said. "Only what made him come back by that round-about way?"

"He always liked doing things in a secret, round-about way," Kitty said. "Poor boy! Father said once he had been dealt a bad hand in the game of life, but that he made it worse by playing it more badly still."

"I expect that's true enough," Bobby said thoughtfully. "I suppose the important thing is not the cards we are dealt, but how we play them."

But what he was really thinking to himself was that almost certainly, from Mr Fletcher's description, any one crossing the forest from the Barsley road to the Threepence road, coming out near Miles Bottom Farm would pass near that hidden cache of petrol now discovered by Mr Fletcher's Boy Scouts.

CHAPTER XXVII
ADVERTISEMENT

THEY HAD REACHED the Skinner cottage by now. Kitty pushed back the door and they entered, the door opening immediately into the kitchen. Mr Skinner was sitting there in his chair, in his accustomed place, near the window. Like a bearded Jove he seemed to Bobby's fancy, dominating this simple room where poverty had taken on a dignity of its own by sheer power of acceptance. He looked up at them frowningly as they came in, his manner not at all that of one with a confession to make or excuses to offer. He did not speak for a moment or two; nor did Bobby, through whose mind were buzzing the many thoughts and speculations roused by what Kitty had just told him.

A duel? A queer, disturbing idea. Could that possibly be what had happened? he wondered. If it were, it might explain much.

"Young man," said Mr Skinner in his most severe, authoritative voice, "what is the meaning of your having put one of your police on watch outside this cottage?"

"You've noticed that, have you?" Bobby asked. "Too bad. I told them they were to be sure to keep out of sight. The trouble is," he added apologetically, "we have to put up with any one we can get these days—men we wouldn't have looked at before the war, and now I hardly dare say 'bo' to one of them. They know I can't sack them, and though they can't clear out themselves, they can go sulky. And what is the good of a sulky policeman?"

"I'm not asking for information about your men," Mr Skinner said in the same severe tones. "Young man, you talk too much."

"Well, you know," Bobby explained with what was meant for his most winning smile, "if there's anything more useful to a policeman than knowing when to hold his tongue, it's knowing when to talk too much."

Mr Skinner gave Bobby a long and searching look.

"I think you seem an intelligent young man," he said finally.

"Well, I've often thought that myself," admitted Bobby, "but I never say so, in case other people disagree—even violently."

"He knows things without any one telling him," interposed Kitty, suddenly and indignantly. "I think it's beastly."

"Oh, I say, come now," exclaimed Bobby, equally indignantly. "What a thing to say."

"At this moment," said Mr Skinner, "you are simply trying to put me off by smart talk."

"You've noticed that?" asked Bobby. "I'm almost afraid I shall have to return your remark about being intelligent. I daresay it was fairly obvious, though. I often am. Obvious, I mean. It pays. The more obvious you are, the cleverer other people think you, and then they start being clever, too, and then you get 'em."

"I don't know what you mean by that," Mr Skinner said, but now not so much sternly as uneasily. "I ask you again: why have you put a constable here to keep observation on us?"

"Because," Bobby answered with a sudden change of tone, " think it proper in the exercise of my discretion as the responsibl officer of police in this neighbourhood." Less sharply, he added "I may remind you that I am answerable only to my immediat superior, the Chief Constable of Midwych, and through him t the Home Office—which in turn is answerable to you, though n doubt at rather a long remove."

Mr Skinner was still looking at Bobby in a somewhat puzzle manner.

"Obvious, you call yourself, do you?" he grunted. "Full c tricks as a ship's monkey, if you ask me. All that doesn't get awa from the fact that you've started a lot of gossip about me."

"Why, no," Bobby said. "No, not I. Ned Bloom."

"What do you mean? Ned Bloom? He's left the place."

"Yes," agreed Bobby, "he's left, and he has not come back, an that is what has started any gossip there may be."

Kitty said from behind:

"It's not that he's left, it's not that at all. What people are say ing is that he's been made away with."

"Is that what you think?" Mr Skinner asked.

"Not what I think, but what I fear," Bobby answered.

"Is every young scamp who leaves his mother and his hom to go off on his own affairs necessarily murdered?" demanded M Skinner.

"Far from it," Bobby agreed. "Very few of them, in fact—ver few indeed."

"He'll come back when he thinks he's been away lon enough," declared Mr Skinner. "In the meantime, there's a lot c gossip going on, and some of it is about me. I don't like it, and expect you to put a stop to it."

This was said so much like an order from higher authorit that Bobby could not help smiling a little.

"My dear sir," he protested, "if you really think that any polic in the world—even a Gestapo working full blast—can stop gossip you must have a good deal less experience of life than I shoul have expected."

"What do you mean by that?" growled Mr Skinner.

Mrs Skinner came into the room from behind. Apparently she had heard and recognized the danger signal in her husband's low, rumbling tones.

"Now, Jerry, now," she said rebukingly. To Bobby she said: "It's very sad if anything has really happened to that poor boy; but, if it has, we know nothing about it. How could we? Mr Skinner is very annoyed."

"Well, I'm sorry about that," Bobby said. "But there it is. It seems certain the young man knew something—or thought he knew something—that some one else didn't want others to know. And now he has disappeared, and as long as he remains disappeared, he can't be asked what it was he knew. It worries me, because he came to tell me he knew something, and I let him go without making him explain. I can't help feeling that with more tact and patience I might have got it out of him. Makes me feel responsible, in a way. His mother says it would have taken more than tact and patience to get him to part with any secret he knew. Perhaps that's so. Anyhow, he has vanished, and his secret with him—if he had one. What's more worrying still is that I don't get much help. People seem to be keeping things back."

"Nothing that has anything to do with his going away," Mr Skinner growled.

"How can I tell that till I know?" Bobby asked. "I don't like secrets. They are so apt to make trouble, mischief. If you know any and would tell me, trouble might be saved."

"An impertinent remark," pronounced Mr Skinner. "We all have private affairs that are no concern of any one else."

"Then there's the story," Bobby continued, "that you had threatened to put a bullet into Ned."

"He's always saying things like that," explained Mrs Skinner, intervening. "No one ever thinks of taking any notice."

"Oh, they don't, don't they?" roared Mr Skinner. "Let me tell you—"

"Yes, of course, dear," interrupted Mrs Skinner soothingly. To Bobby she said: "Wouldn't any one be annoyed if there was a young man prowling about the garden at night with a camera as if he wanted to try to take photographs?"

"Photographs?" repeated Bobby sharply, remembering at once that photograph of heaped-up jewellery he had found in the missing lad's 'den'. Here was the first reference to photographs he had so far come across. "What of? Photograph what?" he demanded.

Kitty had vanished into the back part of the cottage, the scullery. Mrs Skinner gave Bobby a maternal look as if to say: "You're much too young." Mr Skinner growled:

"I had heard of 'em before—country Paul Prys, I mean. The first time I had come across it, though. In the garden. If I could get about, lay my hands on them . . . I can't. Tied to my chair. So I said that—about putting a bullet into the next one. I didn't. If I did, what am I supposed to have done with the body? Boiled it up for soup in the scullery copper?"

"Father. Don't be—disgusting," said Kitty's voice from the scullery.

"Shut the door, my girl," retorted her father, "and then what you don't hear won't hurt you."

Kitty accepted the advice with a most emphatic bang. Mrs Skinner said three times over, each time more reproachfully than before:

"Jerry, Jerry, Jerry."

Taking no notice of this, though thrice repeated, Mr Skinner said to Bobby:

"There's no bathroom here." He seemed to expect Bobby to be surprised by this information. When no astonished comment resulted, he went on: "I don't know why. Easy enough to add a bathroom. It means we have to use the boiler in the scullery—at night generally. Takes too long to heat up in the morning for the three of us. Some young blackguards started hanging about outside in the evenings. I waited for them in my chair. I thought one of them might come near enough for me to get hold of him and shake his life out. I had a stick with a hooked handle I meant to use for a gaff. I didn't manage it. Kept off far enough. But I recognized Ned Bloom by his limp. He had his camera with him. I shone my torch on him and saw it plainly. He cleared out fast as he could. I called after him by name that I would put a bullet in him next time. By gad, sir, I meant it, too, at the moment. But I never saw him again, or any of the rest of the young blackguards either, so I never got the chance. I think they were really frightened, and I hope it did them good."

"Yes, I see," Bobby said. "A bit unlucky it happened just before Ned vanished, and I suppose it explains why there is this undercurrent of talk. Anyhow, thank you for telling me."

He went away then, troubled in his mind. Possible, he thought, that now he had been given the true story with cause and motive. Conceivable, he thought, that an old man of passionate and headstrong temper, carried away by a fury of indignation against village 'peeping Toms', might have fired a shot to frighten them away, rather than with actual intent, and yet by bad luck have killed.

A trifle suspicious even that Skinner had so quickly pointed out how impossible it would have been for an invalid like himself, tied to his chair, to conceal the body. But there was Kitty. Bobby had conceived a considerable respect for her strength of will, resolution and resource. Not beyond her, he thought, when the safety of her father was concerned, to carry out such a task.

He found himself thinking of their garden, a fairly large piece of ground. Graves have been dug in gardens before to-day.

Yet there was that other suggestion put forward almost by accident, almost reluctantly, apparently drawn out by his own questions, but possibly questions provoked and anticipated—the suggestion of a duel between the missing Ned and Captain Dunstan. Both suggestions could not be true, but one might be, and both had to be most carefully considered and followed up. Or was it merely an invention of Kitty's by which she hoped to divert suspicion from her father?

Bobby felt his head was beginning to whirl—too many possibilities, too many considerations altogether. A duel in these days seems fantastic. All the same, Bobby felt the idea could not be too lightly dismissed. Dunstan might have been taunted into compliance by more of such sneers at his courage as Ned seemed already to have been responsible for in trying to hint that Dunstan's wound had been self-inflicted—a story none the less likely to anger a high-spirited young man for being so entirely unfounded and improbable. Dunstan might conceivably have accepted the challenge with some idea of 'teaching a lesson' to Ned, and then by unlucky accident, rather than by intention, a fatal conclusion have resulted.

Two alternative explanations. Either might be true, or neither. But each got over the difficulty Bobby had felt before that neither Mr Skinner nor Captain Dunstan seemed like murderers, even though Bobby knew well that murder is the one crime that almost any one may be guilty of in just one single instant of loss of self-control.

Both were men of passionate and head-strong temperament, and Bobby could easily picture either one of them as trapped by circumstance and his own temper into hasty action, with tragic, unintended results.

Taunts from a spiteful tongue, anger at indecently prying eyes, these at times have roused a height of temper overtopping reason and control.

A hard task, Bobby told himself, to disentangle the truth from so many conflicting considerations, and he was both looking and feeling worried when at last he reached home. Olive, alone in the house—the woman who came in 'as a favour' to help had long since departed—gave him first his belated supper and then showed him a paragraph in the evening paper.

Bobby read it with interest. It was to the effect that a Government grant of £5,000 had been made to Mrs Billings, widow of the late Lawrence Billings, on account of suggestions made by him for the improvement of the detection of sound-waves under water. It was added that Mrs Billings, now a resident of Threepence, near Midwych, was receiving many congratulations on this long-delayed recognition by the Treasury of the value of her late husband's work.

"I suppose it must be true?" Olive said.

"Oh, yes," Bobby agreed. "An item like that couldn't be a fake."

"Well, then," Olive said.

Bobby went to the 'phone. He called up in turn the two local papers as well as the offices of the 'national' papers that produced

ocal editions. Each one he asked to insert in the personal column
of the next issue a notice he dictated. It ran:

"To M. P., from E. X. Dean. Be in the church porch at midnight to-morrow."

CHAPTER XXVIII
NEW SUGGESTIONS

AT LAST BOBBY finished all his 'phoning. Olive had been listening
thoughtfully. She said:

"Even if he is there in the church porch so late—what made
you say midnight?—how much farther forward will you be?"

"Don't know," Bobby answered, "but you've a better chance to
find the right road if you can mark others 'no thoroughfare'. I said
midnight because I want it to be quite dark, so he won't be able to
see who is there and sheer off, and also to make it more difficult
for any one else to stop him from turning up."

"Oh, well," admitted Olive. She held up her hand and told off
each finger in turn. "One," she said. "Mr Skinner and that daughter of his, and why is she pretending to be a waitress, and why is
he pretending to be poor?"

"Miss Kitty is a waitress, and a jolly good one and no pretence," Bobby said, "though I don't know why; and if Mr Skinner
is pretending to be poor, it's a very realistic pretence."

"Only," Olive pointed out, "he can't be, can he? I mean, not
poor, not if what you've worked out about him is right."

"And how in blazes," demanded Bobby, "do you know what
I've worked out? I've never told you."

"You've said quite enough for any one to see what you are
thinking," retorted Olive, "and you've only not said because
you're afraid it's all wrong and then I shan't think you are really
so awfully clever after all. As if," said Olive with quiet scorn, "any
woman ever thinks her husband awfully clever. Poor things! We
get to know them too well."

"Hum," said Bobby. "Huh. Hah."

"Two," Olive went on, without requiring these quaint sounds
to be translated into words—she supposed it was probably Basic
Language. "Two. Mr Martin Pyne, though that's pretty clear now,

isn't it? Only there's still why did Mr McRell Pink run away, and you can't really truly believe it even now, can you?"

"Well, it is pretty incredible," Bobby admitted, "only it does—" He broke off abruptly: "What do you mean by 'it'?" he demanded

Olive had reached her third finger by now, and she made no attempt to answer his question.

"Three," she said, "and that's the Roman Wright family, and what did Mr Roman Wright mean by calling his water-colour the most remarkable picture ever painted, and is it?"

"A daub if ever there was one," declared Bobby—"a daub even among all the rest of his daubs."

"And what," continued Olive, "is the effect it never fails to have on Mrs Roman Wright, and why has Miss Jane Wright taken to going to Mrs Bloom's for her tea?"

"If I knew—" began Bobby, and paused.

"Well, of course, but you don't," Olive said, "and it is still a very big 'if', isn't it?" Her little finger was lifted. "Four, the Theodores business, and who got away on the motor-cycle, and who fired the pistol shot?"

"Not to mention," Bobby added, fixing a stern eye on Olive in case she showed any sign of being amused "that young female who had the cheek and insolence to put out her tongue at me, and where does she come in?"

"Needs a good slapping," said Olive absently; "but don't you think the key to everything is why the poor boy took the Barsley 'bus to go home by, instead of the Threepence 'bus, and walked back across the forest? It's not so very far, but it's awfully rough going, especially for any one lame."

"I shouldn't wonder," Bobby agreed. "But there you are again. All guesswork. There is this petrol dump, of course, Mr Fletcher's boys have found, but there may be no connection. Some one who had petrol saved up or bought on the black market, didn't dare use it or keep it in his garage or near his house, and hid it there for an emergency. Like the story of the chap who is said to have hidden two or three hundred pounds in gold in Wychwood for use in case the invasion came off, and now he can't find it. All theory guesswork. No solid evidence. Shut your eyes, make a dab with a pin, and you may pick a winner and you may not. There's still the chance Ned may turn up smiling any moment and want to know what all the fuss is about, and he never meant anything at all and never had any private secret knowledge."

"If he does—" began Olive.

"If he does," interrupted Bobby, "I shall feel like murder myself."

"If he does," repeated Olive, "there's still a lot to explain."

"The dickens of a lot," agreed Bobby, "but nothing on which to continue police action."

"The photograph of all that heap of jewellery?" Olive suggested.

"What about it? Nothing you can identify. Might be a deliberate fake—Master Ned Bloom's peculiar sense of humour. Or just nothing at all. Can't be sure."

"There's Mrs Bloom," Olive said. "She could tell you a lot."

"Yes, but she won't," Bobby said. "Sends shivers up and down your back looking at you, but won't tell a thing. I can't make her out. Ned was her son and she loved him, and all the more, I think, for his lameness. But I'm not so sure what form that love of hers might not take." He stopped abruptly and looked long and hard at Olive, so that she looked back in a puzzled way. He said slowly: "You know, I think perhaps she might you."

"Me what?" asked Olive.

"Talk to you. She won't to me, but she might to you."

"Oh, I couldn't," Olive exclaimed.

"You did once," Bobby said, thinking of a time when she had persuaded one in great distress to tell things she had hitherto kept hidden.

"But—Mrs Bloom," Olive said uneasily.

"You needn't do anything, ask anything," Bobby said. "Much better not. Only go there and order tea and tell them who you are. If she likes to talk, listen. If she doesn't, come away."

"She frightens you," Olive reminded him still more uneasily. "Doesn't she?"

Bobby nodded.

"She frightens every one," he said. "I expect every one was frightened when Lazarus came out of the tomb. If she says any thing, it will be like that, like some one coming from the grave."

"Very well," said Olive.

It was Bobby who was looking uneasy now.

"No," he said. "You had better not. I wish I hadn't thought of it. It just struck me. I didn't realize."

"Bobby," Olive said, and her voice was a whisper, "Bobby, you don't think there's any truth in—in—"

"In its being what they call a 'mercy killing'?" Bobby asked. "I don't know. Apparently it's one of the two favourite theories in Threepence itself. Two parties at the 'Green Dragon', Young tells me. One says it was Mrs Bloom because she couldn't bear any longer to see the boy a cripple and his telling her it was her fault. The other party says it was Skinner and why don't I have their garden dug up? Because then we should see what we should see, and anyhow that girl of his is a proud piece and walks as if the ground wasn't good enough for her to tread on."

"I think it's horrid of them," began Olive heatedly, "only . . . well . . . I suppose I'm the same. You can't help wondering."

"I believe some of them are making bets about it," Bobby said, "and that is going a bit too far—indecent. Young says he has heard that Roman Wright gave them a lecture the other night. Told them they ought to be ashamed of themselves; and they had no right to say such things about their neighbours, just because Mrs Bloom was a bit queer in her manner and Mr Skinner rather violent in his. Wound up by offering to bet the lot of them they were all wrong, and for his part he would be ashamed to suspect any one of being a murderer—any one at all. And ended by saying that Inspector Owen would be sure to get at the truth in the end, if he were only half as clever as every one said."

"Well, that was very nice of him," said Olive, "very nice indeed."

Bobby shook his head.

"Not too good," he declared. "Getting a reputation for being clever, I mean. Makes people expect too much, and then they are apt to be disappointed. Much safer for them to think you are stupid. Then they don't expect anything and never feel let down. I say, what about bed? Look at the time."

Olive said she had been looking at it long enough, and therewith they retired. Bobby, indeed, slept well—he had the habit—but Olive was pale and red-eyed in the morning from restless and broken slumber.

"Every time I did manage to go sleep," she said, "Mrs Bloom was there, telling me things I didn't dare to listen to."

"See here," began Bobby uncomfortably, "it was only an idea of mine."

But Olive shook her head when he went on to try to persuade her to forget the suggestion he now regretted having made.

"I don't want to a bit," she said frankly, "but I've got to. I don't know why. I suppose it's silly, but I feel somehow as though she were waiting for me."

Bobby repeated that he thought it was better left alone, but after that he said no more.

So, after a somewhat hurried breakfast—for his own feeling was that things were approaching a climax, and the day might not be long enough—Bobby departed for his office. There he found with satisfaction the result of a line of inquiry he had instituted concerning the Skinner family. However, there was no time to follow that up for the present, the less so that now there arrived a plaintive report from the unfortunate Sergeant Young, telling how all that long, long night—the longest in human history—he had waited, waited, waited in the chill drear forest for a relief that never came, never came till long after dawn, and then so exhausted with hours and hours of wandering in the forest, lost and forlorn, as to seem less a relief than a rag.

"Poor devils!" said Bobby, filled with pity and regret, "and it's nothing to grin at, Payne," he added severely to his assistant; "you wouldn't have liked it yourself."

"No, indeed, sir," agreed Payne. "Quite another 'the boy stood on the burning deck' stunt, isn't it?"

"Quite different," pronounced Bobby coldly; and grabbed the 'phone and sent out a soothing message, all honey and sympathy, advising bed for the rest of the day—Young was already there, with no intention whatever of leaving it—and going on to arrange for the succour of the other unfortunate, relief or rag, as soon as possible. Next he rang up Mr Fletcher, the Scout-master, and confirmed arrangements, already completed, for meeting him and the two boys who had made the original discovery, and who claimed as by right permission to themselves show the exact spot to the police. Then as soon as all other necessary steps had been completed or arranged for, he set out for the appointed rendezvous, taking with him in the car Sergeant Payne and large and brawny Constable Watts, this last-named a little puzzled by instructions to bring with him a spade and pick.

CHAPTER XXIX

OAK SEEDLING

AT THE APPOINTED spot Mr Fletcher and two small boys—slouch hats and poles all complete—were duly waiting. Bobby greeted Fletcher, paid the two small boys a grave compliment—as man to man—on their discovery, and then they all started off. As far as possible they went by car, then alighted to continue on foot, though this did not so much mean walking as scrambling, climbing, even crawling in one place to make a short cut through a kind of tunnel of bramble. The large Constable Watts, carrying reluctantly and he thought most unnecessarily both spade and pick, made but heavy going of it. In this part of Wychwood forest the trees were stunted; the undergrowth a jungle; bracken often impassable; here and there sullen pools still lingering in spite of the recent dry weather, the water held in small rocky basins sometimes quite deep under the surface. Sometimes, too, there were bare patches where stone and rock came to the surface in outcrops often steep and rugged. Some miles farther on this formation culminated in a quarry that had been a source of much building material in former days, but here the stone had never been worked. No doubt transport had always presented difficulties.

As desolate and as deserted a part of the forest as any its great expanse could show, Bobby thought. It reminded him strongly of the scene shown in that water-colour of which Mr Roman Wright had boasted that it was the most remarkable ever painted. Some-

here about here, it seemed likely, the original of that scene was
o be found.

Now, not without a bruise or two, some damage to clothing
hat is always so serious in these coupon-ridden days, an occa-
ional fall, and one small boy lost till it was found he had wriggled
is way ahead, they came to the scene of the discovery, where
he relief sent from headquarters was waiting, smoking a med-
ative pipe. For this, he felt, was an occasion when the order
gainst smoking on duty might be considered "temporarily abro-
ated"—"washed out for the time," he said, preferring five short
vords to two long.

In one respect Bobby was disappointed, for a vague hope he
ad cherished that this might prove to be the scene of the wa-
er-colour was plainly unfounded. As lonely, as desolate, as that,
o doubt, but in aspect and surroundings entirely different. He
ermitted himself, too, a faint regret that initiative was quite so
horoughly taught and practised in the Boy Scout movement.
Iost desirable, of course, but this time initiative had induced the
ids to haul out the petrol tins and make a neat pile of them to
ne side, whereas Bobby would have much preferred it if they
ad been left in their original position. Also there had been a
ood deal of running and tramping to and fro, so that Bobby did
ot suppose there would be much chance of signs or tracks being
eft to provide any clue to the identity of whoever was responsible
or this petrol depot in the woods.

The hiding-place selected had been under a huge boulder
vhere the long processes of time and weather had washed away
he earth. The sort of small natural cavity thus formed—it was
lmost a cave—had been further enlarged apparently to contain
he petrol tins, and yet not enlarged enough, since no room had
een found for four, which had merely been concealed close by
nder a covering of twigs and leaves. It was these which had been
oticed first by some sharp-eyed lad, and then further search had
iscovered the rest of the tins in the deep cavity under the great
pstanding boulder.

Bobby was a little puzzled, though, by certain signs which in-
icated that the efforts to widen and deepen the cavity were quite

recent, and yet they had not succeeded in making it big enough to hold all the petrol tins. Moreover, it seemed curious that the four apart under the bushes had apparently not been long in that particular spot, while those under the boulder showed every sign of having been in place some considerable time. An inconsistency there, Bobby thought, and inconsistencies he never liked. He was still puzzling over it when Payne, who had been hunting round on his own account, came up.

"Something to show you here, sir," he said.

He led Bobby to a spot outside the kind of glade where they were standing and showed him tyre tracks on a spot of soft ground where underlying water had kept the ground soft in spite of the recent drought.

"Motor-cycle," Payne pronounced. "Too deep for a pedal machine."

"Yes," Bobby agreed, and went down on hands and knees to look more closely, and especially more closely at a spot Payne had marked by a twig thrust into the ground near. After a very close examination he said: "Yes, it's only faint, but it's the same triangular patch there was near Theodores. The same man who was dodging about Theodores that night was here recently."

"Came for petrol; this is where he got it," Payne said. "Who is he?"

Bobby did not answer.

"Captain Dunstan?" ventured Payne. "It was him before."

This time Bobby had no chance to answer, for Mr Fletcher was calling.

"I wanted to tell you the boys think they have found a place rather like your description of the one you wanted," he said. "Quite close. A hundred yards or so. I expect they would have spotted it before only for being so excited about the petrol tins."

Bobby called Watts, told him to mark off the damp spot where the tyre marks showed, by means of a circle of branches he could cut from the trees near. Then he and Payne accompanied Mr Fletcher to the new discovery. When they reached it Bobby recognized it at once.

Here was the very scene the water-colour had shown, and there the curiously distorted tree to which, in the picture, Roman Wright had drawn attention as, in his opinion, tying the whole composition together.

A dreary place, a queer place, Bobby thought, to choose for subject. Wychwood Forest has many beauty spots, but this was none. Here bracken grew, and weeds, and the trees were stunted and the bushes a tangle, and it seemed as if here the sunlight never came and that here the air was always stagnant and the ground only waiting for a little rain to turn into a foetid swamp.

Payne, who was standing behind, said:

"It looks to me as if no one has ever been here since creation day."

"Oh, I wouldn't say that," Mr Fletcher answered. "Not very often, perhaps. Not attractive—gives one the shivers, somehow. But I think I remember being this way with a few of the elder boys some years ago. It's the smell I remember. There had been a good deal of rain, and there was a smell of rotting, a smell of things decaying. I don't think any of us ever came again."

Bobby was concentrating every faculty of his mind on the scene before him, intently struggling to reproduce mentally every feature, every line of Mr Roman Wright's drawing. It had impressed itself on his mind, and feature by feature he went over it in his memory.

"Why should any artist choose a scene like this?" he asked Mr Fletcher.

Mr. Fletcher said he didn't know. Payne suggested that artists are a rum lot and you never knew. Watts, who now had joined them, yawned. He thought it would be a good idea if they set off home. For his part he was quite ready for his supper. The two lads, equally bored, had been chasing each other through the rock and undergrowth. Now one of them, anxious to show off his woodlore, came up to Bobby and said:

"That's a pine in the middle there. Hasn't it grown crooked? It's a little oak next to it."

"Is it?" said Bobby abstractedly. "Is it now? An oak, is it? You know, that's interesting. Very. How old is it, do you think?"

The boy considered this carefully. Then he gave his verdict. Three years, he thought. He appealed to Mr Fletcher. Mr. Fletcher thought only two years. He gave his reasons. Bobby, listening, regarded the seedling with renewed and close attention. It was beginning to loom large in his imagination, to take on a strange significance. It had not been shown, he thought, in Mr Roman Wright's water-colour, almost photographic in detail as that had been. Presumably, though, it had not been there to show, since, according to Mr Fletcher, it was only two years old, and two years ago was about the time when Mr Roman Wright had painted the scene. Yet Mr Roman Wright had certainly made some remark about an oak being there in that exact spot where this seedling was growing now. He had even said something about its growing tall and big, and had seemed to hope that it would do so. Why? Why had he wished for an oak in that particular spot? Or expected it? Had he planted an acorn there himself? Why? Why should he? Bobby said:

"I'm no woodsman, but I don't remember noticing any other oak as we came along."

Mr Fletcher, wondering at this sudden interest in trees, said he hadn't taken special notice, but certainly there were few oaks in this part of the forest. Ground didn't suit them; he would have been surprised if there had been many. In fact, it was surprising to find even this one seedling growing here. Bobby asked how it had got itself planted. Mr Fletcher, looking a little pained at the use of the word 'planted' for a seedling, said he supposed perhaps a bird might have dropped an acorn. Or even a squirrel. One never knew. Or possibly one of his own boys had thought to push an acorn into the ground here. He had often talked to them about the need for afforestation. Anyhow, he said smilingly, it had got there somehow, and it was pretty certain no one would ever know how.

Bobby said he supposed not, and suggested that Mr Fletcher might like to take the two boys back to Threepence now. Watts would go with them to the car and drive them to the village and then return. He himself, Bobby said, would remain a while with Sergeant Payne and have a further look round. They might find something else. No telling. Mr Fletcher smiled proudly, and said that if anything of any interest had escaped his boys he would be—well, surprised. He indicated that he did not in the least expect to be surprised. Bobby agreed it wasn't very likely, and gave Watts his instructions.

"May as well leave that spade and pick here," Bobby added negligently. "No use toting them around."

Constable Watts smiled gratefully. He was heartily sick of the things. But Mr Fletcher had not added to the experience of the first German War a good many years of still more enlightening and enlarging experience in the company of small boys without learning how to put two and two together. He said aside to Bobby and Payne:

"That seedling hasn't been transplanted recently or anything like that, you know. I'm sure of that. It's been growing there two years at least."

"Two years is a long time," Bobby said vaguely.

Mr Fletcher shrugged his shoulders and departed. If the police liked to waste their time, no affair of his. When they were alone, Bobby possessed himself of the pick.

"Like to do a bit of excavating?" he asked Payne.

"The oak sapling?" Payne asked, puzzled.

"Oh, I'm not going to try to transplant it," Bobby assured him. "Wouldn't like to, somehow. In any case, I don't suppose it would ever come to much. A stunted, twisted, evil growth."

"Sir?" said Payne, startled by this. "Why?"

"Oh, I may be wrong," Bobby said.

He started to work. Presently Payne relieved him. After Payne had been digging for a time he stopped and said abruptly:

"There's something here."

"Dig carefully," Bobby said. "Dig very carefully."

Payne with care lifted another spadeful and yet another, still more carefully. His face had taken on a chalky, sickly hue. He rested on his spade and said:

"In God's name, sir, how did you know?"

"Go on digging," Bobby said. "Shall I?"

Payne worked on, ever more carefully, more slowly. Presently he put down the spade and scrambled out of the hole they had made. He looked as if he were going to vomit. When he had recovered a little, he said:

"It's him all right. There's a foot and part of a leg uncovered now, plain to see. How did you know, sir? How did you know Ned Bloom was buried here? How can he be?"

"I don't think he is," Bobby said. "I think it is a woman we have found."

"A woman?" Payne repeated. "But there's been no woman ever reported missing hereabouts—never."

"No," agreed Bobby. "That was clever, wasn't it?"

Payne had gone back to the hole they had made and was looking down at the dreadful thing uncovered there, so well, so long and truly hidden, now brought at last to the knowledge and the justice of God and man.

"That's why you got rid of the kids, isn't it?" Payne said. "Good thing too, sir. Not fit for any kid to see."

Sounds behind made them both turn. One of the Boy Scouts was there. For some reason, on some pretext, he had come back. His eyes were bright and shining, his cheeks flushed.

"Crumbs," he said delightedly, "if they haven't found a dead 'un."

Bobby turned on him angrily.

"Get out of here," he almost shouted. "Quick now. Hurry." He called after him as the boy scuttled away. "Mind, hold your tongue; not a word to any one."

"Oh no, sir," said the boy.

"If you do," said Bobby, searching in his mind for the most awful penalty he could imagine, "if you breathe a word—I'll ask Mr Fletcher to throw you out of the Scouts for good and all."

"Yes, sir, I promise, sir," said the lad and vanished, having at any rate learnt to know when defiance was possible, when obedience was necessary.

Bobby turned gloomily to Payne.

"All the same," he said, "it'll be all over the place before long. Secrets can't be kept."

CHAPTER XXX

VANISHED WATER-COLOUR

UCH A DISCOVERY as this that had now been made naturally meant that very many different matters had to be attended to. Every one was kept exceedingly busy for the rest of the day; and, whether by the fault of the little Boy Scout, or, more probably, simply because of the many signs of unusual activity to be observed, soon the whole neighbourhood was buzzing with rumours of one sort or another.

It couldn't be helped, Bobby told himself, and he anticipated with resignation the arrival on the scene of various reporters, most of them probably much more keen on securing a front-page story than on consulting the convenience of the police.

One of the first things Bobby did was to send Watts to Prospect Cottage to find Mr Roman Wright. But very soon Watts returned to say that Mr Roman Wright was in London on business and was not expected for a day or two. Watts said also that his knocking and ringing had gone so long unanswered that he had thought no one could be at home till, just as he was going away, he discovered Mrs Roman Wright in the garden.

"She must have been there all the time," he complained to Bobby. "Somehow you never seem to see her. Swore she hadn't heard me knocking. Can't imagine why I didn't see her before."

"She has practised the art of being inconspicuous," Bobby remarked; and wondered if Roman Wright had vanished on account of this discovery, or for fear that it was about to be made.

But that did not seem likely. He could hardly have known so soon what was happening.

Bobby had also rung up Olive to ask her to meet him at the little Threepence police station, but he was delayed in getting there, and when he did arrive he found that she had been and had gone again, leaving word that she was going to the Pleezeu Tea Rooms for her tea.

Presently she returned. She had nothing to report. Everything had seemed much as usual. A fine day and business good. Olive had asked Kitty if Inspector Owen had been, and Kitty had looked disturbed and had answered, no, she had not seen him. She had either not heard any of the rumours with which all the district was alive, or else had not seen fit to refer to them. Olive had asked her to tell Mrs Bloom she was there, but to that request Kitty had made no reply. She had gone away to attend to another customer and she had not come near Olive again.

"Do you think she did tell Mrs Bloom?" Bobby asked.

"I don't know," Olive answered. "Miss Skinner is rather an alarming sort of young person. You feel you don't know why she's there or what to make of her. I waited for a time, and Mrs Bloom didn't come, so I went away. I didn't see Miss Wright either. Everything was absolutely ordinary. People sitting about having tea, talking, and so on. It's rather nice there. So was the tea. Only—"

"Only—?" Bobby repeated, when she paused.

"Oh, I don't know," Olive answered, with an uneasy and unmirthful laugh. "Imagination. That's all. Nerves, I suppose. Only—well, as if there was someone there you couldn't see, waiting. Just waiting. If you know what I mean."

Bobby said he knew what she meant all right. He said if she would wait a little he would be ready to go back to Midwych with her, and then she would have to go on home alone while he came back to Threepence to keep his appointment in the church porch.

"Suppose there's no one there?" Olive said.

"Then I shall have a long wait for nothing," Bobby answered. "Not for the first time, and probably not for the last."

Olive said he must remember to take an overcoat, as it was sure to be cold and draughty in the church porch and he might have a long wait; and Bobby explained how disastrously discipline would be affected if it got about in the force that the inspector coddled himself.

"'Noblesse oblige'," he reminded her, "inspectorship even more so," and Olive said that was nonsense, and very silly as well, and she didn't think much of an inspector whose authority depended on no overcoat. Let him, she exhorted him, pluck up his courage, put it to the test, take his overcoat and a woollen muffler as well, and show himself a real boss.

Bobby, slightly alarmed lest a hot-water bottle and a porta-ble stove should be added to the list, protested still—and the ar-gument was still undecided, or at least Bobby thought so, when Sergeant Young appeared to say that an odd discovery had been made about the petrol tins discovered in the forest. It had now been found that four of them were filled not with petrol, but with water.

"Black-market dodge," declared Sergeant Young; "just their sort of trick—hand out a can full of petrol and let the customer see for himself, and then change it for another full of water, and he daren't complain. Regular black-market style."

Bobby said he supposed that might be it. Sergeant Young re-tired, but left Bobby both looking and feeling worried. Vaguely he felt the cause might well be deeper than any such mere swin-dling trick. But what that deeper cause could be there was noth-ing to show, nor anything, so far as he could see, that he could do about it.

All the same, his mood was troubled as he departed for Three-pence, where he saw for himself the four petrol tins filled with water, and again wondered uneasily what the cause and purpose could be of such a substitution.

There was still no news of the return of Mr Roman Wright, but Miss Jane was back home from what seemed to have been a shopping expedition to Midwych. So Bobby decided to call and see if she could give him any information. She did not seem in any way pleased to see him when she answered his knock. Her uncle was expected back at any moment, she said, but he had not returned yet, and would the inspector call again some other time? Bobby said he had called chiefly about Mr Roman Wright's motor-cycle. Was it still in the shed where it was generally kept? and could he see for himself? as he thought it possible it might once more have been borrowed without its owner's knowledge. Jane said that was quite impossible, but she allowed Bobby to enter, and asked him to wait for a moment in the dining-room. She would take him to the shed, she explained, as soon as she had fetched herself a wrap, and he could assure himself that Mr Roman Wright had taken precautions.

Alone in the dining-room, Bobby noticed with some interest that the water-colour to which that other day Mr Roman Wright had directed his attention, and for which he had made the curious claim that it was the most remarkable painting in the world, had now vanished. Its place was taken by another, also in no way remarkable, unless for lack of skill, nor was Bobby much surprised by this disappearance. He thought it might have significance, though, and when Jane came back with her wrap he said something to her about missing the very interesting sketch Mr Roman Wright had shown him on his previous visit. But Jane merely looked blank and said that the pictures had not been changed. They were just the same as they had always been. The inspector was making a mistake; he must be thinking of something else.

Bobby did not pursue the subject, and followed her out to the back. Mrs Roman Wright was not visible, and Bobby was inclined to suspect that Jane's desire for a wrap to visit a shed only a yard or two from the back door had been an excuse to get the old woman out of the way. In detail she explained the kind of booby trap Mr Roman Wright had rigged up to give warning of any attempt to tamper with the cycle. It was a device, well concealed, by which opening the shed door would set a bell ringing in the kitchen. Jane disconnected it, went outside with Bobby, opened the shed door, and showed the cycle within. Bobby examined it with care. Nothing, of course, to prove that because it was there now, it had been there all the time. It had plainly been cleaned recently; but why not?

So he thanked Miss Jane and went off to return with Olive to Midwych, thence home for a brief meal, and so back again to Threepence well before midnight. He alighted some distance from the church, parked the car by the roadside under some trees, carefully left therein the overcoat he had been obliged to bring with him—though a trustful and confiding wife had forgotten to exact a promise that it would also be worn—posted an accompanying constable in a convenient position to keep further watch, and settled down to wait. It was well before midnight when he heard cautious footsteps approaching. He waited till they were at the entrance to the porch, and then he flashed his torch.

"Dr Reynolds, I presume?" he said.

"Oh," exclaimed the startled voice of the former dean. "Oh. Oh, it's you."

"It is," agreed Bobby and added: "I see you've brought the church keys."

"So I have," agreed Dr Reynolds thoughtfully. "Yes, I have, haven't I?"

"I wonder why," mused Bobby. "Any notion of—er—well, of seeking seclusion within the building? A place of ambush and advantage perhaps? However, never mind that. It was Mr McRell Pink I was really hoping to see. Do you think he is likely to come?"

"I suppose you know all about it," Dr Reynolds said dismally. "I can't imagine how."

"Do you think he will come?" Bobby repeated.

"I have no idea. I suppose if he chances to see your advertisement—I presume I am right in concluding that it was inserted by you?—he may consider it wise to respond. A matter of pure chance, I imagine."

"Hadn't you made any arrangements to communicate with him?" Bobby asked.

"It had not struck us as necessary," Dr Reynolds answered. "Indeed, it had not occurred either to him or to myself or to Mrs Billings that it would be possible to do so. The exceedingly simple method adopted by you had not been thought of by us. I fear we were all three lacking in the wisdom either of the serpent or the dove. I cannot help wondering by what means you penetrated a secret we so carefully guarded."

"Secrets can't be kept," Bobby answered for the second time that day. "It was fairly obvious—your secret, I mean. Mr Pyne was earning enough money to provide for the education of his nephews. How? Literary work, I was told, but his study didn't look like a writer's. A journalist or author generally uses a typewriter. He seemed to have none. Mr McRell Pink was refusing all chances to appear elsewhere than in Midwych or oftener than three days a week. Why? Obviously the answer to one question might be the answer to the other, too. Mr McRell Pink appeared only on Mondays—and Monday is the parson's holiday—Fridays and

Saturdays. On Fridays and Saturdays Mr Pyne went into seclusion to prepare his sermons. What clinched it was that Mr Pyne knew who I was the moment he saw me coming through his garden gate, and immediately vanished. Yet we had never met. But I had had a talk with Mr McRell Pink the evening before. Obvious conclusion. I am afraid I must press for an explanation. We are making inquiries in Threepence, and we can't leave mysteries and disguises unexplained."

"Mr Pyne consulted me," Dr Reynolds said. "I could see no harm in it. I remembered the legend of the juggleur in mediaeval times who praised God and the Virgin by performing alone before her statue in an empty church. The need was great. Had it not been for the money earned in this way, there would have been nothing with which to pay for the education of the boys, not enough even, for that matter, to provide for their daily bread. This is a poor living, shamefully poor, like so many others. I could not think there was ill in the use of the gift God had bestowed on Martin to provide for the widow and the fatherless. Fortunately the need no longer exists. Mrs Billings has been informed by her solicitors that the Treasury is prepared to make a substantial grant in recognition of services rendered by her late husband. But we both realized from the first that every precaution must be taken to avoid unnecessary and distasteful publicity and the ribald comment that might have been aroused if the facts became known. I always felt—and Martin agreed—that the dear bishop would have found it difficult to understand."

"I imagine," Bobby said slowly, "young Ned Bloom had ferreted out all this."

"We feared so," admitted Dr Reynolds. "The young man began dropping hints. Nothing plain, nothing direct, but unpleasant, disturbing. A letter came, making the same kind of obscure, disturbing references. Mr Pyne took no notice. Another letter came—two, I think—registered. Mr Pyne destroyed them both without opening them. But he began to prepare for the elimination of his McRell Pink metamorphosis. I urged that course most strongly. Then the young man left Threepence. A great relief. But you of the police began to make inquiries. We were all much dis-

urbed. We knew that a Treasury grant was imminent, and we
felt it would be indeed unfortunate if at the very moment when
necessity ceased an unhappy and extremely regrettable publicity became inevitable. It seemed to us all that the most advisable
course would be for Martin to depart for a brief holiday. He trusted that before any great efflux of time the whole affair would have
blown over and been forgotten. Unhappily it does not now seem
probable that that will be the case."

"No, it doesn't," said Bobby grimly. "Not at all likely. I suppose one of the 'phone calls asking if Ned Bloom had come to see
me was from Mr Pyne? I asked Mr Pyne—or Mr McRell Pink—a
good many questions, but I don't think I got very candid replies.
For a clergyman he was pretty good at hiding the truth."

"Inspector," said Dr Reynolds, in a very disturbed, embarrassed voice, "that was a most unexpected, most distressing development. One I never anticipated. I still cannot think there was
anything wrong in my acquiescence in Martin's plan to raise the
money required for the education of his three nephews. Nevertheless there was in it an element of deceit. The little foxes that
break in to destroy the vine. As McRell Pink, Martin did begin to
show himself careless of, even indifferent to, the higher stand-
ards. He seemed to forget those ideals to which a priest must ded-
icate himself. Only as McRell Pink. As himself he was as strict,
as punctilious as ever. But as McRell Pink he permitted himself
to—well, to diverge. It was as though he began to develop a second personality."

Dr Reynolds lapsed into silence, evidently deeply disturbed,
even distressed, and Bobby found himself thinking: "A second
personality and of what kind?" Aloud he said:

"What made him take such a roundabout way to let me know
where Ned Bloom was last seen?"

"I think he feared further questioning. But if the facts were
communicated to you by him as McRell Pink, who then ceased to
exist, he himself would not be involved, you would not be able to
interrogate him further, but you would still have the information."

"I must say," remarked Bobby with some asperity, "that
McRell Pink at any rate showed himself a very complete dodger."

"I don't think," Dr Reynolds answered uncomfortably, "tha Mr Pyne felt in any way compromised by any action of his *alte ego*. A secondary personality. A different personality altogether.

And again Bobby wondered if Dr Reynolds understood a that might be here implicit.

CHAPTER XXXI
SAPPHIRES

THEIR TALK FINISHED, Dr Reynolds returned to the vicarage, bu Bobby stayed on in the dark church porch, wondering a good dea what to make of this strange story he had just heard.

In a sense, the revelation made was without significance s far as he was concerned. No business of the police if a countr vicar chose to lead a double life as clergyman and as favourit music-hall performer. What the church authorities would think i such facts came to their knowledge was another matter. Dr Reyn olds had shown himself tolerant and broad-minded; but, then he held now no official position. The bishop of the diocese migh take a different view.

Certain, apparently, that Ned Bloom, with his disastrou gift for ferreting out other people's business, had discovered M Pyne's secret, and what had Mr Pyne been tempted to do abou it? And what had Ned Bloom intended or threatened to do abou it? Difficult, Bobby felt, to predict the actions of a man so un conventional as to double two such different rôles—parish pries and music-hall performer. True, the theatre has its roots dee in religion—from fertility rites on to mediaeval mystery plays But since then the gap has grown deep and wide—to the harm o both. Possible, even, that McRell Pink would care little for thos restraints and sanctions which would be deeply ingrained in th Rev. Martin Pyne. Was it Jekyll and Hyde in real life?

Still deep in thought and moody fears, Bobby's meditation were interrupted by a low and cautious whistle, coming, he knew from one of his men he had posted near by in case help was need ed. He gave an answering signal, and his man approached, pick ing his way with care, and keeping as much as possible in th shadows. For now the moon had risen, and, though the night wa not clear nor the moon at the full, there was enough light to see by.

"Captain Dunstan just gone by, sir," the man reported. "Heading down the road, and going quick and cautious, like he didn't much want to be spotted."

"Are you sure?" Bobby asked, puzzled by this new development.

The constable was quite sure. The light was enough for him to be certain, and the captain had passed close by, and so Bobby thanked him and sent him back to his post. Not likely, Bobby thought, that the Rev. Martin Pyne, alias McRell Pink, would put in an appearance now, and anyhow the question of identity had been cleared up. Unless and until further evidence could be secured, there was no great likelihood that an interview would produce fresh information. More pressing, Bobby felt, to find out what had brought Captain Dunstan hurrying by so late, so far from the farm where he was staying, away from the bed all good, easy, law-abiding citizens should by now be seeking.

So Bobby, too, took the road down the hill, treading, too, as lightly as he could, so that the echo of his footsteps might convey no warning to others, and himself straining to listen for any unusual sound.

All was quiet and calm, all was still—peaceful and still—even though here, as elsewhere, all through the sleeping land at any moment the night might burst into a tumult of roaring guns, of bombs screaming earthward. He came to cross roads and wondered which to take. Nothing to suggest which way Dunstan had gone, if indeed Dunstan it were his constable had seen. Straight on would bring him, he knew, to Mrs Bloom's tea-garden, and already in this business Mrs Bloom had had one midnight visitor: the one who searched the shed Ned Bloom had used for his private purposes. On the right the way led up Love Lane, to where it joined the highroad near Prospect Cottage and its cycle shed. And an open road and a motor-cycle could make any journey easy— or any escape, for that matter. Going to the left Bobby knew he would presently reach old Mr Skinner's cottage, where it stood with open fields behind and no other cottage nearer than fifty yards or so.

He stood still, hesitating, straining to hear any sound that might provide any indication of which way to take. He even thought of giving up the search and returning to the church preparatory to driving home. A searchlight darted to and fro across the sky, a probing finger, as it were, that sought to uncover the secrets of the heavens. Then it went away, and now followed a distant rumbling in the upper air to tell of the wrath of Britain passing overhead to answer those who had so wantonly provoked it.

That, too, passed, and all was still again, when abruptly he heard a pistol shot and then another. They came from his left—the direction in which lay the Skinner cottage. Bobby started to run, swiftly and quietly. He wondered who had fired, who else besides himself had heard. In normal times he would, he supposed, have seen lights appearing in windows, heard sleepy voices asking what was the matter. But now lights could not be shown, for who knew what roaring death might not be hidden, waiting in the skies? Nor did many people care to venture forth in the black-out if they could help it.

From a warden's post some one hailed him as he ran by, but he did not answer. Fire-watchers even here, where houses were scattered and few, might be on duty; but, then, fire-watchers often sleep soundly through everything except the alert that calls to them to be up and ready. Half-way along the lane, it was little more, he saw in the pale moonlight two figures that ran at speed across a pasture field, away from the village, towards the open country beyond. Bobby crashed through the hedge that formed the boundary of the lane and shouted to them to stop. They paid no heed. He ran diagonally to cut them off, if possible. The second of the runners seemed to be gaining on the first, but the first was close to the small wood that lay beyond the pasture. Bobby thought, however, he still had a chance of cutting them off before they reached the shelter of the trees. He burst through a hedge into the same field, but found to his dismay that here ploughing had begun. More pasture turning into grain land, no doubt. There had been some rain, the freshly turned earth was sodden and sticky, it clung to his feet in great clods, his speed diminished by a half. The other two were now at the very edge of the wood. He shouted to them to stop. Futile, of course. Those who ran like that ran no race they would abandon for a shout. The second runner was hard upon the first, the first already escaping from the moonlight to the shadows of the trees. Bobby struggled free from the sodden ploughland and began again to make good speed. It seemed an hour or a day he had run like this. In reality it was not more than a minute or two. Both the other two had now vanished among the trees within the wood. He could hear them crashing through bushes, trampling dry twigs. He plunged among the trees himself, but felt the race was lost. He wondered whether what he had seen had been pursuit or an escape in common. He ran on, for he could still hear, though sight had ceased to count here beneath the trees where the moon could hardly penetrate He was sure the two he followed could not be far ahead. He came to a space where the trees were fewer, where the undergrowth had been cleared, where he could increase his speed. He thought that perhaps now he had outdistanced the other two, hindered and held in this confusion of trees and bush, for sounds he still heard seemed to come from one side and slightly to his rear. He swerved accordingly, got at once into a closer growth of trees, saw emerge from them immediately before him the figure of a man who shouted aloud and ran at him.

Indeed, they almost fell into each other's arms, so instant was their encounter. No time to deliver blows or to avoid them. They grappled, breast to breast. Hard and close they grappled. A good grapple, strong and fierce, to test each nerve and muscle to extremity. An equal antagonist, Bobby realized, and one who knew each device and trick of what is now called 'unarmed combat'. But Bobby knew them, too, though so close the two fought and strained and wrestled there in the pale moonlight beneath the trees, there was small scope for trick or cunning skill. Strength against strength it was, sheer strength of body in closest grip, and then Bobby felt the resistance of the other collapse. He weakened and went down heavily. Bobby stooped over him, ready for any trick. But none was meant. The prostrate man gasped out:

"My arm. It gave." Then: "Why, it's that damn inspector." Next: "It wasn't you before. What are you doing here?"

"Captain Dunstan," Bobby said. "It's you, is it?"

"Help me up," Dunstan muttered. "It was my arm did me. You've done it in. It was getting all right before, but now you've messed it up again."

To this complaint Bobby made no reply. Still wary, still on the alert, he helped Dunstan to stand up. Dunstan did not seem too steady on his feet, and there escaped him a groan he only half suppressed. Bobby said:

"What's all this about? Who was that with you? I heard pistol shots. Did you fire them?"

"No," Dunstan answered. "I don't know who did. I don't know who the other bloke was. I might have caught him if it hadn't been for you," he added resentfully. "Now he's got away."

"What is that you've got there?" Bobby asked.

Captain Dunstan held it up in the dim light of the moon struggling feebly through the branches above. Even in that pale light it shone, it sparkled, was dazzling.

"Blessed if I know," he said.

"Sapphires," Bobby said. "Great sapphires such as I have never seen. The Arlington necklace, I think. How do you come to have it?"

CHAPTER XXXII
EXPLANATIONS BEGIN

INSTEAD OF ANSWERING this question, Dunstan moved a step or two away to lean against a tree, seeking support. He slid to the ground, into a sitting position, his eyes closed.

"Sorry," he said. "Gone dizzy a bit . . . my arm."

Bobby was not sure whether this semi-collapse was genuine or whether it was an excuse to gain time wherein to consider how to answer, He stooped and took the necklace, a river of pale, iridescent light, from Dunstan's grasp.

Dunstan opened his eyes.

"Here, what are you doing?" he protested.

"I was asking where you got this?" Bobby said. "Needs expla-ation. I heard shots. Did you fire them?"

"No," Dunstan answered. "Bloke I was chasing. When I got fter him, he potted at me. Twice. Missed. He didn't again. Pistol ammed, perhaps. Or no more ammo. One went close, though."

"Who was it?" Bobby asked.

"No idea," Dunstan replied. "He could run like a good 'un."

"Where did this come from?" Bobby repeated, holding up gain the necklace, on which the moon shone with a strange and hangeful glamour.

"Bloke swiped me with it," Dunstan answered. "I was just go-ng to grab him. My arm's gummed up still, but nothing wrong vith my legs. I had my hand on his shoulder, and he turned and ung that thing full in my face." He paused and felt it tenderly. Iobby, producing a pocket torch for which so far he had had no se, flashed its light and saw that in fact one of Dunstan's eyes vas bleeding slightly from a recent small cut or scratch and was eginning to swell. A blow from the necklace, perhaps—or equal-y well a blow from, for instance, a branch or twig of one of the urrounding trees or bushes.

Dunstan was beginning to get to his feet again. He went on:

"Slammed the thing flat at me. I tried to dodge, tripped on omething, and went over. Then I saw you. I thought you were he bloke I had been chasing. I suppose you weren't."

"No," said Bobby briefly. "You are sure you have no idea who was?"

"Not an earthly. Smallish bloke. Half your size. My arm let me own, or I would have put up a better show."

"You put up a good enough show to let the other man get way," Bobby said drily. "Please tell me exactly what happened."

"I was over there, by those houses, down the road," Dunstan aid. "I heard shots. I thought I had better see what was up, so went along. There was a bloke running, so I ran after him. 'hat's all."

"Captain Dunstan," Bobby said sternly, "a moment ago you aid the shots were fired at you. Now you say you heard them and vent to see what had happened."

"Oh, yes. Yes," Dunstan admitted. "Hang it all, when a bloke
been swotted in the eye with a sapphire necklace that hurts lik
hell and then been laid out by a damn police inspector with
grip like a bear, you can't expect him to be too clear in the head
I'll take you on again, though, any time you like, once my arm
all right."

"Never mind that," Bobby snapped. "I want your stor
please. It doesn't seem too easy to get it. Why? What are yo
trying to hide?"

"Nothing," Dunstan retorted sulkily. "I'm trying to get it clea
only I'm a bit rocky still. I was down the lane there. I saw a blok
in the garden of one of the cottages. I don't know which. I thougl
he was pinching cabbages or tomatoes or something. I asked hir
what he was up to. That was when he took his pot shots at me. H
said: 'Mind your own business, it's my own garden', and I saic
'Is it? We'll see if it is.' I pushed open the garden gate, and l
fired—one shot came damn close. So I went for him. He didn't fir
again. Good thing, too. I don't know why. Perhaps he only wante
to scare me, and when I didn't scare he didn't try again. He ra
like a good 'un. I told you the rest. I was going to grab him whe
he chucked that thing in my face. It may be worth a lot, but it
jolly hard as well. Stings. Then we had our little scrap."

"Which," Bobby commented once more, "gave the other ma
his chance to get away. And you haven't told me yet what yo
were doing here at this time of night when most people are i
bed—especially people supposed to be convalescing from
wounded arm."

"If a bloke can't sleep at night and chooses to go out for
breath of fresh air, why shouldn't he? Anything wrong about it?

"When the breath of fresh air gets mixed up with sapphir
necklaces, pistol shots, and mysterious pursuits, at any rate
wants explaining," retorted Bobby. "Perhaps you won't min
coming with me as far as the houses you mentioned? Those co
tages at the foot of the lane, I take it?"

"Yes, but you can carry on by yourself," Dunstan said. "M
arm's hurting like hell and my eye is pretty well closed up, to
See you another time if you like."

"I think I would prefer it if you would be good enough to come with me now," Bobby said quietly. "I should like you to point out the exact spot where this happened. I hope you won't mind. I am afraid I must insist," he added, as Dunstan still showed signs of hesitation.

"Is this an arrest?" he grumbled.

"I should prefer not to call it so," Bobby answered.

"The velvet glove, eh?" Dunstan growled. "I suppose it means you think it all highly suspicious?"

"Yes," Bobby agreed.

"Don't believe a word I say, is that it?" Dunstan asked truculently.

"In police work," Bobby replied, "you soon learn you must accept no statement without getting it confirmed. No difficulty about that when people are telling the truth."

"Oh, well, now then," Dunstan muttered, but made no other comment.

"In police work," Bobby replied, "you soon learn you must accept no statement without getting it confirmed. No difficulty about that when people are telling the truth."

"Oh, well, now then," Dunstan muttered, but made no other comment.

They continued on their way across the pasture towards the road, and as they went Bobby asked:

"Have you heard anything about what's been happening?"

"I heard a yarn that you had found young Ned Bloom's body. Is it true?"

"No," Bobby answered. "A dead body has been found, but it's a woman's."

"A woman's?" Dunstan repeated. "A woman's? Who is it?"

"She has not been identified yet. It's probably two years ago at least. Identification will not be easy."

"Do you mean," Dunstan asked slowly, "it's some one who got lost, died from exposure, something like that?"

"She had been shot through the head," Bobby answered. "Twice. Probably an Army point four five five was used."

"A woman. Two years ago," Dunstan repeated slowly. "It can't have anything to do with this other business, can it? Ned Bloom, I mean?"

"Two murders in one district," Bobby said. "They may be connected. Nothing yet to show. Or at least it may be the same murderer. Not so very likely, is it? that one small district should have two inhabitants, each capable of cold-blooded murder. But a killer who has killed once and got away with it is always liable to kill again."

"Custom is all," commented Dunstan, and walked on in silence. Then he said as they drew near the lane again: "You mean if you can find who did the one killing, you will know who did the other?"

"I think so," Bobby said, and he wondered if he were walking here in the faint light of the moon across this quiet and lonely field in the company of that very double murderer.

"Why do you think she was murdered here?" Dunstan asked. "I've never heard of any girl or woman being missing here?"

"I think I have heard," Bobby remarked, "that a young woman, Mrs Veale's daughter, left Miles Bottom Farm two years ago, and that it was not known what had become of her. I understand that at the time there was some gossip, in which your name was mentioned."

"Oh, my God," Dunstan groaned, "have you got hold of that? You don't miss much, do you?"

"We try not to," Bobby answered, a grim note in his voice.

"Well, have some sense," Dunstan urged. "You can't suppose Mrs Veale would have me there if there was an atom of truth in it?"

"Not if she knew," Bobby agreed.

"Oh, well," Dunstan muttered. "Well, how could she help? As a matter of fact, she knows quite well what became of Carrie."

"If she can put me in touch with her," Bobby agreed, "that will be cleared up, of course."

"I don't know if she can do that actually, or if she knows just where Carrie is now."

"Unfortunate," Bobby said drily.

"Meaning you don't believe me?" Dunstan asked. "It's like this. Carrie ran off with a married man. She went to Canada with him. Mrs Veale has old-fashioned ideas. She tried to stop it getting about what Carrie had done. Only made the gossip worse, of course. She wouldn't have anything more to do with Carrie, not as long as she went on living with a married man. I don't think she even knows Carrie's present address in Canada."

Bobby said nothing. All this might be true. Or the girl's mother might believe it to be true. And yet it might well be no more than a cunning tale put about to satisfy Mrs Veale and prevent further inquiry. It was noticeable that Dunstan told his story in an odd, embarrassed, almost hesitating manner. Bobby, in his present suspicious mood, wondered why. If the story were true, why show so odd an hesitation in telling it? Not till some time later did he discover that Dunstan had a brilliant young brother who occupied an enviable position as a leading reviewer on the staff of a well-known London weekly journal of melancholy temperament, advanced views, and a firm conviction that adultery is the first infirmity of noble minds. Dunstan, admiring tremendously his young brother, wondering with awe to see him thus riding in the Bloomsbury whirlwind, directing the Chelsea storm, had come to believe that such an attitude was common to all sensible people, was embarrassed to let it be seen that he and Mrs Veale did not fully share it, and did not realize that to Bobby this show of hesitation and embarrassment appeared as a just possible indication of conscious guilt.

They had reached the lane by now, and were walking towards the houses clustered at the farther end. Dunstan said hesitatingly:

"I'm not sure if I shall be able to show you exactly where it was. Not easy to find places again in moonlight."

"Well, then, I'll show you, shall I?" Bobby asked. "It was here, wasn't it?" he said a moment later.

"How the devil did you know?" demanded Dunstan, a good deal taken aback.

CHAPTER XXXIII
SIR GERVASE ARLINGTON

WITHOUT ANSWERING THIS question, Bobby pushed upon the garden gate of the nearest cottage, one that stood at a little distance from the others. He flashed his torch on the ground, and saw plain traces of footprints here and there, and of broken and trampled plants. He said to Dunstan:

"I think it was here, wasn't it?"

A voice, a woman's voice—that of Kitty, thought Bobby—called from the cottage door;

"Is some one there? What is it?"

As with all these cottages, the front door opened directly on a kitchen that served also as general living-room, the only other apartment on the ground floor being the scullery behind. A kind of light-trap had been arranged with the aid of an old blanket, so that people could enter or leave without risk of breaking the black-out regulations, and now, though the speaker was standing at the open door, no light showed. Bobby went towards her. He said:

"May we come in, please? I am Inspector Owen. Captain Dunstan is with me."

The figure at the door drew back silently. Bobby and Dunstan followed into the kitchen. Within were Kitty, her mother, who looked ill and shaken and was supported in the arms of her husband, sitting upright and angry in his invalid chair. He gave such an impression of energy and power that one almost expected to watch a miracle accomplished and see him by sheer force of will make those withered legs of his once more support him. The attire of all three suggested that they had been roused from their beds. In deep tones, through which reverberated the fury of his physical helplessness, Mr Skinner demanded:

"What's all this? What's happened now?"

"He's got it," Dunstan said, nodding at Bobby. "Grabbed it. I had it, and then he grabbed it. The bloke got away, though."

"That inspector's always there," Skinner grumbled. To Bobby he said: "Well, if you've got it, hand it over. It's my property."

"Is this what you mean?" Bobby asked. He showed the great necklace, holding it up. A strange sight it seemed as it shone in

nat plain labourer's cottage, a dazzling thing, more dazzling still
a these bare surroundings that spoke of so great poverty. "You
laim that it is your property."

"It is my property," Mr Skinner reiterated in his deep-throat-
d, rumbling voice.

"I shall have to ask for proof of that before I return it," Bobby
aid; and Mr Skinner gave him a glare that ought to have blasted
im where he stood, but failed to do so. "Will you please tell me
xactly what has happened?"

"I must get mother upstairs," Kitty said. "She has had a fall."

"Ought you to have a doctor?" Bobby asked.

Kitty said she did not think it was necessary, but seemed
rateful for the suggestion. She got her mother to her feet, and
ith Dunstan's assistance half carried her, half led her up the
arrow stairs. When they had gone Mr Skinner said:

"We go to bed early here. Have to. We were all asleep. My wife
oke me. She said: 'There's a man in the room.' I said 'Nonsense.'
generally keep a candle and matches near the bed. They weren't
ere. I didn't know whether they had been moved or had been
rgotten. It was pitch dark. The black-out curtains were up. My
aughter heard us talking. She called out to ask if we wanted her.
ly wife said she had heard something. Kitty came in with a light-
d candle. There was no one there. I told them to get back to bed.
ly wife said to make sure the necklace was safe. She got it out.
here had been a man in the room all right, and he must have
een hiding at the top of the stairs. Or somewhere. I expect he
new I'm pretty helpless. All right within arm's length, nothing
e matter with my arms. But legs useless. Whoever it was had
een hiding, rushed in, knocked the candle out of Kitty's hand,
natched the necklace from my wife, knocked her over, and was
ff again. All over in a minute. None of us saw him plainly."

Kitty and Dunstan had come downstairs again while this sto-
y was being told. Kitty said:

"He was small and quick. I thought he had killed mother, or
would have tried to follow him. He had got our necklace, and it
 all we have."

"I saw the bloke run out," Dunstan said. "I ran after him."

"How did it happen you were on the spot?" Bobby asked.

"I told Captain Dunstan I had heard some one in the garden at night," Kitty said. "I thought perhaps it might be Ned Bloom come back."

"There seems to be some sort of story going round that his body's been found," Mr Skinner said. "Is that true?"

"No," Bobby answered. He was wondering whether he could accept this story exactly as it had been told. He was wondering, indeed, if Mr Skinner and Kitty, even if they thought they had told the truth, knew the full truth to tell. He wondered this more especially about Kitty. Above all, he wondered what, if he accepted it, were all its implications. He said to Mr Skinner: "I suppose all this means you are really Admiral Sir Gervase Arlington?"

"How the devil do you know?" demanded the self-styled Skinner.

"I believe he knew it all the time," Kitty said. "I believe he knows everything."

"If you know who I am," growled Sir Gervase, "perhaps you'll be good enough to hand over my necklace."

Bobby shook his head.

"I'll give you a receipt acknowledging it is in my possession," he said. "It'll be safer with me. Even if I lost it you could recover full value from the Government. I am acting as a responsible officer of police in keeping it for the present."

He sat down and wrote a receipt on a page he tore from his notebook for the purpose. He handed it to Sir Gervase, who took it, read it, and said:

"'Alleged' sapphire necklace. 'Alleged' indeed. You are cautious, young man."

"One has to be," Bobby answered. "I have no proof it is genuine, and I'm no judge. I shall still require satisfactory proof of your identity."

"You have my word," Sir Gervase said, looking more like an offended Jove than ever. "You said yourself you knew who I was."

"A guess, a deduction, is not proof," Bobby said. "All I have to go on is that it was plain Miss Kitty was no waitress—"

"I am—I'm a very good waitress," interposed Kitty indignantly. "Ask them all at the Tea Gardens."

"Oh, excellent," agreed Bobby, "but none, all the same. Then I was fairly certain your identity cards were faked. The Christian names you and Lady Arlington used to each other were not those on the cards. An offence against the law, by the way. Also I found among Ned Bloom's papers a newspaper cutting about friends of Admiral Sir Gervase Arlington being worried about his safety, as they were ignorant of his whereabouts and he was known to have left for the Continent with his family some time before the outbreak of the war. And I noticed Miss Kitty seemed a good deal disturbed by it."

"I suppose," growled Sir Gervase, "that is why the little brute came sneaking round here at night."

"Probably," agreed Bobby. "Unfortunately you used threats and unfortunately he has since disappeared."

"So you think I may have murdered him?" asked Sir Gervase. "Well, I felt like it, felt like twisting his neck for him if I had got hold of him. I never did, though. Peeping Tom, I thought. Impudence enough, trying to poke his nose into my business. But not like the Peeping Tom idea. I might have murdered him for that."

"Father, don't say such things," interposed Kitty. "The inspector will think—"

"He's thinking already," retorted Sir Gervase. "Thinking hard. But I haven't the use of my legs, and so I had no chance to catch him at it. The other thing only rated a sound thrashing."

"Have you any more jewellery besides this?" Bobby asked, and when Sir Gervase shook his head and looked surprised, Bobby said: "Another thing I found in Ned Bloom's possession was what seems like a photograph of a considerable quantity of jewellery. It is all piled on a table, and it shows the hands of a woman apparently and of a man just above, as if they had just been putting the stuff there or sorting it over."

"I don't know anything about that," Sir Gervase said. "A photograph of a pile of jewellery?" He shook his head again. "You seem to have found plenty in the lad's papers," he said.

"Not so much," Bobby said, "as I should have done if some one else had not been before me, and I wonder who."

CHAPTER XXXIV
MAIDEN AUNT

BOBBY SAT DOWN on a chair near, resting his head on his hand, deep in thought. Through his mind passed one consideration after another, and still behind them all seemed to be shadowed the dark, enigmatic figure of the missing man's mother, her silence, her strange, still, tragic eyes. Dunstan stirred and looked at the clock.

"It's late," he said.

"Yes," Bobby agreed, getting to his feet. "Sorry. I was thinking. I don't see my way. It all seems plain and then it's dark again." He had been speaking more to himself than to them, speaking out of the confused tangle of his thoughts. With an effort he put them from his mind and said to Dunstan: "One of Lord Vennery's guests was a lady owning sapphire earrings and a sapphire pendant. I believe they formed a set at one time with this necklace. There was what appeared to be an attempt at burglary, probably with them in view. Captain Dunstan was on the spot at the time. To-night there is an attempt to get possession of this necklace. It is from Captain Dunstan I recover it."

He paused, watching to see the effect of this on Sir Gervase and his daughter. Neither seemed in any way surprised or disturbed. Kitty said:

"I told you why Captain Dunstan came. None of us ever thought about the necklace. We didn't think any one knew we had it. We haven't had it here very long. I don't know how any one could know."

"I think young Ned Bloom knew, and I think he knew too much," Bobby said. He turned to Dunstan. "At Theodores," he said, careful to give the word its correct pronunciation 'Tedders', "that night when you were there—"

"How do you know I was?" interrupted Dunstan.

"I do know," Bobby answered, though indeed he had no real proof he could have produced if challenged to do so. All he could have said was that Dunstan had known that that night a pistol shot had been discharged. "Never mind how I know. If you care to say anything, I am ready to listen. Later on, I will ask you to make a written statement, but it might be useful if you would tell me now."

"You may as well tell him," Kitty said resignedly. "He'll only find out for himself if you don't."

"Oh, all right," Dunstan grumbled. "Nothing to it, anyway. They had a 'phone call at Theodores—Tedders—telling them to look out, because there was going to be a burglary one night soon. Ned Bloom the bloke said he was. They didn't know him from Adam. Lord Venery said to take no notice, said it was probably just a hoax. Lady Venery was a bit scared, though, and he said if it would make her happier she could ask Scotland Yard about it. Scotland Yard passed the buck. Said it wasn't their pigeon, said consult the county police. So they did, but all they got was a formal printed acknowledgement."

"Not printed," Bobby said mildly. "Typed. And we don't generally give full details of what we are going to do. People are apt to talk too much."

"Well, anyhow," Dunstan went on, "Lord Venery was rather pleased than not. Said he didn't want any damn fool country police knocking about, and they had better leave it at that. Miss Wood—she's Lady Venery's secretary—"

"Yes, I know," interposed Bobby, resentfully reminiscent of a certain protuberant tongue.

"Well, Lady Venery was still more than a bit nervous, and so was Miss Wood, if you ask me, though she swears she wasn't. Anyhow, if they couldn't have a policeman, she told Lady Venery they could have me. So she wrote and asked me to hang around that night, and I did. Anything to oblige, and anyhow that girl— Miss Wood, I mean—she's a tartar all right. You do what she says, or she raises hell. A born bully. She has Lady Venery eating out of her hand."

Bobby, glancing at Kitty, noticed that she listened to all this quite calmly, as if she found the suggestion of close intimacy between Dunstan and Miss Wood perfectly natural. Bobby began to revise an idea that he had come to accept as a certainty. Dunstan continued:

"Then you butted in. Miss Wood told me to get out quick. She's like that. If she doesn't want you any more, I mean. The thing is she and Lady Vennery didn't want Lord Vennery to know they had had me there, unbeknown to him and in spite of what he said. Bit of an autocrat, by all accounts. So I climbed out of the window of her room, and just as I touched ground a bloke went for me like hell. I let him have it back with all I had. Took him clean on the point of the chin. He went down, and when I looked I saw he was a policeman. Well, that was that, and I cleared out fast as I could. My C.O.'s a pretty stiff old boy, and I knew he would take a dim view of one of his officers laying out a policeman. The War Office, too, most likely. Might have meant a court-martial. Not to mention that I knew the two women weren't keen on Lord Vennery knowing anything about me being there. Least said, soonest mended, and I made a bee line for where I had parked my bike. I heard one of your men tearing off on a motor-bike along the main road, so I kept to the lanes and side roads. Mine was a pedal bike, of course. A bit thick though, I thought it, when I heard you blokes start shooting. Only meant to scare, I suppose, but once you let a bullet loose, it's always liable to score a bull somewhere."

"The shooting didn't come from us," Bobby said.

"Well, who was it, then? Was it one of Lord Vennery's people? The women had to own up, with all the fuss and excitement, but Lord Vennery backed 'em up good and hard. Very sporting, too. Though I rather think one reason was that he didn't much want anything in the papers. Sort of private confidential talk he had on—house-party only camouflage. Post-war planning. Big business post-war planning, that is, not the other sort. No harm done, and I expect he was like me, and thought least said, soonest mended."

"Yes, I see," Bobby said, but was not at all sure that in fact he did see. The story might be true as far as it went, but was it all the truth? The collaboration of Miss Wood and Captain Dunstan might easily bear an interpretation very different from that given it in the story just told. He asked:

"Have you known Miss Wood long?"

"Oh, all her life, worse luck. In the nursery. First time I ever saw her she scratched my face and grabbed my slice of cake. She's an aunt of mine."

"A—what?" said Bobby, not quite sure he had heard aright.

"Aunt," repeated Dunstan. "Maiden aunt. Everyone thinks it damn funny. I don't know why," he added resentfully. "She and my mother are sisters. Of course, mother's years older, but they are sisters all right, and Polly—Aunt Theo otherwise-seems to think it gives her a right to boss me about."

"Leads the poor boy an awful dance when she gets the chance," Kitty interposed gravely.

Her father indulged in a chuckle. Dunstan looked sulky and grumbled:

"There's some fool will some old ass of a great-great uncle or something made, and Polly pretends that by it she is my guardian and trustee till I'm thirty. It only comes to about a couple of hundred a year, but she has to sign some silly paper, and she always says she won't if I don't do what I'm told, and promise to go to bed early, keep my feet dry, and always wash behind the ears." He was grinning himself now. "I had to go jolly near to putting a spider down her neck once," he confided, "before she would behave. That did bring her round in a hurry, though."

"I think it was brutal," observed Kitty with severity, "and very ungentlemanly."

"No good being a little gentleman with Polly," retorted Dunstan.

Bobby, from his experience of the young woman in question, was inclined to agree. On the whole he supposed all this made more probable what he had been inclined to listen to somewhat doubtfully. Nevertheless he could not feel completely satisfied. He said presently:

"You are using false identity cards. That is an offence against the Defence of the Realm Regulations. It seems to provide a proper reason for prosecution."

For the first time the seated Jove that was Sir Gervase Arlington looked uneasy.

"Can't you use another name if you want to?" he asked. "Sure ly it's quite usual. I crossed to New York once in the same shi with Mr Montagu Norman of the Bank of England. He calle himself Professor something or another."

"That was before the war," Bobby pointed out. "No identit cards then. Now it is an offence to pass by a name other than tha by which a person was commonly known before the beginnin of the war. My difficulty is that all this is mixed up with the dis appearance of young Ned Bloom. That is what is really serious."

"Why are you so sure he won't turn up again when it suit him?" Sir Gervase demanded. "You say the story that his bod has been found isn't true?"

"The body found is a woman's," Bobby said. "Her deat probably took place two years ago. It is possible we may soo find Ned Bloom's body as well, for now I think I know where t look. But even if I am right about that, I shall still have to as who put it there."

CHAPTER XXXV

WHOLE STORY

There was again another silence. Then Bobby, looking at th clock said he must not keep them any longer from their beds. H began to move towards the door. But Kitty said:

"Father, now it's gone so far, hadn't you better tell hi everything? Now he knows so much he can easily find out th rest. If you explain in confidence, then you can ask him not to te anyone."

"I can listen to nothing in confidence," Bobby said quickl "But I can assure you police do not talk about private affairs un less they have to in the course of their duty. Police know and kee many secrets."

"I daresay Kitty's right," Sir Gervase said. "Probably you ha better know the whole story."

"I'll go, shall I?" Dunstan said, moving in his turn towards th door, but Sir Gervase called him back.

"No, you had better hear it all, too, if you and Kitty are think ing of getting married," he said.

"Oh, I told him I wouldn't," protested Kitty.

"Yes, I know," retorted Sir Gervase. "Your mother said that—went on saying it." To Bobby he said: "There's a son of mine. We have the two children—Kitty and this boy. Some years ago he made a mess of things. The details don't matter. There might have been a criminal prosecution. If it had been pressed, there might have been—well, it might have meant penal servitude. Things could have been made to look that way, though really there had been nothing worse than carelessness and extravagance and muddle. I made myself responsible for a large sum of money. That put an end to any threat of prosecution. We could show the money was still there. But to raise the money I had to scrape up every penny I possessed. It wasn't enough, and I had to borrow on the strength of my half-pay. I gave my lawyers a power of attorney to collect from the bank. A mother will do a good deal for her son, and my wife was more than willing. It meant sacrificing Kitty, too. I had no right to ask that, but—"

"It wasn't sacrifice, father," interrupted Kitty. "I wasn't going to stand by and let anything like that happen to Tom."

Sir Gervase turned in his chair and looked at her. In a voice that sounded almost casual, he said:

"If you ever have children, I pray God Almighty they may be to you as you have been to your mother and to me."

Turning back to Bobby, he continued:

"I felt we had to get away from friends and their questions. It wouldn't have been easy to explain. So we went to live in France. I had enough left for immediate needs, and I bought a cottage near Tours. It had a good garden. I expected to be able to manage with the garden and what money I had kept. Kitty said she would help by teaching English. She did, too; she had several pupils. It helped considerably. Then the war came. We got away just in time, but we had to leave everything. I used our real name in France. I called myself a retired 'fonctionnaire'. No one asked why a retired civil servant had come to live in France. They all felt it only natural that any one who could would come to live in France. I expect the Germans would soon have found me out, though. I've met a good many of their officers, both Navy and Army. I didn't want to risk giving my real name when we got back. I should have had all my old friends asking and wondering why we were living as we are, what it was all about, why Kitty was a waitress in a tea-room. The truth would have come out. Tom is doing his best to get over the past. He is in the Army, hadn't long to wait for his commission. Any scandal would have ruined his chance of making a new career for himself. He's a prisoner in Germany now, but he got his promotion and a D.S.O. first. When the war is over and he gets back he will have a chance of a fresh start. I called myself Skinner when we returned—the name of neighbours of ours in France. They had lived there many years. Skinner owned a small garage. They had no friends or relatives in England, and even when the French looked like folding up they decided to stay on. I made up my mind to borrow their names and identity—I knew they came from Nottingham, and I knew their ages were much the same as ours, so I could give all details. I didn't know there was anything illegal involved. Since then we have heard that Mr and Mrs Skinner and their daughter were all three killed when their garage was bombed. To raise the money to put Tom's accounts right we had to sell the sapphire earrings and pendant you were talking about. We couldn't sell the necklace. Life interest only. It was listed as an heirloom. The earrings and pendant were heirlooms, too, originally, but somehow or another in the last century they got left out of the inventory. Only the necklace is mentioned. My lawyers have been trying to get permission from the courts to sell it as well. Now permission has been given. That is why the necklace is here. The lady who bought the earrings and pendant is willing to buy the necklace and to give what the valuers say is an exceedingly good price—a much higher price than we should be likely to get in the ordinary way. But she wants the sale to be private. I suppose she has her reasons. She may not want the exact price she is giving to be known, or perhaps she doesn't want people to think her extravagant in war-time."

"Polly," observed Dunstan, "says she wants to be able to boast she gave twice what she really did. I daresay Polly's right. She's up to all the tricks, because she knows them all herself. I should guess what she really wants is to be able to sell again without any one knowing what her profit was."

Kitty shook her head.

"No," she said, "no one who has those lovely, lovely things means to let them go again if she can help it," and there was that in her voice which told how she in her time had longed for those exquisite, shining toys, and how much it had cost her to forego her right to them. Then she added: "Of course, only some one very, very rich could wear them ever, and I suppose no one to-day ought to be very, very rich."

"Turning bolshevik," grunted Sir Gervase. "Well, I suppose we all are—me, too."

"Oh, daddy," Kitty exclaimed, "you bolshevik!"

"And why not, girl, why not?" demanded offended Jove. "The Russians can fight, can't they? Not much wrong with bolshevism if it makes people fight the way the Russians do."

A doubtful argument, Bobby thought, since for bad causes, too, that strange animal, man, can fight with ferocity and conviction. But he did not want to pursue the subject. He thanked Sir Gervase for his story, assured him again nothing would be disclosed unnecessarily. But he had to say that the matter of the identity cards must be straightened out, though he thought and hoped that in the circumstances prosecution and consequent publicity might be avoided. That, however, was not for him to decide.

Then at last he left, and managed to get home in time for an hour or two of sleep. Breakfast that morning was a somewhat silent meal, however; for Olive, too, was tired after sitting up most of the night, waiting for Bobby's return. But strong coffee—a veritable Hercules among coffees—and a reckless use of the bacon ration conduced to revival, and Bobby said presently:

"Last night cleared up a good deal. The Rev. Martin Pyne is admitted to be the same person as McRell Pink, the music-hall artiste, and Ned Bloom knew it, and Martin Pyne knew he knew it, and was worried. It's admitted he made one of the three 'phone calls, Mrs Bloom made another; but who made the third? Question, did Mr Pyne fear exposure and a possible scandal to the Church enough to make it possible he would resort to extreme

180 | E.R. PUNSHON

measures? He had a split personality—cleric and music-hall performer. Perhaps he had a third as well—killer."

"Oh, Bobby, it's not possible," Olive protested.

"Anything's possible when it's a question of the human mind,"
Bobby said. "Saints have killed for the sake of the Church before
to-day, and might again. Then the identity of Skinner with Sir
Gervase Arlington is established, and Ned Bloom knew that, too,
and it may be Sir Gervase knew he knew it. If he did, and if Ned
came within arm's length, I think it's possible Sir Gervase might,
as he put it, twist Ned's head off. And if that happened, or something like it, I feel sure Dunstan and Miss Kitty, too, would help
to hide the body."

"Oh, Bobby," Olive protested again, "not Kitty—she's a dear."

"A pretty formidable dear at times, I think," retorted Bobby. "It has to be considered. But there's one thing. I said I
thought I knew where Ned's dead body was concealed. I was
watching them both when I said that, and neither seemed at all
disturbed. But then again—how much did Ned know about the
sapphires? He certainly did know something about the chance
of a burglary at the Theodores place they call Tedders—to make
it easier, I suppose."

"That doesn't implicate the Arlingtons," declared Olive.

"No," Bobby agreed; "and possibly what Ned knew provides
the link between the attempt on the Skinner cottage and the attempt on Lord Vennery's place. But again that link may be provided by Dunstan and his aunt—if she is his aunt. I'll have to check
up on that. You have to remember the possibility that what it all
means is Dunstan and Miss Wood plotting together to get hold of
the sapphires. Dunstan comes into the picture both with regard
to the murdered woman whose body we've found—because she
may be Mrs Veale's missing daughter and the elopement story
put about to keep Mrs Veale quiet—and with regard to Ned, who
may have found out something there, too."

"There's still nothing to show what's really become of Ned,"
Olive said. "There's no proof he isn't alive and well all the time."

But Bobby shook his head.

"I think that he is dead is as certain as anything can be," he said, "and I think I know what happened and where the poor lad's body has been hidden. I am having a watch kept, on the chance the murderer may come to see all's safe still. But we are coaling, if I am right, with a man as cautious as he is dangerous. I'm not too hopeful that the watch will be successful. If it isn't, we shall have to act. We can't wait indefinitely. He can. Only too glad to."

"I suppose it is always the same person," Olive said.

But again Bobby shook his head. It was a point on which he was by no means sure. One more question mark in that maze of doubt and wonder wherefrom as yet he saw no clear outlet.

"There's Mrs Bloom," he said. "I wish I could get her out of my mind. She could tell us a good deal if she wished. But it seems she won't. And Miss Wright. Why is she always going to Mrs Bloom's for her tea?"

"I'll go there for tea again this afternoon," Olive said. "Perhaps one or the other will be ready to talk."

CHAPTER XXXVI
TWO STORIES

IT WAS EARLY, earlier than usual, not yet three o'clock, when that afternoon Olive entered the Pleezeu Tea-Garden. The weather was fine and warm. She sat down at one of the outdoor tables, the only customer who had as yet appeared. The little red-cheeked, smiling, zealous maid who was Kitty's chief assistant came up, and Olive gave her order. It was brought her by Kitty, still at work as usual, till some one could be found to take her place. With the sale of the necklace, necessity had passed, but she did not wish to leave without the due and proper notice to which Mrs Bloom was entitled. Olive thanked her and poured out a cup, but had not tasted it, had neither eaten nor drunk, when she saw Jane Wright appear. Jane saw her, too, and came towards her, stood for a moment as in doubt, and then sat down at the same table. She said:

"I know who you are."

Olive did not know what to say to this, and so remained silent. Liza, the little red-cheeked child, bustled up to take the new-comer's order. To her Jane said:

"Tea. That's all. Very strong. I don't want anything to eat."

"Well, you never eat it anyways, nor drink your tea neither," the girl said; and then, when Jane looked at her, scuttled away in a great hurry.

"You've frightened her," Olive said. "The way you looked at her. Why did you?"

"I know who you are," Jane repeated. "I know what you want. It's no good."

"What's no good?" Olive asked.

"What you are waiting for. For me to talk. I shan't, and you can't make me."

"No one can make you talk," Olive agreed. "How could they? Except yourself."

"Well, I shan't," Jane told her. "Not me. Why should I? Not me. Don't you think it. But I'll tell you why I come here. You want to know that, too, don't you? Because Mrs Bloom and me—we are two. See?"

Olive had no idea what this meant, and so made no answer. Though she did not know it, her silence and her tranquil presence were having their effect. Kitty brought the tea that Jane had asked for.

"It's double strength," Kitty said. "You said you wanted it like that. There'll be an extra charge."

"There always is," Jane said moodily. "That's a thing you can ever get away from—the extra charge."

Kitty looked puzzled, but said nothing and went away.

"Drink your tea," Olive said. "You'll feel better."

Jane took no notice. She might not have heard. Perhaps she didn't. Olive poured herself out a cup of tea. Presently Mrs Bloom came as silently as she had done before from behind the hedge near by. She sat down on Olive's other hand.

Jane said:

"Now we are three."

"If you would drink your tea, it would do you good," Olive repeated.

"No, it wouldn't—not me," Jane answered.

"Leave her alone," Mrs Bloom said unexpectedly. "She and I, we can't keep away from each other. That's all. She knows that she must come, and when I see her I know that I must go to her. It's quite natural." To Olive she said: "It's nothing to do with you, but it makes all the difference, your being here."

"I shan't say a word," Jane declared. "Why should I? I'll go."

But she made no effort to move.

"I think you know that in the end you must," Olive said.

"It's nothing to cry about," Jane said, staring at her. "What are you crying about? That won't make me."

Olive said fiercely: "I can cry if I like, can't I?"

"I never cry," said Jane. She looked at Mrs Bloom: "She doesn't either," she said. "Not now. What's the sense?"

"It's only that I'm so sorry for you both, but most of all for you," Olive said.

"Well, it's silly," Jane said. She looked again at Mrs Bloom and said: "She thinks she'll make us talk, you and I. Silly. She can't. Can she?"

"No," agreed Mrs Bloom. "John was always good to me. The first day I saw him he was cutting wood in his shirt sleeves. He looked wonderful, like a young god come down to earth. John was my husband, you know. Did I say that before? He was always good to me, always till the day I killed him. We both wanted a boy, but we had a long time to wait for Ned. When I knew he was coming we were both so glad. When he came he had a club foot and he cried a good deal. John said a cripple had no chance in a world like this. I think he thought it was my fault, and I thought perhaps it was. Sometimes I thought baby would be better dead and John said: 'That's what you think, too, isn't it?' He said: 'Who wants a cripple? What good's a cripple?'"

Olive interrupted. She said:

"Many cripples are better every way than those who aren't. That is, if they want to be."

Mrs Bloom took no notice. She continued:

"That night when John came home he had had too much to drink. It had always happened now and then, but more often since Ned came. I think sometimes where he went they used to

tease him for having a cripple for a son, because, you see, he had
always been so strong and active, and there was never any one like
him for playing football. But this time he had drunk more than
usual, and he took up Ned from the cradle and he said he would
take him down to the river and throw him in, because that's what
you did to kittens and puppies no one wanted, and who wanted
a cripple in a world hard, and too hard for sound men? I tried to
stop him, but he gave me a push and I fell down, and he ran out
of the house to the river. He ran too fast for me, and I picked up
his gun and I followed, and when he wouldn't stop and when he
was quite near the water I pulled the trigger and it went off and
he fell down. I went to him and I said: 'Have I hurt you?' I said:
'Are you hurt?' and he said: 'You have killed me, and so some day
some one will kill the child, but I never meant to.' When I saw he
was dead I took Ned back to the house and gave him his bottle
because he was crying, and then they came to take me away, and
I said nothing because I couldn't when it was all true. So I never
said anything, though all I ever meant was to make him stop, and
the judge put a black cap on his head and said I was to die. But
that was stupid, because how could I? I had died already, when
I saw what I had done. So I could not die again, could I? I expect
that's why they didn't try, but put me in prison instead, and then
they let me out again. It's all a long time ago now, but I knew what
had happened to Ned, because I always knew it would, because of
what John said before he died."

She stopped. Neither of the other two spoke or moved. She
said presently to Jane:

"Now it's your turn."

"We killed your boy," Jane said, "because he had found out
too much. Why was he so fond of finding things out? It is always
better not to know. It's safer, too. Much safer. It would be safer
for me if I did not know. For you as well," she added, looking at
Olive—"much safer for you if you did not know what I am going
to tell you. I always knew some day she would have to know, and
I would have to tell." Jane was looking at Mrs Bloom now. Olive's
presence she might entirely have forgotten. She went on: "No one
else, only you, and what's it matter, because I can always say I

never did? Roman's line is jewellery. It's funny. Jewellery. That's all right, only mostly you want it so you can sell again. If it's big stuff you go to South America generally and get rid of it there. The best market. If it's small, there's always some thieving swindling fence or another. Never pawn. You soon find that out. Roman is different. He's funny. I mean the way he feels. I mean he won't let the stuff go if he can help it. He has to sometimes for living money, but he hates it when he's got to. Isn't it funny? What he likes best is to put it out and look at it, or let me wear it while he watches how it shines. I liked that, too, but he never let me keep it. I've cooked and cleaned and scrubbed wearing jewels like a duchess would have worn at Court. That's how he got me first. Showing me the stuff and letting me wear it sometimes. In London. Tom—that's the man I had before—had just been sent up. I expect he's in still. He was a swine. Of course, they all are, aren't they? All of them. Men, I mean. It was only after I had run away from home to join Tom that I found out he was married. It was too late then. Everything is always too late."

"Nothing is ever too late," Olive said.

Mrs Bloom said:

"It's too late when you see what you have done, as I saw it when I saw John was dead."

Taking no notice of these two interruptions, Jane continued:

"What made him so fond of finding things out? Your boy, I mean. Roman found out things, too. He found out Ned had been in the garden at night when Roman had out all his jewellery he had stolen over years and years and kept because it was all he ever cared for. Not me nor any one, not his wife—because when I got here I found he was married too, just like Tom was. But this time I didn't care. I had got over caring, and, besides, Mrs Wright—you never noticed her—was there but all she wanted was you shouldn't notice, and Roman never did. It was funny about that, too. Sometimes he would take her into the diningroom and lock the door, so they were alone, and I never heard a sound, not even when I listened at the keyhole; but when she came out she was like dead, and couldn't hardly speak or stand. But what he did I never knew, and she wouldn't tell. And I didn't ask so often, because, you see, even then I thought it was better not to know too much. And all those jewels and things, all shining, all beautiful, all sparkling and most lovely, so Roman was drunk with them, like others are with whisky. I liked to watch them, too, and wear them when he let me, but Mrs Wright, she never seemed to care, only to slip away and not be noticed any more, by him nor me neither. When Roman knew Ned had been snooping round he thought at first he would hide it all again and bluff Ned out, if Ned said anything. But Ned had managed to get a snap of all the stuff spread out, and when Roman knew that, he knew, too, he had to do something. He did think of trying to make Ned believe it was all his own and he was a dealer in jewellery, and at first he thought Ned believed him, and Ned told him the Skinners weren't going by their real name, and really they were some one else. Because one night when he was listening at the window he heard Mrs Skinner say something that made him sure they weren't what they let on to be. That's what put Roman wise about the sapphires, and he began to plan to get them, and he found out, too, that the rest of the set had been sold to a lady who was a friend of Lady Vennery and sure to visit her some time or another. So he made his plans, and he told Ned how Mr Skinner must have stolen the necklace and they would get it back again and ask for a big reward. Only he knew Ned didn't believe it, and he watched Ned, and when he knew Ned had gone to Midwych to the police, he rang up to make sure. He made me speak so it should be a woman's voice, and I said I was his mother."

"That was the third 'phone call," Olive said.

"What third 'phone call?" Jane asked, and without waiting for an answer she went on: "When Roman knew for certain where Ned had been, he told me it all depended on how much Ned really knew and how much he had said, and perhaps we should have to go on the run. He said he would try to get hold of Ned and find out, and I was to wait at the end of Love Lane in case he came back that way. But Roman found him first. He hadn't come by the 'bus, he had come back another way, through the forest, and I don't know why, but that made Roman still more afraid. I think that was when Roman made up his mind. When I saw them coming I went to join them, and Roman told me to give Ned the note I had. The note said Roman had got hold of the big sapphire necklace from Mr Skinner and Ned could have it for proof who was right. Roman said: 'You can ask her if it's true.' Ned said: 'Is it true?' and I said of course it was true, I had seen it; it was on the diningroom table. Ned went with us then. He was very excited. When we got indoors Ned said: 'Where is it?' and he looked all round. Roman said it was in the drawer, and he went to open it, but before he did, he said: 'Now the police will have to believe you. How much did you tell them?' Ned said: 'Not much.' He said they would look foolish now, and sorry they hadn't wanted to listen. He said it would most likely cost that cocky young Inspector Owen his job. People wouldn't think he was so smart, after all. Roman opened the drawer, but he didn't take out the necklace, because of course it wasn't there. He took out a cosh instead. He said: 'Well, that's all right if you haven't told them much, because if I kill you now you won't be able to, will you?' Ned began to laugh. He said: 'What's the joke?' and Roman hit him and he fell down. Roman knelt on him, and he told me to hold Ned's legs to stop him kicking. Roman said: 'There mustn't be any blood.' He put his hands round Ned's neck and squeezed. Presently he said: 'Now it's finished.' He said I needn't hold Ned's legs any longer. I said I never knew he was going to do that, and he said I always was a fool and I had better look out. I thought he was going to kill me, too, because he looked like it, and I think with them like him, when they've once begun, they feel they must go on. I went into the hall, and Mrs Wright was there. She said: 'That's the second'. I think that was the first time I had ever heard her speak unless you spoke to her first. I said: 'Who was the first?' and she said it was the girl he had before me. Because she had been like Ned and said perhaps some day she would tell. We went into the kitchen and we made ourselves a cup of tea. Mrs Wright said it would be us next, because once you've begun you can't stop. I said I thought so, too. Roman came into the kitchen. He asked us for some tea. While he was drinking it, he said he would have to get rid of the body somehow, but he didn't know how. He said most likely Bobby Owen from Midwych would come messing round,

188 | E.R. PUNSHON

but he wasn't so smart but that Roman Wright, Esq., couldn outsmart him, same as he had done others. He went back into th dining-room, and he carried Ned out to the cycle shed. When i was dark we heard him go off. We went to bed then, Mrs Wrigh and I, and in the morning we tidied up the dining-room."

"You'll feel better now you've told some one," Mrs Bloom said

Jane was looking at Olive. She said:

"Well, now then, there you are. Well, now then, what do yo think of me?"

"I suppose it might have been me and not you," Olive said.

"That's a silly thing to say," answered Jane. She jerked a han at Mrs Bloom. "What do you think of her?" she asked.

"I know it might have been me," Olive answered.

"If you ever say a word of what I've told you, either of you, Jane said, "I'll just say you're both liars and you've made it all u yourselves. See?"

"Yes," said Olive.

"I'll never hang," Jane said. "Not me. Never."

"No," said Olive.

"Where did he put my boy?" Mrs Bloom asked.

"I don't know," Jane answered. "He never said, and I neve asked. I knew better." To Olive she said: "Do you know why I never hang?"

"No," said Olive.

"Because he'll do me in first," said Jane.

She got up and went away quickly. The little red-cheeked gi saw her going and ran after her to ask her if she had paid. Jan said she had forgotten, and gave her a two-shilling piece. The red cheeked child came back beaming.

"She said I could keep the change," she confided to Mrs Bloor and Olive as she went by. "I do think she's just sweet."

She hurried on to attend to another customer. Mrs Bloom an Olive watched her. Mrs Bloom said:

"They have taken my boy and I know not where they hav laid him."

CHAPTER XXXVII

FEAR OF SAFETY

THIS WAS THE story to which, as Olive told it, Bobby listened gravely, uneasily, with increasing discomfort. Only once did he interrupt. It was to make the comment that it was small wonder he had thought, the day when he first saw Jane, that she had looked as if she were suffering from a hangover—though little had he suspected then of what kind that hangover was to prove to be. Then he went to the 'phone, to send out fresh orders, new instructions. He returned to hear the rest of Olive's story and to ask a few quick questions. He was looking more troubled, more uneasy than ever as he said:

"The difficulty about a verbal statement is that it can always be denied. A thing's no good unless it's in writing and signed and all that."

"Mrs Bloom was there, she heard it all," Olive said.

"Yes, there's that," Bobby agreed, "but not much help. For one thing, you can't be sure she would be willing to speak. She has a gift for silence. She may exercise it once more. Besides, we can show nothing to prove Jane wasn't inventing the whole story for her own purposes. To put us off, perhaps. Oh, I know, you and I, we know she wasn't," he added as he saw Olive was about to speak, "but it's what other people might suggest. Anyhow, we must get hold of Jane. I think what she said is true enough. Her life won't be worth much if Roman Wright gets to know she's been talking. I expect he will as soon as he sees her. We must find her first and make her understand her best chance, her only chance, is for us to accept her as king's witness, for her to tell in public what she's told you in private. But will she? Or there's Mrs Wright. She could give us the evidence we need. But she won't unless we can get her right away from Roman Wright. He has them both completely under his thumb. No wonder he called that water-colour of his he showed me the most remarkable picture ever painted. Quite true. At least I've never heard before of a murderer making a picture of his victim's secret grave. Or using it to put such fear into his wife as to make him sure she would never tell."

"Wouldn't it be evidence enough itself if you could find it?" Olive asked.

"Yes, if—but a big if. It wasn't there the next time I went, you remember. I suppose he began to feel after I left that day that he had gone just a bit too far, given too broad a hint. He wanted to gloat to himself how he had dangled his secret before the thick-headed police and they never knew. All the same, prudent to destroy the exhibit. He could still enjoy remembering how he had taunted us with the evidence we wanted, pushed it under our nose and drawn it back again. Vanity. It has destroyed before to-day better men, greater men, than Roman Wright. Not but that he isn't remarkable enough in his own way, with his passion for jewels, his influence over women, his painting. He slipped up there, though."

"You mean it was all that silly stuff he talked when you first met him that made you suspect him?"

"Well, not so much what he said," Bobby answered. "All that might have been merely the swank of the incompetent amateur trying to pass himself off as the successful practitioner. Of course, it was a bit difficult to suppose that any one who took any interest in art at all wouldn't know that the Resurrection painting in the Tate Gallery was a Stanley Spencer and not an Augustus John. Or that even if Hogarth's 'Shrimp Girl' had been a John, living artists are not shown in the National Gallery. But the things people don't know, even about their own jobs, are often surprising enough— the strangest gaps in the knowledge of us all. What struck me as really suspicious was his choice of a house facing a main road and so entirely overshadowed by trees so close up behind as to cut off completely the north light. I thought it possible the incompetent amateur might never have heard of the 'Shrimp Girl' or be very clear about the respective works of Stanley Spencer and Augustus John, but the more incompetent he is, the more as a rule he is inclined to be fussy about his tools and his technique, even if, especially if, he doesn't know much about how to use it and them. He likes to impress by talking about the importance of having a north light to work by, for instance. Then, on the other hand, you couldn't help noticing how conveniently placed the house was for secret comings and goings. Easy to slip in and out without being noticed, and if he were noticed—well, he had been studying sunrise effects in the forest. He went out of his way to lay all the stress he could on that, and if any of our men noticed his comings and goings in the small hours—well, there was the excuse to satisfy them, and why should they associate an artist coming home early from painting a sunrise or moonlight effects with a recent burglary? I thought it might be all right, but I didn't like it very much, though at the time there was nothing to show that anything had happened to poor young Ned Bloom. A queer, inquisitive lad, and he might easily have slipped away to try to pry into some one else's private affairs. Besides, he had learned so much about so many secrets of so many other people there was always the possibility that one of them was responsible. Easy enough to lose your temper and go too far with a cheeky, inquisitive lad trying to nosey parker into your private affairs you might have very good reason for wishing to keep' to yourself. And then, in addition, there was the mercy-killing theory. It was all over the village."

"I know," Olive said. "I used to wonder sometimes. I'm sorry, now we know the truth."

"I did more than wonder," Bobby told her. "There was always a look about Mrs Bloom, something—most people felt it. A background, so to speak, a background of horror beyond imagination or experience. Jane Wright knew it, recognized it, understood very well that Mrs Bloom had memories like her own. Their mutual knowledge seems to have made between them such a bond Jane could not keep away; and when she came, then, in her turn, Mrs Bloom could not keep from her. In the end I think it was your presence made them speak."

"It was a dreadful thing to listen to them," Olive said slowly. "Because it made you feel how easily you might have been like them yourself, if you had been in their place. It's so easy to be bad."

"Jane was right in what she thought she saw when she looked at Mrs Bloom," Bobby repeated. "It might have been her son. A mercy killing as they call it. It was her husband instead, but it might have been her son."

"She never meant to," Olive said. "She never meant it."

"'Never meant' is a poor excuse," Bobby said. "You never meant, perhaps, but all the same you did—and what you did, that is done."

"That is a hard thing to say. Hard like stone," Olive answered. "It is all so long ago."

"Facts are hard, life is hard," Bobby answered. "The world God made is hard—stone and iron, too. And I don't think Mrs Bloom feels it is long ago. I think she always feels it only happened yesterday." He began to walk up and down the room. "A race," he said. "A race with all the odds against us. Can we find Jane and get hold of her before she goes back to Roman Wright? For that's what she'll do. She won't be able to keep away now she's told, and that's where the odds are against us. She won't help us. Irresistibly, fatally, he'll draw her. And he'll soon know she's talked. A race, the odds against us, her life the prize, and that, I think, she knows."

"She knows," Olive agreed—"or I think she does—but I'm not sure either how she'll choose."

"Nor am I," Bobby agreed. "Death has its fascination, too. Mrs Wright—but she'll make no choice."

"No," Olive said, "but if you could manage to get her away, then, after a time, I believe she would tell you everything. But she won't let you take her away if she can help it."

"I suppose I could arrest her," Bobby said thoughtfully. "I don't know why. I might think up some charge or another to hold her on. False imprisonment, of course. Action for damages, perhaps. Have to risk it. Or hold her for questioning. Her life won't be safe if I can't manage to get her away somehow. I imagine Roman Wright has only kept her there still alive because he hates her so, and if he sees he can't any longer, then he is altogether likely to give his hate vent in killing. Two women's lives at stake and not too much chance of saving either, for neither of them will help."

The 'phone rang to tell him the orders and instructions he had given were in process of being carried out.

"Now I can go," he said, returning from the 'phone.

He started off at once. At a little distance from Prospect Cottage he left his car and continued on foot to join the two men now on watch, one just arrived as a result of Bobby's recent orders. The other, who had been there since much earlier in the day but till now under strict orders to subordinate closeness of observation to avoidance of attention, reported that he had seen Jane return and enter the cottage. As far as he knew she was still there, but it was possible she had gone out by the back, whence escape into the shelter and concealment of the neargrowing trees was so easy. Bobby asked him about Roman Wright and Mrs Wright, but he had seen neither of them.

"But that Mrs Wright," he said, "she's a queer one. You look and look and you think there's no one, and then all at once you see she's been there all the time. Sort of natural born camouflage, as you might say."

Bobby warned both men to keep very much on the alert. Roman Wright, he told them, was probably armed and certainly desperate, desperate as only those can be who see inevitably closing upon them the doom they have long dreaded but long thought they could evade. The newly arrived constable had brought two revolvers. Bobby put one in his pocket. He went to the house and knocked. There was no reply. He waited and knocked again, and still got no response. He went round to the back, but there, too, his knocking won no answer.

"Can't be any one in, sir," said the constable who had come round to the back with him, the other man having remained on guard at the front.

"I've no search warrant," Bobby said. "No time. Too much red tape about search warrants. An Englishman's house is his castle, but castles can be taken by storm. Are you any good at burglary, Jones?" he asked his companion.

"Well, sir," answered Jones, warily, "I wouldn't say—"

"I am," said Bobby, interrupting. "One of my specialities. Case or not, search warrant or none, I'm going to have a look. You can stand by and watch."

Jones, grateful he wasn't an inspector and hadn't to take the responsibility, watched accordingly, while Bobby satisfied him-

self the back door was bolted as well as locked so that an assaul
on the lock alone would be useless. He turned his attention to th
kitchen window. It had a special patent burglar-proof fastener
Mr Roman Wright, as one of the profession, evidently knew how
to baffle his colleagues. Bobby went back to the front, though h
would have preferred to effect less conspicuous entry at the rea
The front door had a Yale type lock. Such locks enjoy a well-de
served reputation for security, but all the same present no grea
difficulty to those who know how to deal with them, though it ma
be as well not to explain too precisely the method Bobby adopted
Soon he had it forced with little to show what had happened an
with small injury to the lock. Fortunately the door had not bee
bolted, and once the lock had been dealt with it opened easily.

Bobby did not enter immediately. He stood on the threshol
in the open doorway and called.

"Any one at home?" he shouted, and there came no answer.

Once again he called, loudly and clearly, and then again. H
crossed the threshold into the small entrance hall. He entered th
sitting-rooms. They were empty, showing no trace of recent oc
cupation. He gave another shout up the stairs and still gained n
answer. He went on into the kitchen and at first glance though
that was empty, too, till he perceived that the motionless shadov
in the darkest corner was Mrs Wright.

"Oh, how do you do?" he said. "Do excuse me, won't you?
hope you don't mind my barging in like this, but I couldn't mak
any one hear. Fact is, I'm wanting to have a bit of a talk wit
the young lady staying with you—Miss Jane Wright, isn't it? Yo
don't know where she is, do you?"

The silent, motionless figure contented itself with a fain
shake of the head, a gesture so slight as hardly to be perceptible

"Or your husband? Has he got back yet?"

Mrs Wright made again that almost imperceptible gesture o
denial. Then she said in her low tones that were hardly above
whisper:

"I didn't let you in, but he'll say I did."

"Well, that won't matter," Bobby told her cheerfully, "not
scrap. You'll come away with us, won't you? I hope you will."

Again that faint movement of the head that was hardly so much as a gesture, scarcely even an indication of one.

"I can't," she said in her low whisper. "I can't. He won't let me. He won't let you. I can't."

"Oh, that's all right," Bobby said. "Don't you worry about that. We shan't ask him. I'll get one of my men to go to Midwych with you, and we'll find a lady there to look after you. She'll take care of you, and you'll be perfectly safe."

Mrs Wright did not answer. She might not have heard. But she began to tremble. Bobby thought it better to say no more for the moment. He was afraid of a complete breakdown. He had a small brandy flask in his pocket, but when he poured a little out and tried to make her swallow it, she could not for the chattering of her teeth, the tight constriction of her throat. He put it on the table, telling her to drink it when she felt better. He called in Jones from outside.

"I want you to look after her and get her away as soon as you can," he said. "But be careful. She's in a queer state, she might collapse any moment. I told her we would take her to Midwych and take care of her and see she was quite safe, and the threat of safety has been too much for her. Not used to being taken care of, not used to feeling safe. I'll send a car along and a doctor, too, if I can find one. Be as gentle as you know how, handle her like a new-born baby that'll die on your hands if you don't watch out. Do your best."

Jones promised, though uneasily, and hoped the car and the doctor would not be long delayed. Bobby went back to his own car and started off for that spot in Wychwood forest where he supposed that by now, following his recent orders, a squad would be hard at work.

CHAPTER XXXVIII
JEWELS AND DEATH

IN WYCHWOOD FOREST, in the heart of that curious kind of peninsula or spur of rough and lonely land, strewn with rocks and boulders, marshy in places, avoided alike by hikers and holiday-makers and by the tramps and gypsies who occasionally made use of parts of the forest as a base for their operations, there was now busily at work with spade and pick and crowbar a small group of the Wychshire county police; all of them grumbling bitterly at having been called back to duty after dismissal, but all of them equally excited to know the cause and upshot of this emergency call.

"Our Bobby's got something," they told each other, using the nickname his men were beginning to give him among themselves; "our Bobby mostly knows what he's up to."

"Found a corpse last time, so he did," one of them observed. "Now it's another, or I'll stand the first man that asks half a pint—"

"That's me," said one of them quickly.

"Provided he pays for it himself," said the other man.

The pleasantry earned the laugh any pleasantry will when men are at work together. A third member of the party, grave and elderly, rebuked them.

"No time for laughing," he said, "if it's that poor crippled lad from Threepence village lies buried here."

"A queer-like corpse, anyway," yet another said. "Take a look."

They were at work under and around the great outcropping boulder where previously the hidden petrol tins had been discovered. Their task had been to excavate still further the kind of cavity or cave beneath it, partly natural, worn by the long, slow forces of Nature, partly plainly enough the work of other unknown human hands. Now the last speaker had felt the point of his pick strike on a wooden box, and it was a gold watch and chain that he withdrew, caught on his tool. Groping with his hands, enlarging the gap already made in the side of the buried box, he freed still more of its contents. Forth there came a small cascade of shining things, splendid, sparkling, earth-stained. He threw them out to his companions in careless handfuls.

"Here, catch," he said; and tossed over his shoulder a glorious tiara that once had shone upon a duchess's head. Followed more such brilliancies—brooches, bracelets, pendants, rings, all in turn. "Here's another," he said, and out came a diamond necklace, followed by a crimson ruby pendant. "That's the lot, I think," he said. He scrambled out from the cavity they had made under the great rock. "A ruddy jeweller's shop," he said. "Now, how did our Bobby know all that stuff was there?"

A strange sight indeed, all that great pile of lovely shining toys spread out there in the failing light, in that rough and lonely spot on that barren earth, things meant for the adornment of their women when the great of this earth were met to display to each other their riches and their power. Yet these sophisticated toys seemed as lovely—lovelier indeed—in their present strange surroundings as ever they could have done at banquet or ball. It was with a kind of half-embarrassed awe that there stood gazing at them the little group of men who had wrenched them from their cunning hiding-place.

"Now I wonder who put them there and why?" said one of them, and another said, half in jest and all in earnest:

"Wouldn't my old woman like to have her pick? But how ever did our Bobby know?"

"Here he comes," a third man said.

Bobby had in fact arrived, and was in the act of making his way towards them as quickly as permitted the rough and broken ground that made all progress about here a mixture of scramble, climb and crawl.

"We've found it, sir; it was there all right," one man called to him.

"Now we can go ahead," Bobby said; and then, when he came nearer and saw what formed the centre round which the men were gathered, he stood still and looked again and said: "That's not what I thought you would find."

"Well, sir, it's something anyway, isn't it?" one of them remarked. "What's there must be worth a mort of money."

"Enough to stock a jeweller's shop," said another.

Bobby was still looking worried and disturbed. He went on his hands and knees before the great cavity they had scooped out under that enormous rock. Then he lay flat so that he could reach farther; and he groped with his hand first and then with the end of a crowbar he asked should be passed to him.

"There can't be any more of the stuff there, sir," one said to him. "It's solid rock behind."

"Feels like it," Bobby grunted, still probing and feeling.

"Smart idea," another of the men said, "to hide one thing on top of another, the petrol tins on top of the jewellery. When you had found the petrol, well, you had found it, and you didn't think of looking any more, not when it all seemed solid earth behind, well packed and beaten in."

"Smart all right," Bobby agreed, he having now withdrawn himself from his probing and scraping, "and smart once may be smart twice. How would it be if some of you had a try at shifting that bit of rock or stone or whatever it is you touched behind the jewel-box?"

The men looked somewhat doubtful as they obeyed. It was no easy task, but crowbars and picks did their work, and presently, with grunting effort and much strain, they hauled forth the great slab of stone that had been so ingeniously fixed in position as to seem a part of the boulder above it.

"Who ever put that there," they said to each other, "did a job."

"He had cause," Bobby said, a picture in his mind of the grisly task a desperate man had accomplished here, working for his life in solitude and darkness. He said to his men: "Go ahead. That stone was not put there without reason."

A few more minutes, a further clearing away of earth; and then, in the twilight of the declining day, beneath the stunted trees, side by side with the heaped-up, shining jewels, there lay the grisly thing they had at last uncovered.

"It's the lame boy all right," one man said—"young Ned Bloom of Threepence village. See that club foot of his?"

Bobby knelt down by the body, a body already not much more than recognizable. No one now was paying any attention to the jewels, their glitter and their splendour quite forgotten. The body was fully clothed. Bobby thought a doctor would be able to establish the cause of death. From damp and mouldering and clammy pockets, Bobby drew out little things of one sort and another that would help to make identification even more certain. Among them was that note of which Jane Wright had spoken, the note she had been given to hand to the unhappy lad, to lure him to his death. Roman's signature was still legible.

"Even if there was nothing more," Bobby said, "that would be enough."

He gave a few orders to his men and he told them, too, to make a quick inventory of the recovered jewels.

"Mustn't forget them," he said.

Then he left them, for he was eager to get started immediately the hunt for Roman Wright. Two murders, he knew for certain, lay at that man's door, and there was a very grim likelihood that he might soon be guilty of two more if he were not checked in time. But Bobby had not gone more than fifty yards from where these discoveries had been made, fifty yards or less towards where he had left his car, when he heard behind him shouting and running. He turned and hurried back. Most of his men had scattered; he could hear them running and calling. One had remained prudently on guard by the piled-up jewels and the body of young Ned Bloom, whose luck in life had been but ill. Bobby called to this one man left on guard to know what had happened.

"It was a chap," the man explained, "who came up from somewhere so quiet like we never heard him, never saw him, us thinking of the stuff we were writing down and ticking off, and when he saw what we were doing he let out a yell like a madman. 'Oh, my pretties,' he said, 'there's all my pretties.' We all turned round quick, and I said, 'Your pretties? who are you?' and he didn't say a word, but was off like a good 'un, and most of us after him, but I stopped to make sure of things, and it's not in my mind they'll catch him, he ran that light and easy; quick like he ran, as if he knew the place well and where to put his feet."

Bobby listened in silence. He did not much think either that any of his men, none of them young, most of them reservists or pensioners called back to duty, would outpace Roman Wright, for that it was Roman Wright who had thus appeared to them Bobby had no doubt.

All the more reason, then, all the more need for desperate haste to bring to justice, to render harmless, one who had already shown himself so reckless, cunning and remorseless. Yet even before throwing all his energy into pursuit, Bobby felt that first he must return to Prospect Cottage to make sure that Mrs Wright had been removed to safety.

To his surprise and disappointment, however, when he arrived it was to see still standing in the road outside the cottage that police car he had sent there and that he had hoped would by now have conveyed Mrs Wright to safety. Standing by its side was a man whom Bobby recognized as a doctor practising in the district

"It seems my patient is missing," the doctor said as he nodded recognition to Bobby, jumping from his car. "How much longer do you expect me to wait? If she has dodged away into the wood behind the house there won't be much chance of finding her in a hurry."

The constable Bobby had left on guard had seen Bobby's arrival, and came up hurriedly, looking somewhat uneasy.

"It's this way, sir," he explained. "We was getting along fine her and me. Chatting away I was to put her at her ease, sir, if you see what I mean, and offering to make her a cup of tea, what ladies are always ready for and bucks 'em up wonderful, and then I heard the car coming, so I said to her: 'I'll open the front door for 'em,' and my back wasn't turned no longer than needed to do that, and take a look to make sure it was our car all O.K., and so it was, and when I went back to the kitchen to tell her, blessed if she wasn't there any more, and how she managed it beats me, with the back door still locked and bolted same as you said to keep it and me only at the front door and never hearing a sound, so how she done a bunk like that beats me."

"I didn't put you there to be beaten," Bobby said with some severity. "If it's like that, she must be in the house somewhere."

"Well, sir, there's the windows," answered the crestfallen constable, well aware that though Bobby seldom rebuked his men when he did, it meant something. "I looked everywhere, sir, and not a trace of her nowhere."

But Bobby, remembering the strange trick she had of achieving an immobility, an invisibility, gained by long habit of long-felt fear seeking safety in avoidance, thought it not unlikely she was still there, silent in some corner, still and quiet behind a curtain or a door. Her deeply ingrained terror of her husband might well be stronger than any hope of refuge or of safety held out to her by the large, strange, busy men who had so suddenly thrust themselves upon her.

"We'll have another look," Bobby said. "Unless we find her I don't think her life will be worth much."

"She can't be there, sir," the constable insisted. "The young lady looked, too. She said as the old party must have slipped out; said she had a trick of doing that so quiet like no one knew."

"What young lady?" demanded Bobby sharply.

"The young lady that stays here—niece or something," the man answered. "Called her aunt, anyhow: 'Aunt's like that,' she said, when she come in and found me looking. 'Off she goes in a moment, and you never notice she isn't there till you look again.' Miss Jane Wright, she said she was."

"Still time to save her at least, if she's come back," Bobby said with some relief.

If Jane had returned and was somewhere in the house, as he had no doubt Mrs Wright was too, then there seemed a better prospect than he had hoped for of saving both these women from a death they appeared themselves to have so small care to avoid. Because, he thought, it was to them as a thing inevitable, and because all hope or even desire to oppose the strange and fatal will of Roman Wright had long since been drained from them both. He gave the man he was speaking to a sharp, quick order to go round to the rear of the house and to be on his guard, both to prevent either of the women from leaving that way and against the sudden appearance of Roman Wright.

"Can't tell what he'll be up to next," Bobby said. "He'll very likely come back here—for money, perhaps. So look out. If he does come, he'll probably be armed—and he'll certainly be desperate."

The other constable, the man who had brought the car, Bobby called to come with him. The doctor he told to keep out of the way, and the doctor told him a doctor was never in the way, except when presenting his bill. So Bobby said it was an order, and the doctor said Bobby could put his order in his pipe and smoke it, and they all three went on up the garden path together. But not very far, for a shot rang out and then another, and there was

Roman Wright in the half-open doorway emptying his revolver at them.

The light was dim, the shooting bad. His revolver empty, Roman Wright dodged back into the house. When Bobby, the first to reach the door, his own revolver in his hand, threw his weight against it, it held fast. He heard the bolts shot, and then a heavy crash that suggested some piece of furniture or another had been thrown against it for a further barricade. The doctor and the other constable had joined him now. They heard an upstairs window go up, and then a louder discharge.

"Shot-gun," the doctor said. "Double-barrelled gun. I know he has one for shooting rabbits—us the rabbits now," he added ruefully.

Bobby stepped out a yard or two and fired back. He did not suppose his shot would have any effect, but it might serve to check Roman Wright's activities a little, and anyhow it much relieved his own feelings. A couple of shots in reply showed that Roman had reloaded his pistol and was not short of ammunition. Bobby dodged back in the shelter of the doorway, which gave good protection from that upstairs window whence death threatened.

"We'll have to break the door open," Bobby said. "Try to smash a panel," he said to the constable. To the doctor he said: "Bend down, low as you can, hands and knees. Shots always go high. Aim at the feet is the rule, but you never do."

The constable was hammering at the door. He had his truncheon with him, and he was using it to try to force a panel. It was strongly built, and resisted stoutly.

"Why not shoot the lock away?" the doctor asked Bobby.

"No spare ammunition," Bobby said. "I may need the cartridges I've left."

"It's no good, sir," the constable said. "I can't do it."

"Try the lower panel," Bobby said. "Try to kick it in."

He himself took the truncheon and using it as a kind of battering ram continued the assault on the top panel. It split suddenly. The doctor cried out:

"My God, the place is all on fire."

Through the splintered panel they could see plainly where a great river of flame flowed upwards, a cataract in reverse, up the stairway. At the top of the stairs a man stood, coming running from one of the rooms at the sound of the roar of the flames on the stairs. The tongue of flame leaped at him, wrapped him round so that for an instant he stood as in a garment of fire. Then he was gone and they saw him no more. Desperately they strove to tear down the door, and within the flames spread still, leaping up the banister rails, springing hither and thither as they sought fresh sustenance. In the strange glare of that spreading blaze they could see now where an old woman stood in the passage, as yet unharmed. With outstretched arms, as though she waved it on, she watched the fire go roaring up the stairs. The door at which the three men strove, Bobby and his two companions, gave way at last. They ran into the passage. Mrs Wright turned to them and laughed.

"I poured it out, I put a match to it," she cried. "He's up there, and it's all a blaze, a blaze."

Bobby pushed her into the arms of the constable behind him.

"Take her out, look after her," he said briefly. "One saved anyhow."

He was about to try to make a dash up the stairs. The doctor caught hold of him and pulled him back.

"No, you don't," he said. "The stairs are going."

"There's a woman up there," Bobby said. "Let go."

But even as he spoke the stairs fell in, and there was no longer any means of access to the upper floor.

"No, there isn't, not alive," said the doctor grimly. "Come on out of it while we can."

"There may be a ladder somewhere," Bobby said, and ran outside, and the doctor after him, while after them came a long, licking flame as though in baffled rage at their escape, as though in a last effort at pursuit.

But there was no ladder they could find and nothing they could do, for the flames were roaring everywhere and the house alight from floor to roof.

"Well, anyhow," Bobby said, "I know now why four of those petrol tins we found had only water in them. Mrs Wright must have planned this long ago. Who would have thought that old, still, silent woman had such thoughts, such plans behind her stillness and her silence?"

"Petrol-fed, eh?" the doctor said. "I must go and have a look at the old girl," he added.

The house was now no more than a huge flaming torch. The firemen came. Nothing they could do, nothing any one could do, except watch from a distance and keep at a distance the crowds that came hurrying from every direction. In that furnace no life could endure, from it none emerged. Only such relics were ultimately found as proved beyond all doubt that there had perished both the man known as Roman Wright and the woman calling herself Jane and passing herself off as his niece, her true identity never established. There was proof, too, that before the flames reached her, the woman had met from the gun of her paramour that death of which, since the hour she had seen it and known it so near and so dreadfully, she had felt the urge and the fascination, had done so little to avoid.

There still remained much to be seen to, many formalities requiring attention, the necessary inquests to be arranged for and attended, a host of eager newspaper men to be satisfied so far as it is humanly possible to satisfy a newspaper man. Often enough during the succeeding days Bobby had to leave the routine of his daily work to go again to Threepence for one reason or another. On one such visit, as he was alighting from his car before the Threepence police-station, there came hurrying by Captain Dunstan and Miss Thea Wood, both apparently in considerable haste and engaged in a somewhat animated and even heated conversation. On Bobby as they came by Miss Thea bestowed a charming smile of greeting and recognition, and Captain Dunstan a curt nod and a brief good morning.

"You still around?" he said, and then, unable to keep the news to himself: "I've got to get busy. Passed my medical all right, going to join up again, the battalion's got embarkation orders, and Kitty says she'll marry me before we go. I thought I was going to get left behind when the battalion moved, and I thought Kitty wasn't going to have me—and now. Well, talk about bringing off a double. Not so bad, eh?"

"No, indeed," agreed Bobby. "Congratulations. Miss Kitty is worth a dozen of most of us—present company not excepted," and if there was a faint touch of the acid in his tone as he uttered these last words, he was careful not to give so much as the merest glance in the direction of Miss Thea Wood.

"Well, now then," said Dunstan, surprised, "that's about the only sensible thing I've ever heard you say."

"Don't mind me," murmured Miss Thea Wood abstractedly.

"Eh? What? Who? You?" said Dunstan, and quite obviously he didn't.

"Not at all," said Bobby, trying to add a sting to this mild and inoffensive phrase.

"So long," said Dunstan. "Some doings round here while I've been away, weren't there?"

"Some," said Bobby.

"Come on, Polly," said Dunstan, "there's lots to see about, only I tell you straight, bride maid or no bridesmaid, a bunch of lilies of the valley is all a maiden aunt ought to expect."

But he said this in a blustering tone that showed how weak he knew his position to be; and Polly smiled on him with tolerance, turned to give Bobby a farewell smile and then once more put out her tongue at him.

"Well," said Bobby to himself, and said it with deep emotion.

THE END